The World's Craziest Love Triangle

Kayla Powers

The World's Craziest Love Triangle/ Kayla Powers. —1st ed.
ISBN 9781790750597

Contents

CHAPTER ONE

May 11th, 1821

Kallie paced back and forth, twirling the end of her long braid between her fingers. She glanced at the clock on her nightstand, the little hand on the four and the big hand on the three. The sun would rise in about an hour. Kallie knew if she was to go through with her plan she must leave now. She grabbed a satchel and packed what she could. She quietly opened her bedroom door and sneaked down the creaky staircase. She entered the kitchen and packed a few pieces of bread and fruit in the satchel. She walked out the back door, made her way around to the front of the house, and began walking down the dirt road.

It was still dark. Her body was covered with goose bumps from the chilly air. She saw a raccoon disappear into a tree as the sky grew lighter. The thought of her aunt and uncle's reaction to her missing never crossed her mind. She didn't care, because she knew they would be more upset about missing out on all that money than they would be about her disappearing.

She was close to the edge of town when the sun began to rise. She could see the dew on the grass as the morning sun warmed her. It had been silent, until now. Kallie could hear horses as she approached a bend in the road. She recognized the voices and laughter of the men who would turn the corner any second. Kallie knew that if they noticed her trying to leave, they would force her to return home.

Kallie looked around for somewhere to hide, and spotted the forest on the other side of the field she was walking. She took off running through the field, as fast as she could. She made it into the forest just as the men passed by. No one had seen her.

The sun was still rising, the forest still dark inside. Kallie could hear the birds chirping as a new day began. The forest was thick, without trails to follow. Kallie hoped that if she kept walking straight, she would eventually make it to the other side of the forest and be at her destination.

She walked all morning, feeling like someone or something was watching her. She kept turning around to look, but nothing was there.

She wondered what her aunt and uncle were doing. Did they even realize that she was missing? Were they looking for her?

Kallie's thoughts were interrupted by the sound of rushing water. She followed the sound, which led her to a wide river. The water smelled fresh and looked clear. She bent down, cupped the water in her hands, and started to drink.

She heard something on the other side of the river. She looked up. On the other side of the river was a big, angry, black bear. Kallie didn't know what to do. She regretted running into the forest; she wished she were back at home. She would rather marry that awful man than be torn apart by a bear.

The bear growled and started charging. She turned to run but stopped as the ground began to shake. She heard something charging through the woods, then, out of nowhere, a wolf that was much larger than a horse came flying out of the woods and over Kallie's head, landing between her and the bear. The wolf turned its head to look at her. The way the drool was seeping out of its mouth made Kallie feel like she was about to be eaten. Its yellowish eyes wouldn't stop staring her down.

The wolf pushed her back. She went sliding backward on the ground and felt rocks scraping against her skin, her left wrist slamming against a rock. She smacked the back of her head on another. She lay there, unable to move, as her vision slowly faded. She heard a growl come from the wolf, a growl so terrifying it could have made anyone whimper in fear. Last thing she saw were the bear and the wolf fighting in the middle of the rushing water. Everything went black.

Kallie felt like she had been knocked out for days, but the day was just coming to an end. She could hear owls hooting, and crickets chirping. She could smell smoke and hear the popping of a fire. She felt the warmth of the fire on her face. She slowly opened her eyes, not sure where she was.

She was lying on the ground, wrapped in a soft, warm quilt. A fire roared in front of her. She could tell by the sky that the sun must have just set.

Kallie noticed a man sitting on the other side of the fire. He was staring down at the fire and hadn't noticed Kallie was awake. She could see that he was a Native American man. He had dark tan skin, dark-brown, short hair, and big, golden, brownish eyes that were so bright they seemed almost to be glowing. He had on long pants, moccasins, and nothing else. He was muscular. Kallie couldn't recall ever seeing a man with such large muscles before. She thought he was probably somewhere in his mid-twenties. He also had a strange-looking birthmark on his chest, like a paw print.

The man looked up, and his eyes met Kallie's through the flames of the fire. Kallie quickly shut her eyes. She waited a few minutes before opening her eyes again. When she did, he was looking back at the fire. He glanced at her again, and she shut her eyes once more.

He spoke. "I know you're awake. You can stop doing that."

Kallie was surprised to hear him speak English. She smiled and opened her eyes again.

Kallie began to sit up. The man stood and walked toward her. He was easily above the average height of any man. She put her hand on the back of her head. She felt a large bump and could feel it pulsating. She clenched her face and quietly whispered, "Ow."

She glanced down at her arm, her left wrist wrapped up in a bandage. She could hardly move her fingers, but could see that her hand was badly bruised. The man sat on the ground beside her and held a cold, wet cloth on the back of her head.

"You hit your head," the man said to her. "You also sprained your wrist."

"All I can recall is a bear running at me . . . and a giant wolf."

The man interrupted her. "That wolf saved your life," he said.

"But why?" she asked. The man took a few seconds to answer.

"The wolves in this Pennsylvania forest are a little different, compared to the average wolf."

"I agree. That wolf was probably five times the size of a normal wolf!" Kallie said as her eyes glanced over the mountainous muscles stretched over his entire upper body.

The man changed the subject. His left hand was still holding the wet cloth on the back of Kallie's head. He extended his other hand, for Kallie to shake.

"I'm Tucker, by the way," he said.

Kallie shook his hand. "Kallie," she said.

"Why do you look confused?"

"I wasn't expecting you to have an English family name for your first name, or to even speak English."

Tucker smiled and said, "I'm from the Indian reservation on the south side of the forest. My people have been trying to live like the people in the village near there. There's less conflict that way. I've been speaking English my whole life, and most of us now have English names. My mother heard of a family with this last name, and thought it would make a good first name."

"How old are you?"

"Twenty-three. And you?"

"Twenty."

"Well," Tucker started to say, as he removed his hand from the back of her head. He dunked the cloth into a pail of water, wrung it out, and wrapped it around Kallie's wrist. She shivered when the cold cloth touched her skin.

"Would you like to explain to me what you are doing here?" he said.

Kallie sighed and thought about what to say.

"I'm from the east village, and I want to get to the west village."

"You're running from something, aren't you?" Tucker asked.

He watched Kallie like he was looking for the answer in her green eyes.

"My greedy aunt and uncle," she mumbled as her eyes filled with tears.

"What about your parents?" he asked. By the look on her face, he already knew what she was going to say. He regretted asking the question immediately.

"They died when I was young."

"I'm sorry."

"So, what are you doing out here all by yourself?" Kallie asked as she wiped her tears with her good hand.

"Protecting my tribe."

"What are you protecting them from?"

"Bears," he said, fighting back a smile.

"Is that supposed to be a joke?"

Tucker started laughing. Kallie giggled.

The two spent the rest of the night sitting by the fire. Kallie told Tucker about how her aunt and uncle took her in after her parents had passed away, but never paid much attention to her. They became greedy, over the years. Kallie also told Tucker about the wonderful group of friends she had growing up, and how as they got older, and all the boys began to only want her, all her friends grew jealous and would no longer speak to her.

She had one true friend. Her name was Minnie. She was the only woman in town not jealous of Kallie. Minnie had been married for a while, and was already expecting her second child. Kallie explained that Minnie would understand why she had disappeared.

Tucker felt sorry for Kallie. She seemed like a caring person, and he could tell she had spent most of her time alone. He couldn't blame the men in her village for only wanting her. He could see why they were crazy about her. She had beautiful, long, wavy, bright, red-orange hair, gorgeous green eyes that had a little bit of blue in them, little orange freckles scattered over her fair skin, and a smile he never wanted to see disappear. But, he still couldn't understand what her aunt and uncle could have possibly done to make Kallie want to leave and never return.

When their conversation ended, Kallie stood. Tucker had still been holding the wet cloth on Kallie's wrist, so he let go.

"I guess I should be going now," she said, and looked around for her belongings. Tucker shot up and looked at her, confused.

"Where are you going?"

"I just thought I should start heading out."

"You should stay here tonight. You have a huge bump on your head, you have a sprained wrist, and you should not go walking in the forest this late."

"But I have to get to the west end of the forest."

"If you stay here for the next few days, I can take you there once your wrist has healed."

"I just met you though. Thank you for the offer but, I think I will be just fine," Kallie said with a sincere smile. She spotted her satchel and picked it up. Tucker watched her as she left his campsite.

Kallie couldn't see a thing as she continued her journey alone in the pitch black forest. She wasn't even sure which direction she was going in, let alone which direction she should be going in. She ran her hands along the trees as she used them for guidance through the darkness. Her wrist began to ache with pain.

Kallie almost jumped right out of her skin when she heard the claws of an animal scurry up a tree right beside her. Then a crow decided to fly right over her head as it let out a loud "CAW-CAH!" Kallie forced herself to hold in the scream that wanted to escape her lips.

She became very paranoid as she kept walking, not sure if the noises she kept hearing were real, or just the night messing with her mind. Images of the terrifying wolf began flashing in her head. The drool dripping from its huge mouth filled with sharp teeth, the anger that seemed to fill its eyes, the ferocious growl that could have been heard from miles away. The glow of a fire finally made the wolf leave from Kallie's mind.

As she got closer to the area with the bright burning fire she realized that she had walked in a complete circle which had led her right back to Tucker. He looked up at Kallie with a smile as she entered his campsite.

"Have a change of heart?" he asked her.

"No . . . I was just wondering which direction the west village may be in?" she asked. Tucker silently pointed to the right.

"Thank you," Kallie said, trying to make it seem like she wasn't afraid to go back into the darkness. She walked past Tucker's tent; she glanced inside and couldn't help but notice how comfy and cozy it looked inside. She wanted to just dive into it and sleep all her problems away.

As Kallie walked farther into the night, the light of the fire began to dim out from behind her. She was looking down at the ground when she noticed a big wolf paw print pressed into the mud. The paw print could have been larger than her whole head. The growl of the wolf echoed throughout her mind as she pictured it again. She knew Tucker was right, she shouldn't be walking around the forest this late. She quickly turned around and rushed back to Tucker, the fire far in the distance leading her.

Tucker looked up at her surprised when she returned again.

"Does your offer from before still stand?" Kallie asked as she tried to catch her breath.

"Of course," Tucker replied.

Tucker's tent was big enough for two people. He and Kallie crawled in.

Kallie could feel the heat radiating off of Tucker. His body was warm enough to heat the whole tent. A few minutes after they had laid down, Kallie glanced over at Tucker. Even in the dark tent she could see his eyes. She was almost positive they were glowing.

"Did you find me lying by the river, unconscious?" Kallie asked him.

Tucker took a while to answer. "No. I saw the whole thing. Once the bear realized it couldn't beat the wolf, it moved on, and I carried you here."

"Thank you."

The last thing Kallie thought about before drifting off was how relieved she felt. If Tucker hadn't offered to let her stay with him, and escort her to the village, she would have been lost in the forest all night long. After everything that had happened that day, she was afraid of being alone in the forest. For some reason, she felt safe sleeping next to a man she had just met.

CHAPTER TWO

May 12th, 1821

Kallie woke the next morning uncertain where she was, at first. She turned to look at Tucker. He wasn't there.

She sat up and crawled out of the tent. She stood and looked at the bright, blue sky, and watched the clouds pass. The sound of leaves crunching pulled her gaze back to the ground. Before she knew it, the wolf entered the campsite.

Kallie screamed when she saw the wolf's yellow-golden eyes that gazed down at her, although its expression did not look as angry as it did yesterday. Bloody drool dripped down from its jaw as it dropped the dead turkey it was holding in its mouth, then turned around and took off running as the ground lightly shook beneath her feet.

A few seconds later, Tucker came running back to the campsite.

"What's wrong? I heard you scream," he said.

"That wolf was just here. Didn't you see it?"

"I didn't see a wolf."

"But it ran in the same direction you just came from. You had to have seen it."

Tucker shrugged his shoulders, then glanced at the ground.

"Well, it left us a turkey."

"There's a monstrous wolf roaming around, and all you can think about is food?" Kallie said as she wondered how Tucker could be so calm about this.

Tucker chuckled as he picked up the dead bird and began plucking the feathers off of it.

Kallie sat on a log, fearing what would happen if that wolf showed up again. She looked around the campsite and spotted Tucker's bow and arrows. She felt she would be safe, as long as she didn't leave Tucker's side. She looked over at him as he began to build a fire to cook the turkey. His bronze skin glistened in the sunlight. She could see the birthmark on his chest better, now that it was daylight. It was in the perfect shape of a paw print.

Tucker prepared the turkey and threw it over the fire. Kallie took out the rubber band that was holding in her braid, and tousled her hair. Tucker couldn't help but notice how her hair resembled fire. He could see the shades of red and orange, and even some blonde, shining in the sunlight.

"Is there anywhere I can bathe?" Kallie asked.

Tucker smiled. "Yes, I'll show you after we eat."

As the turkey cooked over the fire, Tucker took off the bandage wrapped around Kallie's wrist. Her wrist, hand, and fingers were black and blue.

"Can you move your fingers?"

Tucker held her hand in his. Her hand seemed small in his hand. She wiggled her fingers. She winced.

"At least you can move it," he reassured her.

They ate, then began walking to where Kallie could wash up, a hidden waterfall that was tall and narrow. The pool it landed in was waist-deep, and fed into a stream that continued through the forest.

"Here we are," Tucker said when they arrived. He turned and began to walk away.

"Wait!" Kallie yelled out to him.

He turned around to face her. "What?"

"What if some wild animal shows up?" she asked, fear written on her face.

"Oh, you mean the wolf?" he said with a smile. "Trust me. It won't be showing up anytime soon."

"Can you at least stay near to me?" Kallie pleaded.

"Fine," he said, giving in. Kallie's expression went from scared to relaxed.

"I'll stand right here. I won't look. I promise."

Kallie walked to the water.

She slipped off her boots and stockings, then attempted to untie her dress. Having only one good hand was making it impossible. She kept glancing back at Tucker, to see if he was still there, which he was. She wanted to see if he was watching her fail at undressing herself. She almost wanted to ask him for help, but she was determined to do it herself.

Tucker kept talking himself out of turning around to look at Kallie. He wanted to look. Kallie was beautiful, and Tucker wanted to see just how beautiful the rest of her was. But he was a good man, and he would respect Kallie.

But after a while, when he still hadn't heard Kallie get into the water, he felt like he needed to turn around, to make sure she was all right. A war began inside his head, over whether he should turn around or not.

He finally gave in. He convinced himself that it was only to check on her, not to see her body. He turned around, and just as he thought, Kallie was still struggling to get out of her dress. He could hear her mumbling, "Ow . . . ow . . . ow," under her breath as she tried to use her bad hand.

"Would you like some assistance?" he said, hoping she wouldn't be mad at him for turning around.

"Well . . . yes," she answered. Tucker smiled and walked over to her. She had her back to him. He began untying the back of her dress. Kallie felt butterflies in her stomach as Tucker touched the back of her. The feeling surprised her.

"Thank you," Kallie said when he was done.

He turned back around as Kallie slipped out of her dress, took off her undergarments, and entered the water. The water was freezing. Kallie wanted to get out as fast as she could. She stood under the waterfall and rinsed herself off. The water stung all the scratches on her arms and legs from when she'd slid across the rocks the day before. She finished, then ran out of the water. She put everything back on, then of course tried to tie her dress on her own.

"I can help, if you want," Tucker said, still turned around.

"Oh, fine," she said as he turned. He tied up the back of her dress; Kallie felt that butterfly feeling again. She turned around and looked at him once he was done. He gazed into her eyes. The sun was peeking through the trees, partly shining on Kallie's face, making her eyes half-blue and half-green. Tucker had never seen anyone with eyes like that before. For a second, Kallie thought that he was going to lean in and kiss her. Kallie had been looked at that way by many men before, and it was always followed by them trying to kiss her. Most of the time she'd move out of the way, but if Tucker were to kiss her, she wouldn't move at all.

"Well, ready to go back?" he asked, still staring into her mystical eyes. She nodded yes.

They walked silently back to Tucker's camp. Tucker kept looking down at her. He couldn't understand the feelings that grew inside of him for this woman he hadn't even known for a whole day. He noticed she kept looking around. He knew that she was scared that the wolf would show up again. Once they returned to camp, he noticed his water pail was empty.

"I'm going to get more water from the river. I'll be right back," Tucker said as he picked up the pail and began to walk away.

"I'll come!" Kallie shouted and rushed to Tucker's side. It was then that Tucker realized that Kallie was completely afraid of being left alone, which was fine with him. They headed to the river, which was just a short walk down a slightly steep hill from Tucker's camp, following the worn-out path that was left by him over the past few years. There was a waterfall, about twenty feet tall and ten feet wide. Tucker bent to fill the water pail.

"Why did we have to go all the way to the other waterfall for me to get cleaned up? I could have done it here."

"I thought you would rather be somewhere more private."

He stood with a full pail of water. Kallie was looking at the forest on the other side of the river as she thought about how Tucker already seemed to be the most thoughtful person she knew. The other side of the forest seemed darker and thicker than the side she and Tucker were on. She noticed some strawberry bushes across the river. The strawberries were bright red. Kallie could smell them from yards away.

"Oh! Let's get some strawberries!"

She went to step on a rock to get across the river. Tucker quickly stuck his arm in front of Kallie, stopping her from going across.

"You cannot go on that side of the river . . . ever," Tucker said, his golden eyes locked on hers.

"Why?"

"Because that side is someone else's territory."

"Whose?"

"Don't worry about it."

"But doesn't that side lead to the village?"

"We will go around."

He began walking back to the camp.

"Go around? That's going to take days!" Kallie shouted.

"We don't know that yet."

He continued walking, Kallie following behind him.

They returned to Tucker's camp, where he found another bandage to wrap around Kallie's wrist.

"Come here," he said. She walked up to him and held out her arm, already knowing what he was going to do. He gently wrapped her wrist.

"How do you know what to do?" Kallie asked as she watched Tucker take care of her injury.

"My grandfather is the tribe's medicine man. I've learned a lot from him, over the years." Kallie liked how Tucker's warm hands felt on her skin, but Tucker ruined the moment.

"I'll try to find a way to the west village once your wrist is healed. It should be within the next few days."

"What do you mean, find a way? You don't know if we can get there or not?"

"Listen, in about two days, I will follow the river and see if we can make it to the west village without having to cross over to the other side of the forest."

"I don't understand why we can't go across the river. It's going to take days going all the way around. Can't we ask whoever is over there if we can travel through their side of the forest?"

Tucker didn't look her in the eye. He shook his head.

"If you don't want to go my way, you can go by yourself." He sounded annoyed, but he felt horrible after saying it.

Kallie didn't say a word. She just stared at him, her big, blue-green eyes full of disappointment. He hated that Kallie was mad at him. But if they set foot across that river, only bad things would happen. He wished he could tell Kallie this was to keep her safe. But he knew she wouldn't understand.

Kallie's anger faded throughout the day. All she wanted to know was what was so bad about the other side of the river, but Tucker made it clear he wasn't going over there.

As the sun began to set, Tucker started building a fire for the night. The stars came out, and Kallie had been staring up at them for quite a while. After a long silence between the two, Kallie finally broke it.

"There's a lot of stars out tonight."

Tucker had a huge smile on his face. He had almost forgotten how wonderful her voice sounded.

"You're not angry with me anymore?" he asked.

Kallie's smile disappeared. She had forgotten she was mad at him and that she wasn't speaking to him. That was one of the things she disliked about herself. No matter how angry someone made her, she could never stay mad at them long.

"I guess you are," Tucker said when Kallie didn't answer right away.

"No," she started to say. "I'm mad at myself for forgetting I was mad at you."

"You know, Kallie, you are different from most people," he said between laughter.

"Is that good or bad?"

"It's great."

They spent the early hours of the night sitting by the fire, learning everything they could about each other. Tucker learned that Kallie's favorite color was blue, and that she loved summer because she hated being cold. She also loved chocolate, but only got to have it a few times a year. Tucker had only tried chocolate once. But he agreed that it was the best-tasting thing in the world.

Kallie learned that Tucker also loved the color blue. His favorite season was autumn, because he liked when things finally cooled after a long, hot summer. They learned what things they loved more than anything and things they hated with a passion. They didn't notice that with each passing moment they were slowly falling for each other. Kallie had never had someone pay attention to her in this way. No one had ever asked her questions about herself. Tucker was the first person to ever truly get to know her. It almost made Kallie feel pitiful. The person who knew her best was someone she had met the day before. Minnie, her only friend back at home, had been busy with her own life, which gave Kallie too much time alone.

There was hardly a moment of silence during Kallie and Tucker's conversation. Once there finally was, Tucker couldn't help but do what he had been waiting to do since the moment he first saw her. They were sitting close together. Tucker was staring down at Kallie. She glanced up at him. She couldn't tear herself away from his glowing, golden-brown eyes.

Tucker slowly started leaning toward her. They were inches away from each other. Then Tucker paused for a moment, as if to give Kallie the chance to move away if she wanted to. But she didn't. For the first time ever, she truly wanted to kiss the man in front of her. Finally, Tucker lightly pressed his lips against Kallie's.

An amazing feeling ran through both of their bodies, as if their hearts had gone soaring through the universe together. They felt like they were meant to be in that exact moment. They continued kiss-ing each other as Kallie wrapped her arms around Tucker's neck, and he wrapped his arms around her waist. Their bodies were pushed up against each other.

Tucker had a tight grip on Kallie's body. She could feel his heart beating through his chest, and wondered for a moment if hers was doing the same. Tucker then slowly moved his hand to Kallie's thigh, gently squeezing it. She wasn't sure if the warmth she felt was coming from him or the roaring fire in front of them. Their tongues were slip-ping in and out each other's mouths, both of them gasping for air in between. Tucker continued to move his hand farther up Kallie's thigh as the tension grew between them.

Kallie suddenly became aware of how fast she was falling for Tuck-er. She knew that once she reached the west village she would likely never see him again. She couldn't develop feelings for someone she'd had such limited time with. She didn't want this moment to end. She wanted to see what it would lead to, but she forced herself to pull away from Tucker.

"Everything all right?" Tucker asked, disappointment in his eyes.

"I just don't want to move too fast," she said with a fake smile. Tuck-er believed it. Their foreheads were pushed against each other.

"That's fine."

They sat under the stars, next to the fire. Tucker held Kallie close. Tucker could tell that Kallie was thinking hard about something. She wanted to kiss him again. She talked herself out of it for the rest of the night.

"You look tired. Want to go to sleep?" Tucker asked. She nodded.

They crawled into the tent, and lay down next to each other. Tuck-er had one arm wrapped around Kallie. He wanted more from her. He wanted to kiss her with even more passion than before. But she seemed like she wanted to take things slow, and Tucker wasn't sure just how far he would be able to take things with her without losing control of himself.

CHAPTER THREE

May 13th–18th, 1821

When Kallie opened her eyes the next morning, Tucker was inches from her face, still asleep. His right hand rested on her waist. She couldn't help but stare at his muscular body. He looked strong enough to snap her in half. He opened his eyes and Kallie smiled.

"Good morning," she said as she stretched her legs.

"Good morning."

Kallie felt her knees go weak when he smiled at her. She wanted him. She felt as if gravity pulled her toward him. She tried to talk herself out of it, but the feelings were too strong. She finally told her mind to shut up and let her heart lead the way. She moved in close to him, grabbed his face, and kissed him. He kissed her back with just as much passion. He gripped her waist, their tongues twisting and turning together.

Kallie threw herself on top of Tucker. She ran her fingers through his thick, dark hair. Their hearts were beating faster with each passing moment. They slipped out of their clothes as Tucker rolled Kallie off of him and lay on top of her. He left kisses all over her neck as she breathed short, rapid breaths. They were chest to chest as their bodies dissolved into each other. Kallie lightly traced her fingers over Tucker's back and arm muscles. Tucker grabbed Kallie's arms and pinned them beside her, being gentle with her sprained wrist. If Kallie was to make his adrenaline rush any more than it was, then his true self would force its way out. Kallie's mind was so preoccupied with what was happening between them that she wasn't even aware that she couldn't move her arms.

The next five days were filled with many similar moments like that. Kallie's thighs had become extremely sore from having Tucker between her legs so often. They couldn't even kiss each other without it leading to more. But they couldn't stop thinking about how they were getting closer to possibly never seeing each other again. They were forced to shove that thought deep inside themselves, trying not to let it get in the way of now.

"What happened with your aunt and uncle that made you want to leave your village?" Tucker asked Kallie as they were lying in the tent one morning.

Kallie didn't want to answer Tucker's question. She didn't even want to think about that day, and had been mentally struggling with it since.

"Just some money issues," she said sitting up.

"Is anyone going to come looking for you?"

"Only if there's some sort of reward involved," she mumbled and rolled her eyes.

"I just want you to be safe once you get to the west village."

"I will."

Kallie's wrist had healed. On the morning of the eighteenth, Tucker knew it was time for him to get them to the west village.

He didn't want Kallie to leave him. He wanted her to stay with him. But he knew it wouldn't be much longer until that thing on the other side of the river realized that Kallie was there, and it would no longer be safe for her.

"I'm going to try to find a way to the west village," Tucker said. "Stay here at the camp and don't go anywhere. I won't be gone long." He leaned down and kissed her on the forehead, the warm midafternoon sun beating down.

"I still don't understand how you're going to find a way," Kallie said.

"I'll run along the river, and see where it takes me."

"But the river goes for miles . . . it will take you forever."

"I'll be quick. Don't worry."

He turned and ran off to the river.

Kallie was sitting on a log, staring at the empty fire pit. She kept wondering about the other side of the river. Whoever was over there couldn't be that bad of a person. Maybe if she could find them and kindly ask if she and Tucker could travel through their territory they would allow it. She knew Tucker would be furious; she stood anyway and walked down to the river.

When she arrived at the river, the strawberries looked even better to her than they had a few days before. She decided on getting some strawberries first and then looking for whoever it was who lived on the other side of the river.

She saw a path of rocks a few feet in front of the waterfall. She began to hop across. When she had made it about halfway, she heard rocks tumbling down from above the waterfall. She looked up, and a huge boulder came rolling off the top of the waterfall above her.

Kallie wished she had listened to Tucker. She should have stayed at the camp, like he told her to. And now she was going to be crushed.

Out of nowhere, someone pushed her out of the way. The two of them went crashing onto the ground next to the strawberry bushes. Kallie had thought it was Tucker who saved her. But when she looked at the man lying on the ground next to her, she saw a man who looked nothing like him.

"Are you all right?" the man asked her. Kallie nodded and tried to figure out where he had come from, and who he was. He had bright, blue eyes that matched the sky and dirty-blonde hair. His skin looked almost grayish. He looked to be in his twenties. He appeared to be strong, like Tucker. Even through his shirt, Kallie could see that the man before her had extremely large muscles. He stood and held out his hand, to help Kallie up.

"I'm Jamison," he said, still holding her hand after she stood.

"I'm Kallie. Thank you for saving me."

She let go of his hand. Jamison smiled at Kallie like it was no big deal. He was wearing a white shirt and black pants with black boots.

"So, what is a pretty girl like you doing out in the middle of the forest?" he asked her, looking down into her eyes as he towered over her. Kallie could feel her cheeks turn red.

"I was looking for the person who lives on this side of the river." Kallie looked at his oddly colored skin.

"Well, I live on this side of the forest," Jamison said with a big smile.

"Is this your territory?"

"Yes."

"Well I have a question for you then. I am trying to get to the west village. I met the man on the other side of the river . . . Tucker." Kallie noticed Jamison's hands clench into fists when she said Tucker's name.

"He said he would help me get to the west village. But, he also said that we can't cross the river 'cause it is someone else's territory. So I was wondering if you would be kind enough to let us travel through your side of the forest." Jamison stared at her with a blank expression.

"Well . . . I would let you, but not him."

"Please. I really don't want to travel there by myself. Last time I tried that I went in a complete circle," Kallie pleaded.

"Well then I can help you get there. I promise I know the quickest way there; it would take less than two days."

Kallie looked into Jamison's bright blue eyes. She felt he was trustworthy. His eyes almost made her feel safe in a way.

"I'll have to think about it," she replied.

Jamison nodded his head. "Why do you need to go to the west village?" he asked.

"To live my life the way I want."

"I feel like you have more of a story to tell." Jamison chuckled.

Kallie told him about her awful aunt and uncle, and how she chose to run away. Then just as she was about to tell him about the bear and the wolf, Jamison's gaze darted across the river. His expression went from happy and relaxed to raging anger. Kallie turned and looked at what Jamison saw. She gasped. They both stood.

"Well it's about time! I've been expecting you!" Jamison yelled across the river to the giant wolf, which had once again appeared out of nowhere.

The wolf was staring Jamison down. Jamison stared right back at the wolf, until they charged at each other.

Kallie could not understand why Jamison was going to attempt to take on this beastly animal. The wolf and Jamison began fighting in the middle of the river, and Kallie realized Jamison was not normal. He punched the wolf, and the wolf went soaring through the air. The wolf got its revenge by throwing Jamison high into the air. Jamison stood back up like nothing had happened. They were wrestling in the shallow river, rolling all over, rocks rattling with every move.

Kallie didn't know what to do. She kept looking around for Tucker, but he wasn't showing up. She knew she needed to get out of there, before one of them went flying across the river and landed on her, or before the wolf decided to come after her instead. She hopped back over the river, and as she was about to exit the unsafe area it grew silent. The sound of splashing water had stopped, Jamison was no longer grunting, and the wolf had stopped growling. Kallie thought they had killed each other, until she looked over at them. Jamison's eyes were no longer blue, they were freakishly red, and he had sharp fangs hanging out of his mouth. Kallie already knew Jamison was much stronger than the average human, but now Kallie could see that Jamison was something completely different from the average human.

Tucker knew he could no longer keep his secret from Kallie. After looking Jamison up and down, Jamison looking away in shame, her eyes locked with Tucker's.

He knew that it was time. He transformed back to his human form.

The expression on Kallie's face was complete and utter shock.

"Well, she didn't know, obviously," Jamison said to no one particular.

"I'm leaving," Kallie said as she turned around and began walking back up to Tucker's camp to retrieve her things.

"Kallie, wait!" Tucker shouted as he chased her. Kallie kept walking, both of them leaving Jamison behind. "Just let me explain!" Tucker said as he followed her. Kallie entered the campsite and began to gather her things. Tucker grabbed the satchel from her hands and looked into her eyes. "Kallie, please don't leave," he begged. "Just let me explain this to you."

She sat on a log. Tucker sat beside her.

"Are you going to tell me what is going on, or no?" Kallie said.

Tucker didn't know where to begin. "My people call men like me moon wolves," he said.

"The term you are probably more familiar with would be werewolf."

"A werewolf? So you are half-man, half-wolf?"

"I wouldn't say 'half.' I'm either in the form of a man, or the form of a wolf."

"Why?"

"Why what?"

"Why can you transform into a wolf? What's the purpose?"

"I don't know the exact reason why. No one knows how this all got started. But it's been in my tribe for forever, I guess."

"So are there others like you?" She had been looking at the sky. Now she looked at Tucker.

"All the men in my tribe are wolves. I'm the alpha, that's why I'm out here all alone. It's my responsibility to protect my people—all humans, actually. We have very strong instincts and can sense danger moments before it happens. We can hear things that are miles away."

"Are you protecting humans from Jamison?"

"Yes."

"What is he?"

"A vampire."

"A vampire? You mean he drinks blood?"

Tucker nodded and glanced behind them.

"He kills people?"

She was frightened. Tucker kept looking over his shoulder. He nodded again. Then Kallie heard Jamison's voice.

"That's not true," he said as he entered Tucker's campsite. Tucker stood. Kallie looked at Jamison and couldn't believe he was a killer. There was something about him that made her feel safe.

"I live off of animal blood, instead of humans," Jamison said.

"What are you doing in my territory?" Tucker asked. He was angry.

"I knew you would be telling her lies about me." He didn't look away from Kallie.

"Return to the other side of the river, or I'll throw you over there," Tucker said.

"I was only wondering when Kallie wanted to leave for the west village."

"*What?* You can't go with him, Kallie! What if he tries to kill you?" Tucker's voice echoed through the forest.

"I have never killed a human before! And you know that!"

"Tucker," said Kallie, "Jamison said he can get me to the village in less than two days. The way you want to go will take too long." Kallie said this in a calming tone, trying to get both of them to stop yelling.

"I just told you he's a vampire. You still want to go with him?"

"He saved me. You were gone. If he wanted to kill me, he would have let that rock crush me."

Jamison smiled at her. Tucker's mind raced, to come up with some way to convince Kallie not to go with Jamison.

"That may be true, but please wait a few days. If he plans to kill you, he won't be able to wait more than a day."

Tucker moved closer to Kallie.

"Jamison, can we leave in a few days?" she asked.

"I can take you whenever you're ready."

"Thank you for saving me, Jamison!" Kallie shouted as he started to walk away.

"It was my pleasure," he said, a kind look in his eyes. Then he disappeared back to his territory.

The rest of the day, Kallie and Tucker were silent. Kallie was trying to take in everything that had happened. She had a hard time processing that werewolves and vampires were real. A million questions went through her mind. Once it grew dark out, Kallie finally spoke.

"Tucker?" she said as he poked the fire with a stick.

"Hmm?" he said, looking into the fire.

"Do your eyes glow when it's dark?"

She laughed at her own random question.

Tucker smiled. He moved closer to her, and pulled her into his arms. "How else would I be able to see in the dark?" He chuckled. Kallie's head was pressed up against his strong, warm chest.

"Are you always warm?"

"Yes."

"How strong are you?"

"I have the strength of twenty men."

"You said you're the alpha. Are you bigger and stronger than the other men in your tribe? Have you always been able to transform into a wolf? Or does it not happen until you're a certain age? How did you become the alpha? And is the birthmark on your chest meant to look like a paw print?"

Kallie was almost out of breath after asking so many questions. Tucker laughed at her curiosity.

"Yes, I am slightly stronger than the other men in my tribe. Around a boy's fifteenth birthday is when they can first change into a wolf. And the alpha gene is passed down through generations. Around my eighteenth birthday, my tribe realized I was growing stronger than the rest of them. That's when I became the alpha. And yes, the birthmark is in the shape of a wolf's paw. We all have one. Anything else you want to know?" Tucker kissed Kallie's cheek.

"That's all, for now," she said with a smile.

Tucker couldn't sleep that night. Kallie's head rested on his chest as she slept. He watched her all night, studying every detail of her body. He wanted everything about her to stay locked in his mind forever. He never wanted to forget a single thing about her.

He was glad he was able to convince her to stay a few more days. Now he had to come up with a way to get her to stay with him forever. He knew Kallie had to have real feelings for him. He only hoped her feelings were strong enough to make her want to spend the rest of her life with him.

Tucker had never felt heartbreak until now, and it was awful. It was the worst feeling in the world. Even though he could physically heal in seconds, if he got hurt, he knew this kind of pain wasn't going away.

CHAPTER FOUR

May 19th–22nd, 1821

It had been three whole days since Kallie met Jamison. She had been spending a lot of time with him. She told Tucker that she didn't want to be traveling with a complete stranger and that she wanted to get to know Jamison better.

Tucker laid wide awake in the tent late at night. Kallie had decided on leaving with Jamison the following morning and she still hadn't returned to the tent, to go to sleep. Tucker knew she was with Jamison again. Thanks to his many werewolf abilities he could hear them across the river, talking and laughing. He could hear every word.

"What's it like being a vampire?" he heard Kallie ask Jamison.

"Lonely," Jamison replied.

"Well, why are you out here all alone?"

"I thought I could meet a nice girl out here. Which I did."

Tucker knew that Kallie was probably smiling that adorable, shy smile that appeared when she was complimented. Tucker wished he couldn't hear them. He wanted it to stop. All he could do was hope he didn't have to hear them kiss or touch, and he hadn't—yet. He knew Jamison had to be developing feelings for Kallie, but he couldn't tell if Kallie had feelings for Jamison. He knew Kallie felt some sort of connection with him, and the only reason he could think of was that Jamison knew what it was like to feel alone. Kallie was from a village full of people, but she only had one real friendship, which was slowly fading. And Jamison had lived all alone in the forest since Tucker was a young boy.

Tucker woke up first on their last morning together. All the moments they'd had together in the past twelve days replayed in his mind: every kiss they had, every time they touched, the sound of her laugh, the feeling he got when he held her, the connection he'd felt with her since the moment he saw her running into his forest.

Kallie's eyes had finally opened. She'd smiled when she first saw Tucker, but her smile faded when she realized what day it was, her body flooded with a rush of both excitement and sadness. She was excited to continue her journey to the west village with Jamison, but she felt sick to her stomach thinking of leaving Tucker. Tucker had made her feel things that she had never felt. He knew more about her than anyone else back at home, and he made her feel like she mattered. Kallie had wondered if Tucker would ask her to stay with him, but she thought if he really did want her to stay, he would have asked her by now.

As they lay in the tent, staring into each other's eyes, Tucker knew he had to come up with some way to make Kallie want to stay with him. He just needed one more amazing moment with her, to prove to her just how every day with him could be.

"I'm going to go wash up, I guess," Kallie said as she sat up. Tucker could hear the sadness in her voice.

"I'll come with you," Tucker said as he followed Kallie out of the tent. She smiled. Tucker thought it might be the last time he ever saw her smile. They walked side-by-side to the same hidden waterfall to wash up. Both slipped out of their clothes, once they arrived. They stepped into the water together, then walked toward the waterfall. Once they were both under it, Tucker grabbed Kallie and pulled her into his arms. The water no longer felt cold to Kallie as she was wrapped in Tucker's warmth.

Tucker cupped Kallie's face in his right hand. He kissed her forehead, then her cheek, then her neck, down to her chest, then made his way up to her mouth. Tucker lifted Kallie off the ground, and she wrapped her legs around him. He pushed her up against the rock wall behind the waterfall. Kallie held on to Tucker as tightly as she could, while the water cascaded over them. The mood during this moment, however, was different from the mood of their past lovemaking. They usually felt intense excitement, but this time they were grieving over the relationship they stood to lose. Their sad, tender lips not wanting to separate, their bodies not wanting to release the grip, they held on to one another.

It was as if in that last moment they had said everything they needed to say to each other, without speaking a word. Kallie couldn't think of a better way of thanking Tucker for saving her, and helping her heal. And Tucker couldn't think of a better way to let Kallie know how important and special she was and always would be to him. Tucker hoped it was enough to make Kallie want to stay, but as he gently put her back down on the ground, she looked up at him, her eyes a dark green. Tucker waited for her to say something.

"I have to go," she said, as she began to walk out of the water, leaving Tucker alone under the waterfall. He was crushed. After everything, she still wanted to leave. He ran his hands over his face. He was so frustrated with her. He wanted her more than anything. He wanted to spend forever with her. He wanted to wake up next to her every morning, to spend the rest of his life loving her and making her happy. He was ready to drop to his knees and beg her to stay, but if she didn't want to she wasn't going to.

Kallie waited to hear Tucker ask her to stay. He finally came out of the water once she was dressed. He remained silent and didn't say a word; he wouldn't even look at her. Kallie thought maybe he was glad to be finally getting rid of her. Maybe she didn't mean anything to him.

Then all sorts of crazy thoughts began flooding her mind. She wondered if Tucker did this with all of the women who came passing through the forest. Maybe he would antagonize the bear to make it charge after them, then help them heal from whatever injury they got. Then he convinced them to stay a few days, as he secretly got them to fall in love with him, then he had some sort of arrangement with Jamison to take the girl off his hands.

Kallie honestly thought this could be true. Tucker made it seem like he had strong feelings for Kallie, but Kallie thought her feelings for him must be stronger, because if he felt the same he would want her to stay with him.

But then, Kallie finally realized Tucker couldn't have had all of that planned out. No other women were crazy enough to go running into a forest that goes on for miles, alone, to avoid marrying rich men with bad attitudes. The negative thoughts of Tucker began to disappear, but the thought of Tucker not having strong feelings for her stuck.

They passed through Tucker's campsite one last time. Kallie gathered her things. Tucker escorted her down to the river, where Jamison was waiting on the other side with a smile. Tucker and Kallie stood at the edge of the river, and they looked at each other one last time. They could see the pain in each other's eyes. They were both debating whether they should say how they truly felt. They wanted to tell one another that what they had together meant so much more than a one-time fling to them; that it was real and something they wouldn't ever forget, even if they tried. Kallie stood on her toes to kiss Tucker one last time, their bodies pressed together as they gripped onto one another.

"Thank you for everything, Tucker," Kallie said as her eyes filled with tears.

"You don't have to thank me for anything," he replied. He held her hands in his as a tear ran down her cheek. He wiped it away. Jamison was just a few feet away, still waiting for Kallie. Kallie turned away from Tucker as she started to walk away, her hand slipping out of his the farther she went, until they were no longer touching, and she was no longer in his territory of the forest.

"I'll keep her safe, Tucker," Jamison said as Kallie entered his territory.

Tucker didn't have anything else to say. Kallie wouldn't let herself turn around and look at Tucker; she knew that if she did she would have a breakdown. While Tucker stood on his side of the river, he watched the woman he was most likely in love with slowly disappear into the forest with his worst enemy. His mind was telling him to turn around and go back to the camp, but his heart wouldn't let his feet move. The only direction he wanted to go in was after her.

Once he could no longer see them, he jumped over the river onto Jamison's side. He knew it was wrong, he knew he shouldn't follow them, but he couldn't help it. He had to know that Kallie was safe, and that nothing would harm her. He knew Jamison wasn't going to kill Kallie, but he wasn't sure how well Jamison could protect her from danger. Tucker had caught up to them, but he made sure to stay back far enough and hidden so neither of them would see him.

Jamison and Kallie walked to the sound of nothing but crunching leaves and chirping birds. Jamison could see that Kallie was trying to hold herself together. Her hands were shaking. He wanted her to feel safe and comfortable with him, like she felt with Tucker. He wanted to prove to her that he was better than Tucker.

Jamison had no idea why he felt so drawn to Kallie. They did not know much about each other, but Jamison could sense there was something special about Kallie. There was something about her eyes that seemed familiar. He knew he had looked into blue-green eyes like hers before.

Jamison kept glancing over at Kallie, and each time she looked closer to bursting into tears. He didn't want to see her like this anymore. He grabbed her hand and held it in his as they walked. Tucker saw this. He hoped Kallie would let go of Jamison's hand, but she didn't. As her fingers intertwined with Jamison's, she could feel herself calm down. She was finally able to breathe again, her heart stopped racing, and the urge to cry disappeared. Kallie wondered how just holding Jamison's hand had had this much of an effect on her.

"Are you doing alright?" Jamison finally asked her.

"Yes. I'm fine," she answered with a faint smile.

They walked in silence a little longer. Tucker still followed behind them, which Jamison knew but ignored. He wanted to get to know Kallie more, and acknowledging Tucker following them and starting another fight with him for crossing over to his side of the forest would interrupt his time with Kallie. So he continued to ignore the fact that they were being followed. Jamison wanted to know how Kallie truly felt about Tucker. Did she have real feelings for him, or did she only fall for him because he had rescued her?

"How do you feel about werewolves?" he asked, still holding her hand as they walked.

Kallie let out a laugh.

"Your laugh is the best thing I have ever heard," he said with a smile. Kallie looked up at Jamison with smiling eyes.

"They're definitely different," she answered.

"Well, I'll just make sure you are aware of it now. Vampires are much better than werewolves." He almost whispered this.

"And why's that?" Kallie asked.

Jamison didn't answer right away.

"You can't think of a reason, can you?" she said as he searched his mind for something that would prove his point.

Tucker could hear their conversation, and had already come up with ten reasons why werewolves were better.

"I don't change into something else. I'm always myself," Jamison finally said, sounding unsure.

"But your eyes change red, and you have fangs that disappear, somehow," Kallie said.

Jamison laughed. "That is true."

"Where are your fangs?" she asked.

"They only descend when my adrenaline is rushing, the same as when my eyes turn red."

"Is that all that makes you different? Besides the blood drinking?"

"I'm a lot stronger than any human."

"Oh, right, I could see that when you were fighting Tucker."

"I have strong instincts. I know things are going to happen moments before they do."

"So, you and Tucker really aren't that different."

Tucker wanted badly to yell out his thoughts on that.

"What makes you say that?" Jamison asked.

"You both have incredible strength, both have strong instincts. And . .
. oh! You both completely hate each other, probably for no reason." She
laughed when she said the third thing they had in common. Jamison
stopped dead in his tracks, Kallie's hand slipping out of his as she continued to walk. He was trying to make sense of what Kallie had just said.
He tried to think of a difference between him and Tucker.

"I think my age and Tucker's age make us very different," Jamison
said, catching up to Kallie, grabbing her hand again once he was next
to her.

"Why? How old are you?" Kallie asked, thinking he was going to say
twenty-something.

"217," he answered.

Kallie's eyes went wide.

"I don't age. I will look like this forever," he confessed.

Kallie was at a loss for words.

"Have you ever even heard of vampires and werewolves before you
came into this forest?" Jamison asked.

Kallie nodded. "I've heard the legends and tales everyone has heard.
I've read some books that mention them. I honestly never thought any
of it could be true."

Jamison explained to Kallie how most vampires will kill humans for
their blood, but he had never tasted human blood. He didn't want to kill
anyone, ever. His whole vampire life, he had only hunted animals and
drunk their blood. He said the older a vampire gets, the less sleep they
need, so he only slept once in a while, for a few hours. He ate food now
and then, but didn't need to.

Kallie kept looking up at Jamison as he talked. She felt like she could
get lost in his bright blue eyes for days. She noticed that when Tucker
would speak about werewolves, he had this sort of proud look on his
face, like he was proud to be a part of something so amazing and get to
protect his people. But she could see that Jamison did not feel the same
way about being a vampire. Jamison looked ashamed.

Tucker could see that Kallie was growing interested in Jamison. He
wondered how she could look so sad and heartbroken about never see-

ing him again, but then look so happy holding Jamison's hand not long after they said good-bye. Tucker could feel his heart breaking as the day went on. He thought about turning around and going back to his side, because he was terrified to find out what was going to happen between Kallie and Jamison. But he felt like he needed to stay and make sure no harm would come to her.

As the day went on, Kallie and Jamison grew closer to each other. Jamison could have sworn he was already in love with her. He couldn't stop looking at her eyes, while she talked to him about her life back at the village. Jamison listened to every word as he tried to figure out what color her eyes were. It was like one side of her eyes was blue and the other side green. He wanted to grab her and kiss her so badly, but he had to fight the impulse. He knew if he did what he wanted, Tucker would ruin their perfect moment.

Kallie had confessed to Jamison how alone she had felt her whole life; had told him that even though every man she knew had practically thrown themselves at her, she still felt empty and alone inside. Jamison knew exactly how she felt. He had been alone for a very long time, and had gone years hardly speaking to anyone. But hiding out in the forest was the safest place for someone like him, aside from the werewolf across the river. The only thing Kallie did not mention to Jamison was that ever since she'd met Tucker her lonely feeling had gone away.

The sun was setting when they arrived at the camp Jamison had set up for them earlier that morning. He had built a fire pit with plenty of wood to last through the night, and two soft-knitted quilts for her to sleep with. Jamison started building a fire.

"Thank you for doing all of this for me, Jamison. It's really thoughtful of you," Kallie said with a sincere smile as Jamison lit the fire.

It had grown dark outside, and Kallie was tired after walking all day. She and Jamison lay on top of one blanket and covered themselves with the other. Kallie was looking up at the sky. There wasn't a cloud in sight. The moon was big and bright, and there had to be over a thousand stars. Kallie could have stared up at it all night, and Jamison could have stared at her all night.

He saw she was shivering. "Come here," he said, extending his arms. She scooted closer to Jamison. He wrapped his arms around her and she lay her head on his chest.

Jamison didn't feel as warm as Tucker did. He felt normal. She tried closing her eyes to fall asleep, but the fact that she was cuddling with a vampire, whose kind usually killed humans, made it difficult to fall asleep. When she remembered that if Tucker didn't think Jamison was safe, then he wouldn't have let her go with him, it helped her feel more comfortable. She missed Tucker, though. She missed his warm body against hers. Eventually, she fell asleep snuggled up to Jamison.

Tucker hated what was happening right in front of him. He could see that Jamison did truly care for Kallie. Once, every now and then, Jamison would get up, trying his best not to disturb Kallie as she slept, and throw another log on the fire.

Tucker changed into a wolf. That way, he wouldn't need to sleep, and could watch over Kallie.

Jamison continued to hold Kallie through the night, trying his best to resist the urge to kiss her. That was all he'd wanted to do, since the moment he first looked into her eyes. He knew that if he kissed her, Tucker would come storming out from his hiding spot and wake up Kallie.

Jamison didn't want anything to bother her as she slept. She looked absolutely beautiful.

CHAPTER FIVE

May 23rd, 1821

As the sun began to rise, so did a horrible feeling in Tucker's gut. He could sense that something horrible was going to happen. He didn't know what, or when. He decided to stay in wolf form, so he could save Kallie the second that danger struck.

Jamison usually watched the sunrise every morning. Not this time. Kallie looked more beautiful than any sunrise he'd seen. But as Kallie began to wake up, Jamison quickly turned to look up at the sky. He didn't want to make it obvious that he'd been watching her sleep.

Kallie expected to see Tucker when she opened her eyes. But a smile appeared on her face when she saw Jamison lying next to her.

"Morning, beautiful," he said to her as she sat up.

Kallie felt her knees go weak. He looked so perfect, lying there, one arm behind his head, muscles flexing. Kallie was surprised he hadn't tried to kiss her yet. He was the only man to ever take this long to try and kiss her. Kallie started to wonder if Jamison actually didn't see her in a romantic way, like every other man had. Maybe complimenting her so often was his way of speaking.

They stood. Jamison folded the quilts and packed them. He poured water on the fire and the two of them continued their journey to the west village.

"When do you think we will arrive?" Kallie asked Jamison.

"Hopefully before sunset tomorrow."

Kallie began daydreaming about her new life. She thought about all the new people she would meet. She pictured herself having a group of friends and meeting a wonderful man she could spend forever with. She was going to miss Jamison, though.

She missed Tucker terribly; her heart still ached at the thought of him. She would never let herself forget either of them, or what they did for her. If it hadn't been for them, who knew what would have happened to her.

When the afternoon arrived, Tucker's bad feeling grew stronger. He followed more closely behind them, since he wasn't sure what was going to happen. Jamison felt annoyed. He wished Tucker would go away. He only had a little more than a day left with Kallie. He was hoping he could come up with some way to make Kallie want to stay with him. He was falling just as hard for her as Tucker had, but he was trying his best not to let it show, with Tucker still around. Jamison wasn't ready to let go of Kallie yet; he felt he might never want to let her go. He knew he had to make his move on her soon, whether Tucker was there or not.

"You suppose your aunt and uncle are looking for you?" Jamison asked Kallie.

"Most likely no. If anything, someone could have offered a big reward for anyone who finds me. That would be the only reason anyone would search for me." She sighed.

"You know, you deserve so much better than that, Kallie." Jamison stopped walking and turned to look at her. He stared deeply into her eyes, her orange waves of hair blowing in the gentle breeze. Kallie stared right back at him. He had a strange look on his face.

Jamison seemed to be the type of person to always say what was on his mind, until now. Kallie had no idea what he was thinking. He began moving in closer. Kallie took a step back from him, not sure what he was doing. He was inches from her face.

"This is where you kill me . . . isn't it?" Kallie said with nervous laughter.

He smiled, then shrugged his broad shoulders. "Maybe," Jamison said as their lips met. Their mouths were opening and closing together, as their arms pulled their bodies close together. Jamison lightly bit Kallie's bottom lip, and shivers ran down her spine. He pushed Kallie against a tree. As their tongues explored each other's mouths, Kallie's dress started slipping off her shoulder. Jamison's lips left Kallie's and traveled down her neck to her shoulder, across her chest, back up her neck, then again to her lips.

Jamison knew his eyes had turned red. He could feel his fangs trying to pop out. They both opened their eyes at the same time. Kallie could see Jamison's red eyes. Jamison thought it would frighten her, but it didn't. She continued to kiss him like it was nothing. She ran her hands over his muscular chest, and down to his abs, counting all eight of them. Jamison's adrenaline rushed more as Kallie ran her fingers down his body, which was making it even harder to keep his fangs in. He grabbed her arms and pinned them to her sides. It reminded Kallie of Tucker. He also did that every time she ran her hands over his body. She almost felt guilty for kissing Jamison, but she was never going to see Tucker again, and after tomorrow she would never see Jamison again, either.

Tucker's heart shattered like a piece of glass. He thought to himself that this must have been what the horrible feeling was about. He hated seeing Kallie with another man—especially with the man he hated more than anything. Kallie was his, then Jamison came and stole her. Tucker and Kallie had only met two weeks before, but he felt like he loved her, and Kallie had felt the same way. Out of everyone in the whole world, Tucker knew her best.

Tucker couldn't watch anymore. He didn't want to see what would happen next. He changed back into human form and headed to his territory. He began walking back, dragging his feet and staring at the ground. That bad feeling grew stronger with every step he took. He wanted to rip every tree he passed out of the ground and whip it at Jamison for causing him all this pain.

Kallie and Jamison's magical moment had finally come to an end. They continued walking. Jamison had a huge smile on his face. He'd finally gotten to do what he had been dying to do, and Tucker had finally gone, which made Jamison even happier.

"Are you thirsty?" Jamison asked Kallie. She nodded. "Let's head this way," he said as he guided her with his hand on the small of her back. "There's a stream over there."

They reached the stream. Jamison got a bad feeling in the pit of his stomach. He looked around at their surroundings, trying to find what caused this. Kallie was bent over the stream, drinking the water cupped in her hands.

"We have to get out of here." Jamison sounded worried.

"Just one more sip," Kallie said.

"No, we have to leave now!" Jamison shouted. Then out of nowhere Kallie felt someone grab her. She screamed at the top of her lungs. He was squeezing her so tight, she could hardly breathe. She felt hot breath on her neck. Jamison looked horrified.

"No!" Jamison yelled.

Tucker was only a few miles away from his side of the woods. That bad feeling hadn't gone away, it had only grown worse. He thought this must be what heartbreak felt like. He had never had his heart broken, until he met Kallie. He was still walking slowly. Then he heard a scream.

He knew it came from Kallie. He transformed into a wolf and took off. Following the path that Kallie's scream had traveled, he hated himself for leaving her alone with Jamison. He should have listened to what his instincts tried to tell him. The closer he got, the more he could sense what was happening. There were four vampires, not counting Jamison. And Kallie was in danger.

"Samuel, let her go," Jamison said to the one who held Kallie. Then three more people, with the same grayish skin as Jamison, appeared. It was like they had come out of the trees. There was a man and woman, who looked to be in their fifties. There was a girl who looked almost twenty.

"Oh, come on, Jamison. Your brother's hungry. We've come a long way," the older woman said. The ground began to shake. It reminded Kallie of what had happened right before Tucker appeared when the bear was coming after her. *Please be Tucker*, she thought to herself. The person holding Kallie released her.

"You haven't killed that werewolf yet?" the older man said to Jamison, looking angry. The ground was shaking more and more with each passing second.

Tucker came flying off a cliff. He didn't slow down, but went right after the vampires. All four of them took off running in the opposite direction. Tucker followed close behind them. Once everyone was gone, Jamison pulled Kallie into his arms.

"I'm so sorry, Kallie. I promise I won't ever let anything hurt you." He looked into her eyes. He could see she felt confused and scared. Tucker had come back and was walking up the stream. Neither of them had noticed him yet. Jamison softly kissed Kallie on the forehead. She opened her mouth to speak, but she couldn't find the words to say.

"Why was Tucker able to scare them away so easily?" she finally said.

Jamison didn't say anything right away. He didn't want to explain it. He was surprised that after everything that had happened, this was her first question.

"Werewolves are stronger than vampires," he answered.

"Oh, finally you admit it!" they heard Tucker yell.

Jamison rolled his eyes. A smile spread across Kallie's face the moment she heard Tucker. She turned around and ran to Tucker with her arms wide open. They hugged each other tightly.

"Thank you, Tucker," she said to him.

"Anything for you," he said, then kissed her head while holding her in his arms.

"Are they gone?" Jamison asked Tucker.

"Yes . . . I chased them all the way out. Come on, Kallie, I'll take you the rest of the way."

"What?" Jamison asked with a look of anger and confusion.

"You can't protect her. I will take her the rest of the way."

Jamison's eyes started turning red. "You didn't even give me a chance!" He walked toward Tucker, his hands clenched in fists. He shoved Tucker.

"Is that the problem, Jamison? What were you going to do next, if I didn't get here?"

Tucker said, stumbling backward. Jamison swung and punched him in the face. Tucker pushed Jamison as hard as he could, and Jamison went sliding across the ground.

Kallie's body felt strange. Her head began to hurt, and she felt like her legs could no longer hold up her body. She was going to collapse any second. She had goose bumps all over her body, and could feel the back of her neck sweating. Then her vision started fading away.

She could hardly hear the men yelling at each other. Everything was gray and fuzzy, then all she saw was black. Her knees gave in and she began to fall.

Tucker and Jamison stopped their arguing. They had both noticed Kallie collapsing to the ground. Both rushed to her side and caught her right before she hit the ground. Tucker picked up Kallie and held her in his arms.

"Kallie! Kallie! Can you hear me?" Tucker shouted, hoping she would open her eyes. But nothing happened. Jamison felt her forehead.

"She's burning up . . . bad," he said.

"I have to get her to my tribe," Tucker said. Both of them tried to think of the fastest way to get there.

"How about you change into a wolf? Kallie and I can ride on your back. I'll hold her up."

Tucker looked at him like he was crazy. "I'm not going to let you ride on my back like I'm some sort of horse."

"How else are you going to get her there fast enough?"

"How about . . . you don't come?" Tucker rudely suggested.

"Alright then, you carry her for miles—maybe you will get her there in less than four days. That is, if she doesn't die before then!" Jamison argued back.

Tucker looked down at Kallie's pale face as he tried to think of what to do. He finally handed Kallie over to Jamison, then transformed into a wolf. Tucker then walked over to a tree. Jamison was unsure of what he was doing, until Tucker growled and motioned his head for Jamison to walk over to him. Jamison placed Kallie on Tucker's back, and leaned her against the tree; then he climbed onto Tucker.

Tucker took off running through the forest as fast as he could. Jamison held on to Kallie as her body leaned against him. Jamison couldn't believe how fast they were going. Vampires could run fast, but not this fast. Everything they passed was a blur.

Tucker dodged every tree. They were jumping over creeks and soaring off of cliffs. They passed the river that separated their territory. Jamison thought they had flown through Tucker's campsite. He thought he saw a tent, but by the time he realized where they were, they were somewhere else.

As Tucker and Jamison rushed Kallie to Tucker's tribe, Kallie was having a strange, vivid dream. She was standing on a rock in the middle of the river, right in front of the waterfall. She was high enough that she could see all the way down the river. It led into a green valley. She heard something come from the right side of the forest. She looked over. Tucker was standing there, and he smiled at her. Kallie felt her heart skip a beat at the sight of him. Tucker's expression went from happy to angry. He was looking at something across the river. Kallie turned to see what it was. It was Jamison. His eyes were bright and blue. Kallie's knees went weak when their eyes met. The ground started shaking. Kallie could see the river cracking in half in the valley. The earth was breaking, and Kallie was standing right in the line of it. She heard Tucker and Jamison both yell, "Jump!" They held their arms out, to catch her. It was like everything moved in slow motion. The ground splitting, Tucker and Jamison yelling and motioning her to jump into their arms. She realized she had to choose one of them. She couldn't possibly choose either. The thought of having to pick one and leave the other behind seemed more painful than falling into the crack that traveled toward her. She couldn't choose.

They had arrived at the edge of the forest. Tucker's tribe lived in a wide-open field where the forest ended. There was a small village off in the distance. A dirt road separated it from the Indian reservation. The sky had been bright and sunny all day, until now. It grew dark and gray. Storm clouds came rolling in.

Jamison climbed off of Tucker. He slid Kallie off with him and held her in his arms.

Tucker transformed back into human form. Jamison passed Kallie over to him. There was a bright flash of lightning, followed by roaring thunder. Tucker was about to walk out of the forest with Kallie.

"I'm going to stay here," Jamison said before Tucker left.

Tucker turned around to face Jamison. "Why?" he asked.

"I want to make sure she's all right. It will torture me, to not know how she's doing, if I leave."

It started getting very windy. Tucker knew what Jamison meant. He couldn't blame him for wanting to stay. He knew this wasn't the time to start an argument.

"Don't come too close to the edge of the woods. And stay hidden, or the others will sense you're here," Tucker warned him. Jamison shook his head and walked deeper into the forest. It started raining. The winds picked up and lightning flashed. Thunder boomed through the forest.

Tucker carried Kallie out of the woods. Children were playing in the rain. When they noticed Tucker, they all started running to him, shouting, "Tucker is here!" As they got closer, they realized what Tucker was carrying, and they stopped running.

"We'll go get Edudu!" one of the older boys shouted. They turned around and ran to the teepees. Tucker's mother came rushing to him as he got closer.

"What happened, Tucker?" his mother asked as she approached him.

"She collapsed, her forehead is extremely warm," Tucker answered.

"Take her into our teepee. Hurry, get her out of the rain," his mother said, motioning to their teepee. Tucker rushed Kallie inside. They were soaking wet. He dried Kallie off with a quilt. Her dress was still soaked, so he took her out of it. The shift she had on underneath was dry. He wrapped her in a dry quilt and pulled her close, trying to keep her warm.

Tucker's grandfather, the tribe's medicine man, whom Tucker called Edudu, entered the teepee. "Where did she come from?" he asked as he started setting up his medicine supplies. It was raining so hard they had to yell at each other.

"She is from the east village. She ran away two weeks ago, and has been staying with me."

Edudu began examining Kallie. The wind crashed against the teepee.

"Why did she run away?" Edudu asked.

"I'm not exactly sure."

"Does she know?"

Tucker knew what he was talking about.

"Yes."

"Don't let your brother find out she knows about the wolf situation. If he does, he'll most likely force you two to get married."

Tucker looked down at Kallie and smiled.

"It seems like you wouldn't mind that," Edudu said, smiling.

"Has you-know-who discovered her yet?" he asked Tucker.

Tucker wasn't sure what to say.

"I'll take your silence for a yes," Edudu said.

"If she was involved with him, could that cause her to become ill?" Tucker asked. He hoped he could blame Jamison for this.

"Don't tell me. You and the vampire have both fallen for her . . . haven't you?" Edudu guessed.

Tucker didn't answer again. Edudu knew what that meant.

"Wow . . . well . . . I think that's the craziest love triangle to ever occur," Edudu mumbled to himself.

Tucker laughed. Edudu was right. Tucker knew he and Jamison both had strong feelings for Kallie. And they were both willing to do whatever it took for them to make Kallie theirs.

Werewolves and vampires are sworn enemies. The fact that they were able to work together and get Kallie to safety was remarkable. Vampires and werewolves never work together. All they try to do is kill one another.

"But Jamison is very different from other vampires. He's never tasted human blood. He's dedicated his life to protecting humans, just like we have. He is a good person, Tucker," Edudu explained, as he began throwing plants and herbs into a pot over the firepit, which wasn't lit.

"What's wrong with her?" Tucker asked Edudu, hoping Kallie would be all right.

"She has what the English call scarlet fever. Has she said anything about a sore throat recently?"

Tucker tried to recall if she had. Their last day together, she didn't say much. Tucker shook his head.

"Well, some people don't show symptoms at first. Anyway, she's going to be fine. Hopefully, she will wake up by tomorrow evening. She'll be back to normal in a few days. She has a rash on her back. We have to wait for it to clear up before she can leave. The same with the bumps in her throat." He finished mixing the ingredients in the pot.

"Start a fire. The mixture in the pot will help her fever go down. And you should go tell the vampire she's all right. I can sense his presence from here . . . he's worried about her, too. Did she hit her head when she collapsed?" Edudu gently opened Kallie's eyes, checking for a concussion.

"No, I caught her before she hit the ground."

Edudu's eyes grew wide when he looked into Kallie's eyes.

"Huh," he said, as he grabbed his belongings and started to leave the teepee.

"What?" Tucker asked.

Edudu was already outside. Tucker followed him. The rain and wind had slowed, and there was thunder in the distance.

"What was that about?" Tucker asked.

Edudu turned around to face him. "Are her parents alive?" he asked Tucker.

"No. They died when she was young."

"Do you know what happened to them?" Edudu asked.

Tucker shook his head no.

Edudu whispered as quietly as he could, "Jamison saved her life, the night her parents died. A home in the east village caught fire, late one night, about seventeen years ago. We tried to get there as fast as we could. When we arrived, Jamison had made it there before us. He was carrying Kallie out of the house. She was holding onto him tightly. She was screaming and crying. The sound of it would have broken your heart. He put her on the ground, then went running back in, to try and save her parents, but the whole house came crashing down. He knew Kallie was too close to the house. The debris could have harmed her. He came running back out and threw himself on top of her, to protect her as the house collapsed. Then he saw us. He carried Kallie to us. She was crying hysterically. She didn't want to let go of him. He said the adults were already dead when he got there, that he only went running back in to show her he tried to pull them out. The townspeople finally came out, and Jamison ran back into the forest. We gave Kallie to two people who claimed to be her aunt and uncle."

"How do you know it was her?" Tucker asked, not wanting to believe the story.

"I would know those eyes and that color hair anywhere," Edudu explained.

Tucker didn't know what to do with this new information. If Kallie found out that Jamison saved her when she was a little girl, she would definitely want Jamison more, Tucker thought.

"Why hasn't Jamison told her this yet?" Tucker wondered aloud. He looked to Edudu for an answer.

"Maybe he hasn't realized it's her yet," Edudu said, then continued walking away.

Tucker returned to Kallie. He kissed her forehead, then softly whispered, "I think I'm in love with you." He held Kallie all evening, debating whether he should tell her what he had learned.

Night arrived. Tucker's parents decided to sleep in his brother's teepee with his family, so they wouldn't disturb Kallie. Edudu entered the tent to check on Kallie one last time before going to sleep.

"Can you stay here with her for a little while . . . so I can go talk to him?" Tucker asked.

"Are you going to tell him what I told you?" Edudu asked.

"No. Why would I tell him something that would make him seem better than me?"

"Tucker, you were only six years old when that happened. What could you have done? I know your brother and your cousins have been trying to convince you that you have to kill Jamison, ever since you became the alpha, but they didn't see the true side of Jamison that I, your father, and your uncles saw, the night of the fire. I know that Jamison is truly good."

Tucker left the teepee when Edudu had finished his speech. Edudu looked at Kallie as she continued sleeping and whispered to her, "He really likes you." He chuckled at himself.

Tucker sneaked around the teepees and made his way to the forest, to tell Jamison that Kallie would be fine. He hoped Kallie didn't wake up while he was gone. He knew she would be terrified, waking up in a new place with someone she didn't know.

Jamison had climbed to the top of the tallest tree he could find. He had been up there through the whole storm, swaying back and forth as the treetop moved with the wind. He kept his eyes on the teepee he knew Kallie was in. Then he saw Tucker run into the forest. Rain was still falling.

"Jamison!" Tucker shouted in a whisper. He didn't want any of the other werewolves to hear him searching for the vampire.

"Jamison!" he shouted again. Jamison dropped from a tree and landed on his feet, right in front of Tucker.

"How is she?" Jamison asked as soon as they were face-to-face.

"She has scarlet fever. She's still asleep. My grandfather said she should wake up sometime tomorrow evening, and she should be back to normal in a few days." Jamison felt relieved to know that Kallie would be all right.

"Let me know when she wakes up . . . please," Jamison said.

"I will."

Tucker was staring at Jamison, like he had much more to say to him. And he did. But instead he turned around to go back to the teepee.

CHAPTER SIX

May 24th, 1821

Tucker woke to the sound of pouring rain. He glanced over at Kallie. She still hadn't woken up. She hadn't even moved. She was in the same position that Tucker had laid her down in. He pressed his forehead against hers. He held her face in his hands, his thumbs stroking her cheeks. Although Kallie was right in front of him, he missed her. He missed her voice and her smile. He missed the sound of her laughter.

Jamison was at the top of the same tree. He had been there all through the night. It was raining on and off, all night long, and he was soaking wet. But he dealt with it, and watched where Kallie was, waiting for her to wake up. He also missed her. He was jealous of Tucker. Tucker got to hold her and sleep next to her, while Jamison froze in the rain at the top of a tree.

He wanted to be the one to hold Kallie. He wanted to be the first thing she saw when she finally opened her eyes. But Tucker would be there instead.

The rain had turned to a light drizzle. Tucker's mother walked into the teepee. She carried a plate of food, and handed it to Tucker.

"I cooked breakfast for you," she said as Tucker took the plate from her.

"Thank you," Tucker said with a smile, and sat up. His mother sat down. Tucker began eating.

"You have feelings for her . . . don't you, Tucker?"

He sighed and said, "I do."

"Have you told her yet?" she asked.

"About being a wolf?"

"No. Does she know that you love her?"

"I—" Tucker started to say. His mother interrupted him.

"Does she have feelings for you?" she asked.

"I hope." He didn't sound optimistic. Edudu came inside and added more stuff to the pot over the fire. He checked on Kallie. Tucker had finished eating.

"How is she?" Tucker asked Edudu.

"Her temperature has gone down . . . she'll wake up soon."

"She's going to be hungry. I'll start making soup," his mother said, and walked outside, Edudu following.

The gray clouds were moving out, and the rain had finally stopped. Tucker's mother had come in the teepee with all the ingredients for the soup and began cooking it in another pot over the fire. Tucker hadn't left Kallie's side. He could tell the sun was starting to shine. He could hear the members of his tribe gossiping outside the teepee. They were talking about how he had shown up with a sick girl the day before, her hair the color of fire.

As it became late afternoon Tucker noticed Kallie finally shifting into a new position. He hoped she was going to wake up. She kept tossing and turning.

As she started to wake up, she could smell something amazing. She also had a headache and stomachache. She was starving and wanted to eat whatever made that wonderful smell. But her throat hurt too badly to eat anything right then. She opened her eyes. She wasn't sure where she was, but she recognized the heavy arm that was wrapped around her waist. It was Tucker. She turned to look at him. She had never seen him look so happy.

"How do you feel?" he asked as she looked around, trying to figure out where they were. Kallie groaned and asked, "Where are we?" Her throat burned as she spoke.

"At my tribe's reservation. Do you remember what happened?" Tucker asked. Kallie's head was pounding. She continued talking with her eyes shut.

"I remember those other vampires . . . and then you and Jamison were arguing . . . and that's the last thing I remember seeing." She started to remember the odd dream she'd had about both of them.

"As we were fighting, you fainted. Jamison and I rushed you here."

Kallie was shocked to hear Tucker say the words "Jamison and I." It was such a simple phrase, but it sounded strange coming from Tucker's mouth. Kallie wondered how many times they must have argued with each other on the way. She was glad she was unconscious during it.

"Where is Jamison?" she asked Tucker, her eyes still shut. She thought he was going to say he had returned back to his side of the forest. She felt even more shocked when she heard him say what he said.

"He's hiding out at the edge of the forest over here."

Kallie almost wanted to open her eyes and check if it was still Tucker she was talking to. It didn't sound like him.

"Were those other vampires his family?" Kallie asked.

Family, Tucker thought to himself. *Jamison has a family?*

"Oh, I don't know, Kallie. I've seen them before . . . but only to chase them out of my territory." Kallie buried her face in Tucker's warm chest, and he softly rubbed her back as she fell back to sleep. He shut his eyes and also fell asleep.

Kallie woke again in the early evening. Her head and stomach felt better, but her throat still felt like it was on fire. She was starving, and whatever was cooking over the fire smelled even more appetizing than before. She sat up. Her movement woke Tucker.

"You look like you're feeling better," he said.

Someone else walked into the teepee. Tucker sat up and smiled when he saw who it was.

Before Kallie could turn to see who it was, Tucker said to her, "Would you like to meet my mother?"

"I'd love to," Kallie answered. She turned and saw a tall, thin woman with long, dark hair and tan skin. She looked like she was in her mid-forties. She was wearing a light-brown dress that stopped just below her knees. It had the outline of a wolf stitched on the front. She had a smile on her face.

"Kallie, this is my mother, Lydia."

Tucker's mother bent down and pulled Kallie into a hug.

"It's so nice to finally meet you, Kallie! Are you hungry? I made soup," Lydia said.

"It's nice to meet you, too. And yes, I'm starving," Kallie said with a smile.

Tucker's heart practically melted when he saw Kallie's smile. He felt like he hadn't seen her smile in forever.

As Tucker's mother was getting them bowls of soup, Edudu came walking in. "Oh, look who is finally awake," he said.

"Kallie, this is my grandfather. I call him Edudu. Edudu, this is Kallie."

"Does Edudu mean grandfather in your native language?" she asked Tucker. He nodded.

Edudu stuck his hand out for Kallie to shake. "Nice to finally meet you, Kallie. How are you feeling?"

"I've been better."

Tucker's mother handed both her and Tucker a bowl of soup. They thanked her and she left.

"Edudu has been taking care of you," Tucker explained to Kallie.

"Oh, right. You're the tribe's medicine man."

Edudu nodded. "You have scarlet fever, Kallie. But you seem to be getting better. I think you'll be back to normal within the next two days."

"Thank you for taking care of me," she said.

"It seems like Tucker was taking good care of you, too," Edudu said as he felt Kallie's forehead and the back of her neck, to make sure her temperature was going down. Then he switched the herbs out of the pot on the fire and put in new ones.

"What is that?" Kallie asked.

Tucker knew she had to be feeling better if she was back to her curious self.

"Different types of herbs and plants. The aroma they produce helps the fever go down."

"And they're only found at the top of the highest mountain in the forest," Tucker added.

"You have to be a wolf to get there. Did Tucker tell you who used to be the alpha before him?" Edudu asked Kallie.

She shook her head.

"Me," he said.

"You're the medicine man and you used to be the alpha?"

"And the chief," Tucker added.

"Who's the chief now?"

"My father is, but my brother is planning to take over within the next year," said Tucker.

"How old do you think he is?" Tucker asked Kallie, pointing at Edudu.

Kallie looked at Edudu, who smiled proudly. His hair was white, and he had wrinkles on his face. His voice was somewhat raspy.

"You look like you're in your fifties," she said, "but I have a feeling you are both trying to trick me . . . so you must be older."

Edudu and Tucker chuckled.

"I am eighty-five years old," he said.

"No!" Kallie said.

"I sure am."

"Then why do you look so much younger?"

"As moon wolves grow older, our aging process begins to slow down. Most of us can live past a hundred years, looking like we are only about eighty years old," Edudu explained.

"Have you started to age more slowly, Tucker?" Kallie asked.

"No. It won't begin until later in life," Tucker answered.

Kallie and Tucker had finished eating. Edudu went back outside. Kallie felt a little better now. Tucker thought about going to tell Jamison that Kallie was awake. But he didn't want to leave Kallie's side.

Tucker and Kallie had been lying next to each other all day. Kallie was staring at the hole in the top of the teepee that the smoke from the fire escaped from. The sun was setting.

Tucker could hear his mother in the distance. She was telling the rest of his family to come meet his future wife. Tucker chuckled, turned to Kallie and said, "You ready to meet my brother and father?"

Kallie's eyes grew wide.

"My brother cannot find out that you know about us being wolves," he said.

Seconds later, Tucker's mother and two other people were standing in the teepee. Kallie sat up.

"This couldn't wait till tomorrow," Tucker said to his family.

"It's all right, Tucker . . . I want to meet your family," Kallie said.

"This is my brother, Thomas, and my father, Arthur." They shook her hand, said it was nice to finally meet her, and that they could see that Tucker cared an awful lot about her. His brother and father looked a lot like him. They had the same bright, golden-brown eyes. Both were tall and strong, shirtless and wearing long pants, like Tucker. They even had that same paw print birthmark on their chests. His brother was in his late twenties, and his father was in his mid-forties, like his mother.

"So, we've heard you are traveling to the west village," his father said.

"We've been there before, it's a very nice village," his brother said.

"Good people there, too," his father added.

"That's what I've heard. I thought it would be a nice place for me to begin again," Kallie said.

"Well, we've also heard that Kallie is your future wife, Tucker!" his brother said, laughing. His parents also started laughing. Kallie felt her face turn bright red. Tucker quickly stood up.

"All right, time for you to go!" Tucker said, pushing them outside. Once they had all left, Tucker sat next to Kallie. "Sorry about that," he said.

"It's fine. It must be nice to have a family embarrass you."

"It is."

Tucker thought how, if Kallie and he did end up getting married, he could give her a family. And his family and tribe members would treat her like one of their own.

Before going to sleep, Edudu came to check on Kallie. While he was in the middle of checking the rash on Kallie's back, he and Tucker exchanged worried looks, their eyes glowing in the dim lighting.

"Is he being serious, right now?" Tucker asked Edudu. Kallie looked at them, confused.

"He's a brave man," Edudu said.

"What is going on?" Kallie asked. No one answered.

"I'll be back," Tucker said, then stormed outside.

"What is happening?" Kallie asked Edudu, looking at his big bright eyes, hoping he would answer her.

"You'll find out very soon," he said, laughing.

Tucker spotted him as soon as he stepped outside. They were heading right for each other.

"Jamison, are you trying to get yourself killed?" Tucker said, once they were face-to-face.

"She's awake, isn't she?" he said to Tucker, sounding angry.

Tucker didn't say anything.

"I asked you to tell me when she woke up!"

"Shh! If the others sense you are here, they will kill you!" Tucker shouted in a whisper.

"I think I can take them. Now, where's Kallie?" Jamison demanded.

"I will let her come see you tomorrow, now go back into the forest."

"I'll go back to the forest once I see her," Jamison said.

Tucker knew Jamison wasn't backing down. He turned around and went back toward the teepee. He knew Jamison would follow.

Tucker entered the teepee. Kallie looked at him, confused. Then she saw who was behind him. Her face lit up.

"Jamison!" she practically squealed.

"Shh!" Tucker and Edudu said at the same time.

"No one can know he's here," Tucker told her. Kallie stood as Jamison rushed to her. He wrapped his arms around her.

Tucker and Edudu kept looking at each other. Edudu tried to hold in his laughter from the unbelievable situation that Tucker had gotten himself into. Tucker tried his best to resist the urge to pull Jamison off of Kallie. He wanted to be the only one to hold Kallie. Jamison finally let go of her, and turned to face Edudu.

"Nice to see you again, sir," Jamison said to Edudu and shook his hand.

"Nice to see you, too, Jamison."

Kallie wondered how in the world these two knew each other.

"Time for you to go, Jamison. Someone is going to realize you're here." Tucker motioned for him to walk outside. Jamison walked up to Kallie, cupped her face in his hands, and kissed her on the forehead.

"I'll see you soon," Jamison said, then left. Tucker followed behind him, making sure he went back into the forest.

"How do you know Jamison?" Kallie asked Edudu while Tucker was gone.

"Back when I was the alpha, one day I sensed that there was a vampire somewhere in the forest. I went running in there, thinking I was going to have to kill this vampire that was probably planning to come after my people. When I got to him, he swore that he had never killed a human, and that he never would. He said he needed to stay in the forest. It was the best and safest place for someone like him.

"He promised to stay far away from the tribe and to never bother us. I could see how strong he was . . . I knew that if I even tried to fight him, I would lose. I have always been able to sense others' feelings. I can tell if people are happy or sad, or in love. I know if they are trustworthy or not. I sensed I could trust Jamison, and that he meant what he said. And he has yet to prove me wrong.

"Everyone thought I was crazy to allow a vampire into our forest. Tucker's brother Thomas still doesn't understand how I could let a vampire come near us. When Tucker became alpha, everyone begged him to stay in the forest and protect us from Jamison. Tucker is the strongest alpha we ever had. And he's also very good at sensing danger, or when someone is in trouble. But I know his instincts are also good at telling him who to trust. Or else he would have never told you about being a wolf. He also would never have left you alone with Jamison, or let Jamison stay close these past two days, if he didn't seem trustworthy."

Kallie said, "So, you and Tucker were both able to sense Jamison's presence . . . but the other wolves didn't sense him because they're not alphas?"

"Right. If he were to stay a little longer, they would know he was here. I could sense that he was close to us, when Tucker brought you here, but the others still have no clue. All werewolves have strong instincts, but the alphas have stronger instincts. We know when something big is going to happen sooner, we know who to trust, who is good and who's not. The rest of the wolves look to us for answers when there is an issue."

"When they were bringing me here . . . did you know we were coming?"

"I did. I knew that Tucker was bringing someone here he cared very deeply for, and that she would need my help."

"Thank you for helping me," Kallie said.

Tucker came walking in. Edudu told them good night then exited the teepee. Kallie yawned and lay down. Tucker came to join her. And just like always, Kallie fell asleep in Tucker's arms, as he fell asleep holding her.

Jamison spotted Edudu coming into the forest. He was with another man who looked a lot like Tucker but older. He figured it must be Tucker's father. They were both collecting firewood.

"Kallie's a star person isn't she? No one has eyes like that." the man said to Edudu.

"Yes, Arthur. She most definitely is," Edudu replied.

"And Tucker doesn't have a clue," said Arthur.

"I don't think she does either."

"What would she be here for?" Arthur questioned.

"Something that involves a werewolf and vampire working together obviously . . . " Edudu mumbled to himself.

"What did you just say?" Arthur asked even though he heard it loud and clear. Edudu remained silent.

"Tucker has been speaking to the vampire, hasn't he?"

"If that is the path the star people are leading them down, then we must let it be," Edudu reminded him.

"I know Jamison is not a bad person, it's Thomas I'm worried about," Arthur confessed.

"He just needs to be reminded that if he is to ever turn against the alpha he will lose the tribe."

And with that they exited the forest. Edudu turned and looked right at Jamison before leaving the forest, knowing that he had heard every word.

CHAPTER SEVEN

May 25th, 1821

Tucker's instincts woke him early in the morning. Something was coming. He got up without waking Kallie, then went outside. He started walking to the entrance of the reservation. He glanced behind him. All the other men were right behind him. They had woken with the same feeling.

Tucker reached the entrance. He stood on the edge of the dirt road, looking back and forth. Whatever it was, it was coming down the road any minute.

"What do you suppose it is, Tucker?" his brother Thomas asked as he stood next to him.

"A group of men. They're going to come from this way." Tucker pointed east. The rest of the men stood beside Tucker, watching the road.

They could hear a horse and carriage off in the distance. Then they could see it coming down the road. It began to slow as it neared the reservation's entrance. Then it stopped right in front of the group of men. There were four men in the carriage. They all looked to be in their early twenties. One man got up and stood on the edge of the carriage steps. He looked down at all of them.

"It's like you were all waiting for me," the man said with a laugh. Tucker and his men stared back at him, trying to figure out what he wanted.

"Oh! Do you even understand me?" the man asked and turned to the others in the carriage for help. They shrugged their shoulders. The man began to speak slowly and loudly, with lots of hand motions.

"I . . . am . . . looking . . . for—"

Thomas interrupted him.

"Actually," he said, "we speak English just fine."

All the men in the tribe snickered. The men in the carriage also started laughing. The man turned and gave them a mean look.

"I am looking for my fiancée. She has been missing for almost two weeks. We have checked our whole village and decided to start checking the surrounding areas. May I speak to the one in charge?"

Tucker's father stepped forward. "I'm the chief of this tribe," he said.

"Would it be all right if we took a look around?" the man asked.

Tucker's father looked to Tucker for the answer. Tucker shook his head no. The man gave Tucker a dirty look.

"Sorry . . . private property," Arthur explained.

"All right, then," the man began to say as he grabbed papers from another man in the carriage. He held up a poster for everyone to see.

"This is what she looks like. She has red hair and blue eyes."

"Most gorgeous woman you've ever seen!" one of the men in the carriage shouted out.

The first man rolled his eyes. "Her name is Kallie Davis. Has anyone seen her? Or heard of her?"

"No, we do not know of her," Tucker answered before anyone else could. He thought that Kallie seemed to be running from more than just her aunt and uncle. And Tucker's instincts were telling him that this man was not to be trusted.

"I will leave these posters with you," the man said as he gave the papers to Arthur.

"We are going to check the village over here, and then we are traveling to the west village to look there. If anyone happens to find her, please send someone to our village to tell her family. There is a $200 reward for anyone who finds her—though you men would probably rather get some corn, or something, instead of money."

Every man in the crowd did his best to resist launching himself at the man in the carriage for speaking to them in such a way.

"I think it's time for you to go," Tucker said, glaring. The man sat back down, and the carriage took off. Tucker watched the carriage ride away.

He could feel his heart breaking. He couldn't understand why Kallie would keep this from him. All he wanted to know was if Kallie was in love with that man or was she also running away from him? He turned around to find all his men staring at him.

"You never mentioned anything about her being engaged, Tucker," Thomas said.

"She never mentioned it either," Tucker mumbled.

"That man didn't seem trustworthy . . . Kallie must have a good reason for leaving him behind," Edudu chimed in.

"What are you going to do?" Thomas asked.

"For the first time ever, I honestly don't know what to do," Tucker answered.

"Whether it is him she is running away from or not . . . you must tell her that he is searching for her," said Arthur.

Tucker took the posters out of his father's hands and walked away to the big fire that was burning in the main fire pit in the center of the reservation. He yelled and tossed the posters into the fire as anger took over his body. But he kept one poster, folded it, and stuffed it into his pocket.

His mother approached Tucker as he was watching the papers with Kallie's picture burn.

"She's engaged," Tucker said as he took a deep breath trying to calm himself, but it was useless.

"And she never told you?" Lydia asked. He shook his head.

"Well then whoever she is supposedly engaged to must mean nothing to her."

"How could you know that?"

"'Cause I see how she looks at you, Tucker. If she looked at that other man that same way . . . then she wouldn't have been able to leave him." Tucker sat down on a log and dropped his face in his hands.

"Maybe you should ask her to stay with you . . . tell her your true feelings for her."

"And then what do I do when she rejects me?" Tucker asked, looking up at his mother.

"You can't think like that, Tucker. Maybe she feels just as strongly for you as you do for her. You're never going to know unless you try."

His mother walked away. Tucker remained seated, staring down at the ground. He had fallen in love with Kallie. He already had to worry about Jamison stealing Kallie's heart, but now another man might have already had Kallie's heart. Of course he wanted to talk to Kallie about this, but he was too angry to speak to her. Tucker stood and made his way to the forest.

As he got farther in, he called out, "Jamison," trying not to say his name too loudly. Jamison dropped from a tree and landed behind Tucker. He could sense that there was a problem.

"What's wrong? Is it Kallie?" Jamison asked Tucker.

"Yes, actually it is Kallie," Tucker began saying. "Did she ever mention anything to you about having a fiancée?"

"What? No."

"Well apparently she's engaged."

"That's impossible."

"How could it be impossible?" Tucker asked. "Some man showed up. Said he's looking for his fiancée and then gave us these," Tucker said, taking the poster out of his pocket and handing it to Jamison. Jamison unfolded the piece of paper.

"They got her eyes wrong," Jamison said. Kallie's name was in big letters under the word "missing." Under her picture it said, "$200.00 reward for anyone who finds her."

"What did you say to him?"

"Made it seem like I've never seen her before."

"Why?" Jamison asked, sounding surprised.

"I got nothing but bad feelings from this man," Tucker answered.

"Why wouldn't she say anything to either of us?" said Jamison. "She's only talked about how greedy her aunt and uncle are. But that doesn't seem like enough to make her want to run away. This man has to have something to do with it," Jamison suggested.

"That's what I keep telling myself. But I can't help but feel like a fool," said Tucker.

"And I thought you were going to be the only man I was going to have to fight for her." Jamison chuckled.

"I just hope this man hasn't put her in danger, and that's why she left," Tucker said.

It was silent for a while as both men let everything sink in. Jamison felt hopeless; he was never going to be able to win Kallie over. But, maybe if he offered protection from her so-called fiancée who could have caused her to leave her life behind, then maybe he could finally have her all to himself.

Then, at the same time, both men said, "I'm going to ask her to stay with me."

They looked at each other like they were about to kill each other. And they considered killing each other. But they both knew that if one of them did successfully kill the other, Kallie would hate them for the rest of her life.

Jamison sighed and ran his fingers through his hair. "I'm not going to argue with you about this. Tell Kallie what is going on. She will decide who she wants to stay with, and the other will have to step back. Or both of us will have to step back."

"Fine," Tucker said, then turned around and began to walk away.

"Did you just agree with me?" Jamison asked, sounding shocked and confused.

Tucker stopped walking. "This girl. She's making me do things I never thought I would. Even though she most likely has been lying to me this whole time."

"Agreed," Jamison said as Tucker resumed walking away.

Tucker was almost back to the teepee. As he got closer, he could hear giggling coming from inside. He wondered what was going on. As he stepped inside, he saw all the little girls in the tribe crowded around Kallie. A few were his nieces. She seemed to be in the middle of telling them a story.

"And then a big bear came out of nowhere!" she shouted at them.

"And Tucker saved you!" one of the little girls shouted back at her.

"He did," Kallie said. Her eyes met Tucker's as he walked in. She smiled.

"What is going on?" Tucker asked, trying to act natural.

"Kallie is telling us how you saved her," one of the other girls said.

"You must be feeling better." Tucker sat next to Kallie, avoiding eye contact with her.

"I am."

Kallie kissed his cheek.

"Ew!" all the girls shouted, laughing, as they covered their eyes.

Tucker spent the rest of the day away from everyone as he fought all the different emotions that were growing inside him. He was trying to think of how to handle the situation, but he was so angry and heartbroken that he couldn't even think straight. His heart ached at the thought of how he could possibly lose Kallie forever.

Kallie laid in the teepee alone most of the day. A few of Tucker's tribe members came and introduced themselves to her. His mother, father, and grandfather came to check on her every now and then, making it seem like Tucker was very busy during the day, although they knew he was off fighting with himself.

As evening came, everyone gathered around the fire in the center of the reservation. Lydia convinced Kallie to join them. She sat down next to Tucker who was trying to ignore her, but it was becoming more and more difficult as the night went on.

The tribe told all stories about their brave ancestors. Thomas would put a stop to any story that had to do with a wolf before the story could begin.

Kallie found the stories so interesting. She couldn't believe how brave this group of people was.

It had become late. Everyone went off to bed. Kallie and Tucker were sitting by the fire, alone.

"I can't believe all the things your people have done," she said, looking up at Tucker.

"This tribe has been through a lot," he said as he wouldn't let himself look at her.

"Why doesn't your brother want me to know about the werewolves?"

"He doesn't like the idea of any outsiders knowing about it."

"I won't ever tell anyone." Kallie looked up at Tucker waiting for a response, but he remained silent. "Is everything alright, Tucker? You seem different today."

"How does your throat feel?" he asked, ignoring her question.

"It still hurts, a little. Everything else feels fine," she said, staring at him, trying to read his emotions.

"We can leave tomorrow then," he said, not even wanting to think about what tomorrow might bring.

CHAPTER EIGHT

May 26th, 1821

Kallie couldn't wait to get to the west village. She impatiently waited for Tucker to wake up, her throat hardly hurting. Edudu came in, which woke up Tucker. Edudu checked Kallie's back to see if the rash from the fever was gone, and it was. He checked her throat to see if all the bumps were gone, and they were.

"Well, Kallie, you seem to be back to your healthy self," Edudu said.

She smiled and looked at Tucker.

"Let's gather our belongings," he said to her, avoiding eye contact.

Once they were ready to leave, they went to say their good-byes. Kallie thanked everyone for their kindness. She thanked Edudu for taking care of her. Everyone kept pulling Tucker aside, to say he needed to tell Kallie about the man searching for her. And he knew that. He just wasn't ready to let her go yet, even though he was completely furious with her. Tucker hugged his family good-bye. Edudu pulled him away one last time.

"If, for some reason, she ends up staying with you or Jamison—make sure someone builds her a shelter before all the leaves have fallen to the ground. She won't be able to survive the harsh winter in a tent. And remember, there is more goodness inside of Jamison than there is evil. And try to understand Kallie's reasoning for all this."

Tucker and Kallie walked into the forest, until Kallie could see Jamison about ten trees away. He began walking toward them. As he got closer, Kallie could see he had a huge smile on his face. Once they were close enough Kallie leapt into his arms. Tucker felt jealousy wash over him. He wanted to destroy Jamison. And he couldn't understand why Jamison looked so happy knowing that Kallie had been lying to both of them.

"You feel better?" Jamison asked Kallie as he let go of her.

"Yes. I can't believe I got scarlet fever."

"Probably caught it from a vampire," Tucker said. He meant to only say it to himself, inside his head. But it was too late to take the words back now.

"Of course you are going to try to blame me for all this. And how could she have gotten it from me?" Jamison said.

"What does it matter? She still kissed you," Tucker said, looking at Kallie.

"I thought I was never going to see you again! And how do you even know that?" Kallie shouted at Tucker.

"You see, once she crossed over to my side, she was probably expecting you to stay on your side, where you belong," Jamison said. Tucker turned to face him.

"It's a good thing I didn't, because you weren't handling the situation with those other vampires!"

Tucker stepped closer to Jamison. They were looking at each other like they were about to attack each other. And then they did.

They launched at each other. Tucker transformed into a wolf, and Jamison's fangs came out. They were tumbling around on the ground trying to pin each other down. Jamison threw Tucker into a tree, and the tree cracked in half. Tucker charged toward Jamison, tossing him high into the air.

Kallie wished they could have just one simple conversation without getting into a fight. She was becoming annoyed and fed up with their anger.

"I have had it! I don't need either of you! I can get there by myself!" Kallie said, then turned around and stormed off.

They stopped fighting, once they heard what she said. Tucker changed back to human. Once Kallie was far enough away from them, Jamison whispered to Tucker, "You haven't told her yet?"

Tucker shook his head.

"Tell her right now, or I will," Jamison said. Kallie was a few yards ahead of them. Tucker took a few steps forward.

"Kallie, before you continue to your destination, you should probably know that your fiancée is looking for you," Tucker shouted to her.

Kallie stopped. She didn't turn around. "I don't have a fiancée," she whispered. Any normal person wouldn't have been able to hear her. They both slowly walked toward her.

"Well, then why did some man show up yesterday morning, saying that he is looking for his missing fiancée Kallie Davis?" Tucker asked. Kallie and Jamison could both sense the anger that filled his voice.

"You don't know if that's my last name," she said, trying to remain calm.

"He gave this to us!" Tucker shouted as he pulled the folded piece of paper out of his pocket. Kallie turned around. Tucker held the poster in front of her face.

"How could you keep this from me?" Tucker's voice was now filled with hurt instead of anger.

"No . . . " Kallie mumbled as she stared at herself on the missing poster.

"Why is he doing this to me . . . " she said to herself as tears filled her eyes, then they quickly disappeared.

"Wait, he came here *yesterday*?" Kallie asked, looking up at Tucker.

"Yes."

"Then why didn't you tell me yesterday? Why am I not finding out until now?" She raised her voice at Tucker.

"Do not get mad at me for hiding something from you for a day. You've been keeping something much worse from me for weeks now," Tucker yelled back.

"I was keeping my own secret. You keeping this information from me makes me want to believe that you are not the man I thought you were, Tucker."

"This man that is looking for you, do you love him, Kallie?" Jamison finally spoke. He didn't want to argue with Kallie, he only wanted answers.

"No," she said without hesitation.

"Are you running from him?"

She nodded silently as tears blurred her vision.

"Why?"

Kallie shrugged her shoulders, her eyes stuck on the ground.

"Kallie, I can't help you if you don't talk to me."

"This is his way of finally getting revenge on me."

"Revenge for what?" said Jamison.

More emotions filled Tucker's body. He was angry with himself for assuming that Kallie was playing with his feelings. And that Jamison was the one to get her to finally open up.

"For all the times I've rejected him," she finally answered.

"So, what did he do?"

"The day before I left, Christopher kept trying to touch me, just like he always did when he would trap me into being alone with him. I've always been able to get away, except this time. He had me cornered; no one was around. When I finally got the chance, I slapped him right across the face as hard as I could, and then made a run for it. Later that day he showed up at my home. He promised my aunt and uncle a large sum of money for my hand in marriage. And they agreed to it. But, I can't marry him." Tears began to roll down Kallie's cheeks.

"He's not a good person. He uses money to get what he wants, thinks he is better than everyone, cares about no one but himself." She began crying more.

"I can't marry someone like that. So, I left. That's why I need to get to the west village, I need to be as far away from him as possible."

Tucker and Jamison both looked at each other.

"He said he is going to the west village to search for you next," Tucker said to her.

Kallie's heart sank. All she wanted to do was start over somewhere new, but Christopher was making it impossible for her to do so.

"What am I supposed to do? I can't go there anymore. If someone recognizes me from the posters, they will forcefully return me home so they can get their reward," she said, looking to Tucker and Jamison. They were silent for a while. They both knew that the moment they had been waiting for was about to happen, the moment when Kallie would choose whom to spend the rest of her life with. Or maybe she wouldn't choose either; maybe she would return home and live a miserable life with a man she hated.

Kallie waited for one of them to say something. She wondered why they had both been quiet for so long. Then they both finally spoke at the exact same time, and said the exact same thing.

"Stay with me." They were the three words they had both been dying to say to her since the moment she entered their lives.

They watched her, waiting for her to respond.

"What?" she asked, as a tear ran down her cheek. She wasn't exactly sure what was happening. Tucker took a step toward her.

"Please stay with me. I am truly sorry for everything I just said. And I feel awful for everything you have been through. I am so in love with you, Kallie. I promise to protect you and take care of you. I will give you the amazing life you deserve. Please, stay with me," Tucker said.

"I can give you a better life than he can, Kallie," said Jamison. "I know you may know him better than you know me. You've spent more time with him. But I promise, if you give me a chance, I can show you how I will love you more and better than any man ever would."

"If you choose him, he's going to change you into a vampire," Tucker said, trying to make Jamison look bad.

Jamison stared at him. "Why would I do that? You honestly think I would ever wish this kind of life on someone? I wouldn't even wish this on my worst enemy—which is you!" Jamison shouted.

Kallie had no idea what to do. She had feelings for both of them. They both made her feel amazing, in two different ways. They were both staring at her, waiting for her to say something—anything. But she didn't know what to say. She felt overwhelmed.

She threw herself down on the ground. She pulled her knees into her chest and buried her face in her lap. She was practically sobbing.

Tucker and Jamison exchanged looks, unsure what to do. Jamison crouched. "What's wrong, Kallie?" he asked.

"How am I supposed to choose one of you? I don't even know if you both only want me for the same reason every other man wants me."

"Kallie, I've known you for more than two weeks, and I think I already know you better than anyone else," Tucker said as he also crouched. Kallie didn't respond.

"I know you love the sky," Tucker said.

"You look up at the sky every chance you get. You would be perfectly happy watching the sky all day long, whether it's clear or stormy, day or night."

Jamison tried to think of something, quickly. "I know that you are the only nonjudgmental person I have ever met," he said. "Tucker and I are very different from the rest of the world. Anyone else would have run away screaming when they found out what we are. You didn't. You saw past the red eyes and sharp fangs and saw the person I truly am."

Kallie finally lifted her head. Her face and eyes were red and puffy from crying. She groaned and lay flat on her back.

"I guess we are lying down now," Jamison said as he lay next to Kallie. Tucker did the same. Jamison put his hand on Kallie's upper thigh, rubbing his thumb back and forth. Tucker held Kallie's hand in his. He brought it up to his lips and lightly kissed it.

"Everything you both said has made it very hard to choose," she said as the three of them stared up at the sky. Big, white, fluffy clouds were passing by. Both men had just said things about her she hadn't even known about herself, until now. She liked how things felt in this moment, both of them next to her. She felt safe between the two of them.

"I can't make a decision right now. I can't decide until I know for sure. And I won't know for sure until I know both of you equally. I don't want to spend forever wondering if I made the right choice, I want to know that I did."

Neither of the men said anything. They continued looking at the sky. Tucker felt upset that he was going to have to wait for Kallie to make a decision. He knew that if Kallie were to pick right now, she would choose him. But if she wanted to wait to make her decision, then Tucker was going to have to be patient with her.

Jamison was relieved that Kallie wasn't picking one of them yet. That meant he had more time to show Kallie just what a wonderful person he was. Both men stood up, and each extended a hand to help Kallie up. She grabbed both their hands as she stood. Then they walked off to Tucker's camp.

When they returned to Tucker's camp, Jamison sat on a log. Tucker looked at him, outraged.

"What do you think you're doing?" he asked.

"I thought I'd stay here while she works on her decision," Jamison answered, knowing he was making Tucker furious.

"Why?"

"To make things easier for you."

"What are you talking about?"

"You really want her to have to travel back and forth over the river all day long? You want her to come over to my territory, far away from you, where you can't see or hear her? Wouldn't you rather have both of us over here? Where you can keep your eyes on her—and me?" Jamison stood, and was face-to-face with Tucker. Tucker wanted to punch him, but he didn't want to make Kallie even more upset. So he ignored everything Jamison had said and let him have his way.

Jamison couldn't believe that Tucker didn't argue with him. He knew that if he stuck around long enough, Tucker would most likely be nothing but angry all the time. And then Kallie wouldn't want him anymore.

Tucker dumped out the water in the pail. Then he started walking down to the river to get more.

Kallie followed him. Jamison stayed put.

They reached the river, and Tucker began filling up the pail with water.

"I'm sorry for assuming the worst before hearing your side of the story," he said, looking up at Kallie. "And I'm sorry for how you have been treated. You are not some piece of property that someone can buy."

"Well, just answer this honestly, Tucker, when you said you were in love with me earlier, did you mean it?" she asked him. Tucker stood and stared into Kallie's blue-green eyes, which were looking more green than blue that day.

"Yes," Tucker said.

Her eyes were focused on the ground. "Well, even though I am still angry with you for not telling me right away about Christopher, I still think I might also be in love with you," she said.

She looked up at Tucker, who was filled with happiness. He knew Jamison couldn't stand a chance. He pulled her in and leaned down to kiss her. Kallie wrapped her arms around his neck as their lips were finally reunited. It seemed like forever since they had kissed each other. Tucker's hands traveled down Kallie's back to her lower waist. Kallie ran her hands over Tucker's strong shoulders, down his smooth chest, to his muscular back. She pulled their bodies together as close as she could.

Things would have gone farther if Jamison hadn't lost his temper. They heard a loud grunt followed by an even louder thud. Kallie pulled herself from Tucker and walked back to the camp. Tucker groaned as he watched Kallie walk away. He picked up the water pail and went in the same direction.

Jamison was sitting on a log, looking at the ground, acting natural. But when Kallie looked closer at what Jamison was sitting on, she realized it was not a log, it was a whole tree. Jamison had ripped the whole the tree out of the ground, roots and all. And he was sitting on it like nothing had happened.

"Jamison . . . what happened to the tree?" Kallie asked, looking confused. Jamison stared blankly at her and shrugged. Tucker laughed as he joined them and saw what Jamison had done.

"Maybe you only want to stay over here so you can keep your eyes on me," Tucker said to Jamison. "You saw what was going on between us just now . . . did you hear it, too?"

Jamison approached Tucker. "I don't care how much she says she loves you. She doesn't love you enough to know if she wants to be with you or not. Why would she choose someone who lied to her anyway?"

Tucker clenched his fists as he moved closer to Jamison, and Kallie knew what was about to happen. Kallie stepped between them before they could start throwing punches.

"Stop! I cannot tolerate your constant arguing! Jamison, I don't think you should stay here."

Tucker and Jamison stepped away from each other. Jamison walked up to Kallie and held out his hand for her to take.

"Walk with me?" he asked her. She took his hand and they walked away, leaving Tucker alone.

They hopped across the river and walked deep into Jamison's territory. Jamison was trying to get far from Tucker, so he wouldn't be able to hear them. Once Jamison thought they were far enough, and was sure that Tucker was not following them, he sat on a big rock and pulled Kallie close. She was standing between his legs, his hands resting on her waist. He looked up at her. Her eyes were a deep green color, with little flecks of blue. When she looked up and the sun hit her eyes, they changed to bright blue with flecks of green. He loved how interesting her eyes were, which reminded him of Tucker's grandfather and father, talking about how they suspected Kallie was a star person. He remained quiet as he gazed into her eyes and wondered what a star person was.

Then he snapped out of his daze and finally spoke. "I heard what you said to Tucker."

"Why were you listening?" she said.

"I can hear everything surrounding me. It's not like I was listening on purpose."

Jamison waited for Kallie's response, but she didn't have anything to say.

"All I need to know is if I stand a chance with you," he said.

She remained silent.

"Can you see yourself falling in love with me?"

Jamison thought this might be the last time he saw Kallie. He felt like Kallie's next words were going to be that she wanted to continue her life with Tucker. She would ask him to leave her alone. Kallie looked into the distance, saying nothing.

"Kallie, please say something," he pleaded.

She smiled, looked down at Jamison, and said, "I could see myself falling madly in love with you."

"You mean it?"

She nodded. Jamison grabbed her face and kissed her. He pulled her onto his lap as his fingers tangled in her long hair. His lips moved down to her neck and his hand traveled far up her thigh. Kallie ran her fingers through his hair. Things were moving fast between them; they were breathing heavily, their pulses racing. There was a loud thud in the distance, followed by another.

"What was that?" Kallie asked as she pulled away from Jamison.

"Just a werewolf throwing a tantrum. Ignore it." He pulled her back in and went to continue kissing her, but Kallie moved away.

"Maybe I should go back," she said.

"Please don't."

"I'll return after sunset."

Jamison walked her back to the river. Tucker was sitting on a rock, watching the water go by, waiting for Kallie. And just as Jamison suspected, Tucker had taken his anger out by knocking down a couple of trees. Jamison kissed Kallie good-bye before she hopped across the river. Tucker had a look on his face that Jamison did not recognize, though Jamison had only ever seen Tucker angry.

Tucker was lost. He almost just lost Kallie to another man and he couldn't stand the thought of losing Kallie to Jamison. And with each passing second, the chances of that happening seemed better and better. All Tucker could do was try his hardest to prove to Kallie how important she was to him, and hope for the best.

Tucker cooked a wild chicken over the fire for him and Kallie. Kallie was staring at the sky, watching the sunset. She asked, "How did you meet Jamison?"

Tucker wasn't exactly sure what to say right away. "You want to hear the story of the first time Jamison and I encountered each other?" he asked, just to be sure. She nodded. "Jamison began living in the forest about twenty years ago." Tucker paused for a second. He remembered how Jamison had saved Kallie's life, the night her parents died. He knew that telling Kallie would be the right thing to do; she deserved to know. But he also knew that if Kallie found out it was Jamison who saved her, she would choose Jamison instead of him. Tucker continued his story.

"When my grandfather first saw Jamison, he could sense that Jamison would never harm us or other humans, so my grandfather let him stay. Then, five years ago, when I became alpha, I chose to live here, in the forest. My brother told me I had to kill Jamison . . . and I was going to. Once I found him, I was prepared to rip him apart. We fought each other all day. It seemed as if it was impossible for either of us to win. But there was a moment when I could have killed him. I had him pinned, and he couldn't move. I was about to take his head off . . . but the look in his eyes made me stop. I could see he was still a human; he didn't look like a murderer. We gave up on trying to defeat each other. We agreed to split the forest in half, and never cross over the river. And we've both broken that rule, recently."

"Have you ever killed anyone?" Kallie asked him.

He shook his head. "Jamison is the only person I ever wanted to kill."

"What about other vampires? Besides him."

"The only other vampires I've encountered are the ones that appeared that day. And they seem to be much more afraid of me than Jamison will ever be."

"Are you glad you didn't kill him?"

"You wouldn't like my answer."

She looked at him, disappointed.

"I wouldn't have to worry about losing you if I had killed him when I had the chance."

Kallie stood up. "I told him I would meet him after sunset."

Tucker hung his head. Kallie lifted his chin and kissed him on the lips, then walked to the river where Jamison was waiting.

Jamison lay out a quilt for him and Kallie to sit on. Kallie finally ate some strawberries off the bush that had been taunting her for weeks. They were worth the wait. Jamison knew he shouldn't ask the question he was about to, but he had to know where she was with this decision.

"Have you gotten any closer to making a choice yet?" he asked.

"No. It seems I become more confused as the day goes on."

"Is there any way I can help you decide?"

Kallie bit her lower lip before she spoke. "There is one thing Tucker and I have done a lot of . . . but you and I have not." She felt her cheeks grow warm after she finished her sentence. Jamison smiled, and his eyes lit up. He stood and held out his hand to help Kallie up, then picked up the quilt, threw it over his shoulder, grabbed Kallie's hand, and took off running far down the river.

Jamison lay the quilt on the ground and took Kallie into his arms. She kissed down his neck, then unbuttoned his shirt as her lips traveled down his chest. Jamison's shirt floated to the ground, followed by Kallie's dress. They lay down on the quilt together.

Jamison removed Kallie's undergarments, then she undid his pants and he kicked them off. Jamison looked over Kallie's gorgeous body, her pale white skin glowing in the moonlight. His fingers traced her. Her hands began to do the same but then Jamison quickly got on top of her, grabbed her arms, and held them down next to her head. Her mind began to wonder why both men always did this to her when she would touch them during intimate moments. Then as she caught a glimpse of Jamison's red eyes she finally realized why. Jamison's lips traveled all over Kallie's body.

She was doing with Jamison what she had only done with Tucker. They were both sweaty, even though the air was chilly. Their hearts were racing.

Kallie hoped, that in some strange way, making love to Jamison would help with her decision. But that's not at all what happened. Making love to Tucker or Jamison felt equally amazing. They both made her feel like she was the only woman in the world. They sent feelings through her body she had never felt before.

Their intimate moment ended. Kallie was filled with happiness, but also frustration, since she was still nowhere close to making a choice. She and Jamison lay on the quilt, their skin touching. They were both looking up at the thousands of stars in the sky. Then Kallie asked Jamison the same question she had asked Tucker, earlier that day. She wanted to hear Jamison's side of the story.

"How did you meet Tucker?" she asked him.

Jamison thought for a moment, then spoke. "I came to this forest about twenty years ago. Tucker's grandfather was the alpha then. When he found me, I swore to him that I am not anything like the average vampire. I told him I had never killed a human and never would. He made me promise to stay far away from his tribe, and never cause any issues, and as long as I followed those two rules, he and the other wolves in his tribe would not come after me.

"And then Tucker became the alpha. I knew he was determined to do whatever it took to kill me. He was running all over the forest, trying to find me. Then he finally did. We looked each other right in the eyes. He said this was his forest now, and I had better leave or else.

"I laughed in his face and said no. Then he transformed into a wolf and launched himself at me. We fought for what seemed to be forever. It was becoming impossible for either of us to win. When Tucker first approached me, the sun was out. By the time we stopped fighting, it was after midnight. There was a moment when I could have killed him, but I couldn't do it. Although I was fighting with this beast, I knew there was a human inside there, who was only trying to protect his people.

"So after we had both finally given up on our endless, exhausting fight, we agreed to split the forest in half. We knew the main river ran all the way down the middle of the forest. We agreed that Tucker would remain on the east side of the river, and I would get the west side. And we swore to never, ever cross into each other's territory. Obviously, that rule has been broken, these past few weeks."

"I find it unbelievable that you two were actually able to agree on something," Kallie said, laughing.

They got dressed and walked back down the river to Tucker's camp. When they arrived, Tucker was waiting on the other side. He had heard everything. He knew exactly what had just happened between them. He could hear them touching, and breathing heavily. He could hear Kallie moaning. He could hear them kissing. It was making him mad, so he changed into a wolf and took off running as far away as he could from them.

As he ran through the forest, his mind raced. Kallie was continuously putting him into situations where he did not know what to do. He tried to come up with a plan, something that would win Kallie over completely. But he realized there may be no way to win her.

Tucker thought about what things would be like if Kallie chose Jamison. And if Kallie did choose Jamison, Tucker would not be able to stay away from Kallie, whether she was with another man or not. He would continue to see her and spend time with her and love her. When Tucker realized this, he also realized Jamison would do the exact same thing. He knew that if Kallie chose him over Jamison, Jamison would react the same way Tucker would. It didn't matter who Kallie picked; Tucker and Jamison would fight over her the rest of her life.

Tucker returned to the spot at the river just as Kallie and Jamison did. Jamison kissed Kallie good night, then she joined Tucker on his side. She began walking back to the camp, but turned around when she realized that Tucker was not following her.

"I'll be right there . . . you go ahead," Tucker said. She walked up the hill to the camp as she waited to hear them begin to argue, but she didn't.

"If she was to choose me . . . would you leave her alone? Or would you continue to spend time with her and still try to be with her?" Tucker asked Jamison.

Jamison laughed and shook his head. "If she picks you, I'm still not giving up. What if she picks me? Are you going to be able to just walk away from her?"

"No."

"Just promise me one thing," Tucker began to say to Jamison.

"If she does choose you and doesn't want me around, I know she might be a part of your life, since you can live forever. But remember you will be her whole life. So, make sure you give her the best life you can."

"I will," Jamison replied.

CHAPTER NINE

May 27th–31st, 1821

Days passed. Kallie tried to spend as much time with Tucker and Jamison as she could. She tried to be with them both equally. She learned more about Jamison as the days went on. She knew his favorite color was green, because the forest is full of thousands of different shades of green. She knew his favorite season: spring, because in spring it was like the forest was reborn, and everything got to start over.

She wanted to know more about his past. She wanted to know how he became a vampire. She wanted to know who those other vampires were. She wanted to know about his life before he became a vampire. But every time she tried to get him to open up, he changed the subject. Or he kissed her, partly because he wanted to, but also because he wanted her to stop asking. She eventually gave up wanting to know about his past. She would stay up late with him each night, and as they lay next to the fire he built for them by the river they counted the stars together. They talked about how fast the world was changing, and what life would be like hundreds of years from then. Also how Jamison would get to experience what life was like in a hundred years, since he would still be around.

Tucker would fall asleep to the sound of them laughing as they kept losing count of the stars. It would break his heart. He could hear everything. He could hear them whispering to each other. He could hear them kissing. He could even hear Jamison's hand running along Kallie's body. It drove him crazy. When Jamison disappeared, to go hunt for some animal's blood to drink, Tucker had Kallie to himself. He spent every second alone with her, kissing her. He didn't want her to forget the chemistry they had.

Both men had paid close attention to how Kallie behaved with them. She seemed happy and in love when she was alone with either of them. But when they saw her with their competitor, she acted the very same way. They had no idea whom she would choose, and neither did she. She found herself in love with both of them. She had formed a deep, strong connection with Tucker. But since she now knew Jamison better, and had spent more time with him, she felt the same connection with him.

She felt lost and confused. She did not know who she wanted to spend forever with. She wanted to spend forever with both of them. She couldn't picture her life without either of them. Three weeks before, she never thought she would fall in love. And now her heart was torn between two incredible men.

On the night of the twenty-ninth, Tucker woke up in the middle of the night to the sound of Kallie crying. He could tell she was trying desperately to be quiet. He pretended to still be asleep and pulled her close. He hoped his embrace would help her calm down, but it only seemed to make her cry harder. He still continued to hold her, though. He could feel her body shaking. Her heart was racing, her pillow soaked with tears. Tucker wanted to ask her what was wrong. But he knew that if she wanted to talk about it, she would have woken him up, and would not have been trying to be so quiet. So he continued to hold her as he pretended to sleep, while she quietly cried herself to sleep.

Ever since that night, Kallie had not been herself. Tucker and Jamison noticed right away. She was quiet and would hardly say a word. Both men saw how sad her eyes looked. They tried their best to get her to smile, but when she finally would, they knew it was fake. They both missed her smile, they missed her laugh. Her sadness was becoming contagious. Even the sun had not shone; the forest was under a constant gray blanket of clouds.

They would try to kiss her, and she would hardly kiss them back. At first, they thought she was only acting this way with them individually. They thought she must have made up her mind, and it was obvious she would choose the other. But when they saw her act the same way with both of them, they felt relieved that she wasn't only behaving this way with them.

But it also made them wonder even more why she was like this. They wanted to ask her what was wrong, but they knew she would break down in tears. They didn't want to see her like that.

It was the night of the thirty-first, and Kallie had cried herself to sleep again. Tucker knew he couldn't let Kallie feel like this anymore. He knew that he and Jamison were going to have to figure out what was bothering her and do their best to fix it.

He crawled out of the tent. He walked down to the river, hoping Jamison was there, and he was. He stood next to the fire he had built, looking in Tucker's direction. It was almost like Jamison was expecting Tucker, waiting for him there. They spoke softly, and could still hear each other over the rushing water.

"Kallie has cried herself to sleep for the last three nights," said Tucker.

"I don't understand, she was fine before," Jamison said.

"Has she mentioned anything to you? Anything about what's bothering her?"

"No. At first, I thought it was me. But then I saw her act the same way with you, and I didn't feel so bad."

"It has to be because she doesn't know who to pick," Tucker suggested. Jamison let out a long sigh and sat on a rock, then dropped his face into his hands.

"I finally found a girl who accepts me for who I am . . . but then it just so happens that a werewolf is also in love with her." Jamison's voice sounded muffled from behind his hands.

"We should probably start building her a shelter soon. We can go look for spots tomorrow. Maybe that will cheer her up," Tucker said.

"But she hasn't chosen yet," Jamison said, looking at Tucker like he was an idiot. Tucker jumped across the river and joined Jamison on the other side.

"Does it matter? If she picks you, I'm still going to be there every day. I'm still going to hold her, and kiss her, and love her. And I know you are going to do the same thing, if she picks me. You're still going to be here every day, you're not going to stop loving her. So it doesn't matter who she picks, or where we build her a home. We are going to fight over her for the rest of her life!" Tucker said, raising his voice. He sounded very frustrated as he stared deep into the fire. Jamison couldn't believe what Tucker had just said.

"So, what? We both get her? We're both going to love her? Share her?" Jamison said.

"Ugh! This is so messed up!" Tucker shouted as he rubbed his face with his hands and sat on a rock.

"This is one crazy love triangle we have gotten into," Jamison said, laughing and shaking his head.

"My grandfather said the same thing."

They were both silent for a long time. Both looked into the fire and thought about the future.

"You really want to do this?" Jamison asked.

"If it will make her happy . . . then it's worth it."

"Are you sure?"

"Are you?"

"No. But if it will make her happy, then it's worth a try."

"All right, so, we will both agree to love her," Tucker said as he also stood.

"And take care for her," Jamison added. He was pacing now.

"And protect her."

"And keep her happy," they said at the same time.

"Agreed?" Tucker asked as he stuck his hand out for Jamison to shake.

"Agreed," Jamison said as he shook Tucker's hand.

And there, in front of the roaring fire, under thousands of stars and a big, bright moon, in front of all the nighttime woodland animals, history was made. A vampire and a werewolf agreed to love the same woman until the day she died.

For the last five years, they had hated each other more than anything, and wanted each other dead. And now they agreed to love the same woman, just to see her smile again. They knew they couldn't live without her smile. But they promised each other one last thing. If, one day, she realized she loved one of them more than the other, and asked the other to leave, then they must go, and leave her alone.

CHAPTER TEN

June 1st, 1821

After sunrise, Tucker gently moved Kallie's sleeping body over as he headed outside and went to look at a spot he thought would be good to build a cabin. When Jamison saw him leave, he sneaked into the tent.

He couldn't help but smile when he saw her there. She didn't look sad anymore. He could tell she must have been dreaming about something wonderful by the expression on her face. He kissed her on the forehead. He could see that her hair had gotten lighter. He also noticed she was getting more freckles on her face. He figured it was probably from being in the sun so much. Even though the sun seemed to be nonexistent for the past few days.

He felt jealous of Tucker in this moment. He got to sleep next to her each night. And that's how things were always going to be. Tucker would get to sleep next to her, and Jamison wouldn't. He wondered if he was actually going to be able to do this. How could he possibly share this amazing woman with a man he hated?

Kallie woke up. She had a smile on her face when she opened her eyes, but then it quickly faded. She looked at Jamison, surprised to see him.

"Good morning," he said with a smile.

Kallie sat up. She looked at Jamison with the most heartbreaking expression, it made him feel like his soul was about to be crushed.

"I think I need to leave," she said to him. Jamison shot up.

"What? No. Kallie, you can't," he started to beg as Kallie crawled out of the tent.

"I have to, Jamison," she said as he joined her outside.

"Where are you going to go?"

"Home." She turned away from him.

"Why would you do that to yourself?"

"Because I can't choose either of you. If I can't make a decision then there is no reason for me being here. And if I were to go to one of the other villages, I would be forced to return home anyway, so I might as well just go."

"What about Christopher?" Jamison asked as he stepped in front of her.

"I'll tell him to leave me alone."

"By the way you described him, do you really think he is going to listen? I bet you've told him to leave you alone plenty of times, and he's never listened."

"I can't stay here, Jamison, all it is doing is breaking me." Kallie began to walk away.

"Just wait for Tucker to return, we can figure this out Kallie, I promise." He was getting ready to drop to his knees.

"It doesn't matter what either of you do or say. It can't convince me to stay. I care so deeply for both of you, and it's tearing me apart. I need to go, Jamison."

"At least let me walk you back."

"I can find my way back. I need to be alone right now."

"You've been alone practically your whole life, Kallie."

"Maybe that's just how things are meant to be for me." And with that she left.

Jamison dropped his sad body onto a log as he tried to hold himself together. He made an agreement with a werewolf all for nothing. Kallie was the only reason for them trying to get along, and now she was gone. Jamison felt completely empty inside knowing he would never get to be with her.

Moments later Tucker returned. He could see that Jamison was upset.

"Where's Kallie?" he asked Jamison.

"She left."

"What do you mean she left?"

"Said that she cares too deeply for both of us, all it is doing is breaking her."

"Did you tell her what the plan was?" Jamison could sense the anger in Tucker's voice.

"I told her to wait for you, but she said that it didn't matter what either of us do or say, she can't stay here anymore."

"Well you should have made her stay!"

"She wanted to go home, Tucker! We can't make her do anything!"

"Home? She can't go home! That jerk is going to make her life miserable!"

Tucker began walking in the same direction that Kallie had gone; Jamison followed behind him. They both continued arguing on the way to Kallie. A strong wind blew through the forest, sending all the leaves flying wildly by them. They both sensed that a storm was coming.

Kallie stood at the very edge of the forest, staring at the village that she hoped to never see again. She knew the moment she stepped out of the forest she would never see Tucker or Jamison again. The thought of how she didn't even say good-bye to Tucker killed her. She didn't want to go through life without them. She wanted both of them by her side until her final breath, and if she were to go back to her old life it would be filled with people who didn't truly care about her.

Kallie's eyes were fixated on the horrible storm brewing off in the distance. Thunder rolled and lightning flashed as the black clouds moved quickly across the sky. She watched all the farm animals run for shelter in the barn nearby. A man on a horse ran down the dirt road, trying to get home before the storm.

Kallie felt as if she were frozen to the ground, her mind telling her to go one way, her heart and soul telling her another. A strong gust of wind blew toward her, making her take a step back. She could hear the deep voices of men bickering coming up behind her.

"Why would you just let her leave?" she heard one voice say, as thunder crackled.

"'Cause it's what she wanted," another voice said, as lightning struck the dirt road.

Kallie gasped. She looked up at the sky, as huge black clouds hung over her.

"There she is!" one of the voices shouted. She knew whose voice that was.

"Kallie!" Tucker shouted as he and Jamison approached her from behind.

"What are you doing?" Tucker asked as they both stood in front of her.

"I'm going home!" she yelled over the wind.

"Is this really what you want?" said Tucker.

Kallie was silent.

"Look me in the eyes and tell me that that is what you want!"

She stared at him.

"If this is not what you want, then don't do it, Kallie. Don't go back to the life that you hated so much you ran away from it. You have to let your heart lead the way."

"It keeps leading me to both of you!"

"Then be with both of us!"

Kallie's eyes grew wide. "What?"

Tucker placed his hands on Kallie's shoulders, forcing her to look at him.

"Be with both of us," he repeated to her.

"What do you mean, both of you?" she asked. Her eyes were stuck on Tucker's; she couldn't even tear herself away to glance at the crazy sky behind him.

"You don't need to choose one of us anymore, you can be with both of us."

Kallie looked at Tucker as if he had lost his mind.

"That's insane! How could that possibly work? You hate each other." Thunder boomed right above their heads.

"It doesn't matter. If it's what you want then we will do it, for you."

"You would never agree to this, would you, Jamison?" Kallie said, looking past Tucker and into Jamison's blue eyes, which seemed even brighter under the dark sky.

"I already have." Jamison smiled at her.

"We both have," Tucker added.

"No," Kallie said.

"It's going to be too hard, you are both going to be fighting with each other every day. No, I don't want to deal with that."

"You can't think of it like that, Kallie," said Jamison.

"Don't try to take the easy way out just because you are afraid of the unknown. Don't think about us or how we would feel. Only think about yourself right now. What do you want? What would make you happy?" Tucker asked her.

Kallie looked back and forth at both of them. No one had ever asked her what she wanted or what would make her happy before. She couldn't even recall the last time she had gotten what she wanted. And right now everything she could ever possibly want was standing right in front of her. Waiting for her to choose them, together. But, she felt that if she were to choose both of them it would make her seem selfish. Torturing them by forcing them to watch her with another man, while she's as happy as ever.

Then, she realized that she had never been selfish in her whole entire life, and maybe it was finally time for her to be. She was going to put her own happiness before anyone else's and go for what she truly wanted. The two men before her. The most passionate, courageous men the world had ever seen.

"You deserve nothing but the best, Kallie," Tucker said to her.

"And who could possibly be better than both of us together?" Jamison added.

Kallie smiled. The black clouds began to fade away, leaving a crystal-clear sky.

"So what is it going to be?" Jamison asked.

"Us? Or a life you hate?" Tucker asked, pointing toward the village. The sun finally began to shine.

"Us," Kallie answered. Tucker immediately pulled her into his arms.

"We will figure this out; you don't have to worry about a thing," he assured her. Kallie let go of Tucker and moved to Jamison.

"It'll all work out, I promise," Jamison whispered to her as he held her close to him.

"One more thing," Tucker began to say as Kallie and Jamison let go of each other.

"If you ever feel that you love one more than the other, let us know. And whichever one of us it is . . . we will go, and leave you and the one you want alone, forever."

"Let's go back now," Jamison said as he turned around and began walking in the direction they had come from.

Kallie went to follow behind him, but as soon as she took a step, Tucker grabbed her hand. She looked up at him, and he smiled down at her. Kallie's stomach filled with butterflies, just like every other time he looked at her. Tucker bit his bottom lip, then leaned down to kiss her. Kallie felt all her stress disappear as her body was pushed up against Tucker's shirtless chest. Tucker lifted her off the ground and she wrapped her legs around his waist.

Jamison was still walking back to the camp. He knew Tucker and Kallie were not following behind him. He knew exactly what was happening behind him, and he refused to turn around and look.

Jamison had made it back to the campsite. Kallie and Tucker arrived five minutes later.

"Now what?" Jamison asked as they entered the campsite.

"We look for somewhere to call home," Tucker answered.

"What do you mean?" asked Kallie.

"You want to live out of a tent?" Tucker asked. Kallie cracked a smile.

"Are you going to build a house?"

"Yes," both men answered.

"How was the area you looked at earlier, Tucker?" Jamison asked.

"Not that great. There has to be somewhere better. But if not, then it will have to do."

"So, you are *both* going to build a house that we are *all* going to live in together?" Kallie asked, looking at both of them.

"You don't think we could build a decent log cabin?" Jamison asked Kallie.

"No, I think you would both do fine with that. It's you building it together and then living together I'm worried about."

"Don't worry about it," they both said to her.

"This should be interesting . . . " Kallie said under her breath, knowing they both heard her.

"I don't think she believes in us," Jamison said to Tucker, trying to sound hurt.

"All the more reason to get along," Tucker said, attempting to sound positive.

Kallie tried to hold in her laughter. "Now this is just getting weird," she said, failing to hold back a smile.

"Don't worry, we will get in an argument sooner or later," Jamison jokingly reassured her.

"Great," Kallie said with sarcasm.

"Well I'm going to go collect more firewood," said Tucker. He glanced at both of them, feeling weird that he was going to have to be alright with them being alone now.

"I'll be back soon." He sighed and walked away.

Kallie couldn't help but start laughing at how strange and awkward things felt.

"What are you laughing at?" Jamison asked as a smile appeared on his face from Kallie's contagious laughter.

"I just can't believe this," she said, lowering herself down on a log.

"What are the chances of two enemies agreeing to love the same woman, and that woman being me?"

"Because, there is no one else like you, Kallie. There will never be another soul in the whole universe that could ever come anywhere close to being as amazing as you are. There's a reason why every man can't help but feel drawn to you. 'Cause you have the most purest form of love to offer. And I guess I must have done something right in my life if I deserve even half of it." Kallie smiled up at Jamison, then he sat down next to her.

"I've always admired how well you speak your mind," she said, holding his hand in hers.

"Do you honestly think you are going to be able to do this though?" She looked deep into his eyes.

"Stop worrying about what I think or what Tucker thinks. Today was the first day you smiled in what seemed to be forever. And if I had to go one more second without your smile, then I don't know what would have happened to me." Kallie wrapped her arms around Jamison. Her embrace made him feel weak. She leaned in and pressed her lips on his. He could feel her smiling as they kissed and couldn't help but also smile.

It was about midnight. Tucker and Kallie were sound asleep. Jamison left the camp. He was searching the whole forest, running back and forth, from end to end, trying to find a spot to build their cabin. Kallie deserved the perfect home in the perfect spot.

He looked along the river, on the sides of the small mountains throughout the forest. He knew the sun would rise soon. He wanted to be back before either of them woke up.

He was at the bottom of a steep hill. He could see the land was flat at the top, and he wondered what was up there. He climbed the hundred-foot hill with ease.

He reached the top. He thought he saw a grassy area through all the vines hanging between the trees. He walked through the vines, and his jaw dropped at what he saw. The sun was rising over one of the mountains. The light was shining on the wide-open field Jamison had found. He turned around, jumped down the hill, and went running back to Kallie and Tucker.

CHAPTER ELEVEN

June 2nd, 1821

Jamison returned to Tucker and Kallie. He had to tell them about the amazing place he had discovered. He couldn't wait for them to wake up. He felt that if he didn't tell them right away he would explode. He walked up to the tent and began shaking it.

"Wake up! Wake up!" he shouted.

Tucker angrily stuck his head outside. "What could you possibly want?" Tucker said as he peeked his tired head outside and looked up at Jamison.

"I found it!" Jamison shouted back at him.

"Found what?"

"The most amazing place you'll ever see!"

Tucker sighed. "Time to get up, Kallie," Tucker said to her. But she was wide awake, after Jamison's outburst.

Tucker and Kallie both crawled outside. Jamison began leading them in the direction he had just come from. They dragged their tired bodies behind him.

They walked for miles and stopped a few times to eat and drink. Tucker had noticed Kallie becoming tired from all the walking; he kept asking her if she wanted him to carry her but she insisted that she was fine.

It was the middle of the afternoon when they finally made it to the steep hill.

"It's right up there," Jamison said, as all three stood at the bottom, staring up at the top.

"I'm not climbing up that," Kallie said immediately.

"I'll help you," said Tucker.

He changed into a wolf, and Jamison helped Kallie climb onto Tucker's back.

It had been a while since Kallie had seen Tucker in wolf form, which meant it had been a while since a fight broke out between him and Jamison. Kallie found it strange, how Tucker changed into a wolf. All he had to do was blink, and he went from being a human to being a monstrous animal. His fur was a mix of dark grays and black, with a few white patches, and the fur on his stomach was also all white.

Tucker and Jamison both took a few steps back to get a running start up the hill, then took off. Kallie gripped on to Tucker's fur as they went climbing up. Jamison was practically swinging from the trees that grew out of the hillside. Tucker jumped from rock to rock. He tried his best to move smoothly so Kallie could hold on. They reached the top before Jamison, who joined them a few seconds later. Jamison helped Kallie climb off of Tucker, and then Tucker changed back into a human.

Kallie noticed sweat dripping down the sides of Jamison's face. She looked at Tucker, who wasn't sweating at all. Kallie tried to think if she had ever seen Tucker sweat, and she hadn't. Not when the sun was beating down on him, not during their romantic moments, not even when he was fighting with Jamison.

"Tucker, do you sweat?" she asked. Tucker smiled and shook his head.

"He pants . . . you know . . . like a dog," Jamison said, laughing.

"Now where do we go?" Tucker asked, ignoring Jamison's comment.

"Right over here," Jamison said, as he approached the vines hanging between the trees. He pulled them back like curtains, and Kallie and Tucker walked through.

Kallie gasped and covered her mouth with her hand. Tucker's eyes grew wide. They couldn't believe this amazing piece of land that was right in front of them. It was like it had just been sitting there, off the side of a small mountain, waiting to be discovered.

The field was in the shape of an oval. It was probably one acre of wide opened land. There were bunnies hopping through the tall field grass. Butterflies were fluttering around the wildflowers. At the far end from where they stood was about an eight-foot-high waterfall, which led into an open pool, then let out into a stream that continued running through the forest. They could see the sunlight glistening off the crystal-clear water. A weeping willow grew right over the natural pool. The tree's leaves were inches above the water.

Jamison walked up next to Kallie and put his arm around her. Kallie looked up at him.

"How did you find this?" Kallie asked, amazed.

"I searched the whole forest last night. I went from end to end, then I finally found this at sunrise."

"How did I not know about this place?" Tucker mumbled to himself.

"What do you think, Tucker?" Jamison asked.

Tucker looked at him and smiled. "You did well, Jamison," he said.

Kallie could see the pride in Jamison's eyes.

"So . . . will this be the place?" Jamison asked them.

"Yes!" Kallie shouted, as she could no longer contain her excitement.

"Do you agree?" Jamison asked Tucker.

"I do," Tucker replied. Then they shook hands, to agree that this would be their home.

Kallie thought that was out of the ordinary. Tucker being a were-wolf, and Jamison a vampire, she found normal. But seeing these two get along was what she called crazy.

Tucker pointed to the middle of the field. "We could build a cabin right there in the middle," he suggested.

"When should we start?" Jamison asked.

"Tomorrow."

Kallie couldn't believe how fast this was happening. Just yesterday morning, she thought she still had to choose one of them, and now they were all going to spend forever in this hidden field, deep inside the forest.

They started walking back to Tucker's camp. They climbed back down the hill the same way they got up.

It was late when they got back to the campsite. The sun had completely set. Tucker and Kallie ate a late supper, then went inside the tent to sleep.

Tucker couldn't believe this was the last night he would spend at his camp. He never thought he would leave this place to go spend forever with the woman of his dreams. And he never, ever would have thought he would share that woman with the vampire across the river.

Jamison watched the moon rise over a mountain. It was so big and bright. He wished he were with Kallie right then. He would have given anything to trade places with Tucker.

Then, as he was looking up at the moon, he noticed it was close to being full. He realized the next night would most likely be a full moon. Jamison usually found himself feeling annoyed when there was a full moon, but this time he looked forward to it. He knew what happened to Tucker when there was a full moon. He would have Kallie to himself, on the night that followed.

CHAPTER TWELVE

June 3rd, 1821

Kallie woke before Tucker. She went outside to see what Jamison was up to. She didn't see him right away, but then she heard him call her name. He had just come up from the river and was motioning for her to come follow him. They walked down to the river. Jamison pointed to something across the way. Kallie looked to see a family of deer drinking water, and she smiled as they tried to be as quiet as they could. But then Kallie accidently kicked a pebble over, and the deer took off running. She looked at Jamison. He was staring at his side of the forest.

"You miss it?" Kallie asked him.

Jamison shrugged. "Now the whole forest is mine," he said as he pulled her in and hugged her. Then he softly whispered in her ear, "Do you want to come with me to gather all my belongings I left on my side?" He was trying to speak as quietly as he could, so Tucker would not hear. "We can stay there overnight," he added.

"What about Tucker?" she asked him.

"Shh . . . " he said, hoping Tucker was still sleeping and couldn't hear their conversation. "Trust me. I don't think you are going to want to be around him tonight." She looked at him, confused. "I'll let him explain it to you," he said.

They walked back up to the camp and heard Tucker yawn as they returned. Jamison hoped Tucker was asleep during their conversation. Tucker crawled out of the tent. He kissed Kallie good morning.

"I think we should pack up everything here, then go up to the field. And I was also planning on going to the reservation and gathering some tools and supplies. You can come with me, Kallie, and we can sleep there."

Jamison spoke before Kallie could answer. "Isn't there a full moon tonight, Tucker?" Jamison asked, trying to hold back his smile. Tucker didn't say anything. He stared off in the distance, then looked up at the sky.

"What happens if there's a full moon?" Kallie asked them.

"All I know is that he howls at the moon all night long . . . it's very annoying."

"As soon as the sun sets and the full moon rises, I'm forced to turn into a wolf. It's like the full moon hypnotizes us . . . all we do is howl at it until the sun rises and the moon disappears."

"You can still come with me," Tucker said to Kallie.

"Well . . . " she began to say. "Jamison already asked me to go with him to get his belongings."

"No. You have to come with me, Kallie. The last time you were over there that long, you almost didn't come back."

"Well, then, why don't you just follow us again?" Jamison sounded annoyed.

"If there wasn't a full moon, I would!" Tucker shouted.

"If you two start fighting right now, I will spend the night by myself!" Kallie shouted before they could start fighting.

"Tucker, I'm not coming with you if you're going to howl at the moon all night," Kallie confessed to him.

"If you don't come with me, everyone will ask where you are. If I say I left you with the vampire, they will be furious."

"Edudu will understand . . . won't he?" Kallie asked.

"Yes . . . but my brother will not. He's been waiting five years for me to kill Jamison."

"Tell them she decided to spend the night alone at your campsite," Jamison suggested.

Tucker shook his head. "All the wolves meet at the same mountain-top every full moon. The other wolves are going to be in the forest all night . . . they won't be far from you. Eventually, they will sense where you are, and who you are with."

"Kallie, you have to come with me. You don't understand what will happen if the tribe finds out about the agreement Jamison and I have."

Tucker had a worried look on his face. Kallie didn't respond.

"If she doesn't want to go with you, Tucker, she doesn't have to," Jamison said.

Tucker looked furious. "Well, when a pack of angry werewolves comes to kill you, don't expect me to stop them."

"I can stop them on my own. Besides, aren't you the big, powerful alpha? Why does it matter what they think? Aren't you the leader?" Jamison said. Tucker glared at him.

Everyone remained silent for a while, trying to come up with a solution.

"Go ahead and spend the night with Jamison. The tribe was bound to find out about this at some point. I won't say anything until one of them brings it up." Tucker began to take down his tent. Jamison and Kallie didn't say a word. They didn't want to do anything to make Tucker change his mind.

They spent the rest of the morning packing everything up for Tucker to take to the field. His tent was taken down and folded up. All his belongings and supplies were packed away. All they left behind were the ashes in the fire pit. Tucker couldn't believe this would be the last time he was there. The small area that had been his home for the last five years would now be a memory.

Once everything was packed up, and they were all ready to go, Kallie hugged Tucker good-bye. They kissed on the lips. Tucker squeezed her tight.

Kallie's hand slipped out of Tucker's as she began walking away from him. He held onto it for as long as he could. Then they went their separate ways. Kallie and Jamison headed west, out of Tucker's camp, and Tucker headed south, toward the field.

Tucker felt strange, being alone. He hadn't been alone for almost four weeks. Once he had arrived to the field, he put up his tent and built a fire pit. He spent the rest of the day waiting for the sun to set and imagining the cabin they were going to build.

As soon as the sun set and the forest began to grow dark, Tucker transformed into a wolf. He tried his best to fight it, like always, but it never worked. He took off running to the highest place in the forest, and waited for the full moon to appear with the rest of the wolves.

Jamison and Kallie walked all day long. They finally reached the area that Jamison had called home for the last twenty years. It was evening, and the sun was setting. She heard Jamison say, "We're here."

Kallie had no words for what she saw. There were twenty yards of roses, growing all over the ground and around the trees. They were thousands of different colors, every shade imaginable. There were dark blues, light blues, bright blues. And it was like that for every color—a huge patch of rainbow flowers. It was the most beautiful thing Kallie had ever seen.

"What are these?" she asked Jamison.

"They're called vampire roses."

"Why are they called that?"

"Because they never die."

Kallie bent down to examine the flowers. They were roses, but they didn't grow on bushes like normal roses. They grew out of the ground, individually.

"They're beautiful," Kallie said.

"That's why I surround myself with them."

Kallie looked up. There was a huge hammock hanging from one big oak tree, across from another big oak tree. It was made of many different quilts, woven together. There were many different patterns and colors.

"Is that where you sleep? Or don't sleep?" Kallie asked.

Jamison smiled and nodded. "Want to go up there?" he asked. She nodded.

There were logs cut in half and nailed into the one oak tree, like steps. Kallie climbed up first, and Jamison followed. Once Kallie reached the top, she climbed onto the hammock. There were many books. Jamison climbed on after her. Kallie looked out into the sea of roses underneath them.

"So this is . . . was? My home." Jamison sounded unsure. He laughed at himself for not knowing what to say.

"It's really amazing up here," Kallie said.

"Did you make this?" she asked, running her hand along the hammock.

"Yes. I took all the quilts I've collected over these years and made them into one giant hammock."

"What are all these books?" She picked one up.

"Some are actually books. I read a lot. And some are full of blank sheets of paper I use for drawing." He picked up one of the books and opened it to a page. He showed Kallie. It was a drawing of her. He got her bright orange hair and blue-green eyes perfectly. He even placed all her freckles. Kallie felt her cheeks turn bright red. Jamison turned to put the book back down. As he turned, Kallie noticed four little black dots on the back-right side of his neck. They made the shape of a perfect square.

"What is that?" Kallie asked as she ran her fingers over the dots. Jamison froze as she touched his neck. He knew what she was talking about, and didn't know what to say.

"That's where I got . . . bitten," he said to her, feeling uncomfortable.

"By another vampire?"

Jamison knew that it was time for everything he had been holding in for last two hundred years to come out. Whether he wanted to talk about it or not, this conversation was going to happen. For the first time ever, Jamison was going to tell his story, and he wouldn't have wanted to tell it to anyone else. He was falling more and more deeply in love with Kallie each day. And he knew she deserved to know everything about him.

"You want to hear about my whole life . . . don't you?" he said, as his bright blue eyes looked into hers.

"You know everything about my life," Kallie said back to him. Jamison sighed and closed his eyes. He opened his eyes and mouth at the same time, trying to think of where to begin.

"I was born in Scotland on January fifth, in the year 1604. I was the youngest of three boys. My family ran their own farm . . . just like everyone. Growing up, my family was always very close with our neighbors. They had a daughter my age; her name was Annabel. She had long brown hair, and deep brown eyes. We grew up together and were best friends. I always planned on marrying her. Then, when I was eighteen, her family became rich. They bought a better piece of land on the other side of the mountains and moved away. We always wrote to each other. After a few years it slowed down, though. Then, when I was twenty-five, I received a letter from her about how she still wasn't married, and she always thought we would get married, and she was wondering if it was too late. But it wasn't. I planned on traveling to her and proposing." Jamison paused for a while. Kallie could see by the look on his face that this was hard for him. She wondered where this was leading.

"Everyone said, never go through the passage in the middle of the mountains, you must travel over the mountains. When someone traveled through the passage, they never made it out. Search parties went looking for them, and when they found the bodies, each one had bite marks in the neck.

"Theories were passed around, that there was some huge snake or serpent living in there, preying on humans. It was a dark, foggy, swampy area. As I traveled, I knew I should go over the mountains, but going through the passage in the middle would be quicker. So that's what I did."

Kallie could see Jamison grow emotional as he spoke. She gripped his hand as he continued.

"I was halfway through. For a while, I felt like I was being watched. Things didn't feel right. Even my horse could sense it. Then all of a sudden . . . "

Jamison swallowed before going on.

"An extremely strong force knocked me off my horse. My horse ran off and disappeared. I hit the ground, and someone was on top of me, holding me down. They were so strong, but by the looks of them they didn't seem strong. Then the most unbelievably piercing pain struck me. I realized that whoever this was, their teeth had ripped through my skin, and were stuck in my neck. I could feel the blood being sucked out of my body. I began feeling weaker and weaker. Then, seconds before I should have blacked out and died, I felt this incredible strength run through my body. I was able to throw the person off of me . . . and when I say 'throw' I mean, launch a thousand feet into the air."

Kallie's eyes filled with tears. She knew Jamison didn't deserve to have to go through that.

"I stood up. I felt so . . . different, in good ways and bad. I felt this strange urge to sink my teeth into something and drink its blood. And I had no idea why. I was terrified. I had no idea what had happened to me. Then I could sense there was a big buck nearby. I knew exactly where it was, my instincts led me right to it. I tackled it to the ground without a problem. I was impressed with my new strength, and then I killed it, and drained it of its blood.

"When I realized what I had just done, I felt so scared. I looked down at my hands . . . they were a different color. My skin used to be just like yours." He looked at Kallie's hands.

"But after that, my skin became strange, almost gray. I knew I needed to get help. All I had to do was get to Annabel, I thought she would be able to help me. I went running out of the woods . . . it should have taken me hours to get out, but I made it to Annabel's village in seconds. I didn't even know how I made it there so fast. It was like I blinked and I was there. So I made it into town, and anyone who saw me looked terrified. They would scream and run away. And I was yelling for help and no one would help me. I didn't know my eyes were a piercing red, and that I had fangs hanging out of my mouth. There was blood all over me. I didn't know I looked like some sort of monstrous creature."

Jamison looked Kallie in the eyes, wondering what her reaction was. She stared back at him, waiting for him to continue his story. He wondered if her silence was a good or bad sign.

"So I started walking down this dirt road. No one was around, it was the middle of the day. I saw this house farther down the road. And there was a woman outside. As I got a little closer, I could see that it was Annabel. I was still far away from her but I could see so well. I could see that it was her. I yelled her name, and she stared at me for a few seconds. As I got closer, she finally realized it was me. She had a worried look on her face. I reached her yard, and her expression went from worried to completely mortified." Jamison's eyes grew watery.

"It's all right . . . keep going," Kallie whispered to him as she squeezed his hand. He sighed, then began talking again.

"She screamed, then shouted, 'You're not Jamison!' She ran inside, and locked the doors. I was standing outside, yelling at her to help me. I tried to explain what had happened to me, but she kept screaming for me to go away, and that she never wanted to see me again. I couldn't understand . . . I thought she loved me . . . I thought she could help me. But she saw me for this hideous thing I had become. But I was still me.

"So I gave up and left. I decided to go back home . . . maybe my family could help me." Jamison blinked, and a single tear rolled down his cheek. Kallie wiped it away.

"So I traveled back through the passage between the mountains. I was able to run back home in probably under twenty minutes. It should have taken me all day. So I made it home . . . same thing was happening to me that happened in Annabel's village. Everyone was running from me, screaming. But these people knew me my whole life. All my neighbors and friends wouldn't help me. I got to my family, I hoped they would listen to me. My parents and brothers were standing before me, staring me up and down. I explained my story to them. They told me I had to leave before an angry mob came after me . . . my brothers wouldn't even let me say good-bye to their children, so all my nieces and nephews thought I disappeared. I begged my parents to let me stay, but they refused. They didn't want anything to do with me anymore. So I grabbed what I could and left."

A few more tears came flowing out of Jamison's eyes.

"They were my family . . . and they abandoned me when I needed them most. Families are supposed to love and care for each other unconditionally . . . they were supposed to help me. I didn't know where to go. I had no one. I traveled through Scotland for a couple of days, staying as far from humans as I could. All I wanted to know was what I had become. I had no idea. I was sitting at the top of a mountain, looking out into the sky, trying to figure out my life. Then these four people appeared before me. Somehow, I knew they were coming. Their skin looked just like mine."

"Were they the vampires we encountered that day?" Kallie asked. Jamison nodded. Kallie could tell by the look in his eyes that he still felt bad about that day.

"Andrew is the older man, Fiona is the older woman, Nessie is the younger woman, and Samuel is . . . " Jamison gulped before finishing his sentence. Kallie already knew who Samuel was.

"He was the one who grabbed you, Kallie. Their story was that Andrew was turned into a vampire fifty years earlier. When he realized he wasn't aging, he turned his wife Fiona into one. They were never able to have children, so they picked a young woman and man in their early twenties, changed them into vampires, and called them their children. They had heard the villagers being scared to death by me. So it turns out, the vampire that attacked me was someone they had been after for years. Apparently, he stole something from them, I never found out what. And when I threw him off of me, he was injured. When they approached him, he couldn't get away . . . and they were able to get their revenge on him. They knew they could use someone that was strong enough to injure another vampire that bad. They had been looking for me since that day. They told me they could help me. They explained to me I had become a vampire. That I survive on blood, now, instead of food and water. They taught me how to get my eyes back to their regular color and undescended my fangs. They taught me everything I needed to know about being a vampire. They helped me grow stronger. They said I might be the strongest vampire ever. Are you getting tired of me talking so much?"

"No. Keep going. I want to know everything."

"They took me in as their own, just like they did with the other two. We were supposed to be some sort of family, but it never felt like one. I still felt empty and alone inside. And then it turned out they were thieves, mostly robbing other vampires of their treasures. And they needed someone strong like me, to kill anyone who got in their way. But I didn't want to kill . . . ever. And I didn't. Instead I would knock out whoever it was they were robbing. Then they would also rob humans. They'd kill them and take everything they had. They have killed many innocent human beings. They tried to force me to, but I couldn't. They tried telling me I was going to die if I didn't. But I'd rather hunt animals and drink their blood instead."

"So you've never tasted human blood?"

"Never. They said it was the most amazing thing I could taste. But I didn't care, I wasn't going to end someone's life just so I could live. Animal blood has done me just fine all these years.

"I spent the next hundred years with them. Helping them do their dirty deeds. I knew it was wrong, but I didn't want to be alone. Then, one day, I couldn't take it anymore. I left. They were furious with me. I spent the next seventy-one years traveling the other side of the world. I tried my best to blend in. I would grow close to a group of people, then disappear before they noticed I didn't age. Soon, I felt like I needed to find a place to call home. I didn't want to move from place to place anymore. People were always talking about the new land, the United States of America. I heard how wonderful it was. I decided to go. I found my family and told them where I was going, in case they ever needed me.

"I truly regret telling them. But they warned me they had heard of tribes that could shapeshift into vicious wolves, and that alphas are usually ridiculously strong. And they hunt vampires.

"I wasn't too worried. I got on a boat and traveled here. I knew I should stay in a forest, where I could hunt animals and be far from humans. Every place I tried, I could sense the werewolves, and they could sense me. They would try chasing me away, and I would give in and leave before someone got killed.

"Then I finally found this place. I made an agreement with Tucker's grandfather so I could stay. And now I've made an agreement with Tucker, to share a beautiful woman, with an amazing soul. And keep her as happy as we can."

Kallie let everything she had just heard sink in. She leaned into Jamison and kissed him on the lips.

"Thank you for opening up to me," she said, and leaned her forehead against his.

"Thank you for listening," he said to her.

Jamison couldn't believe he had just told someone his whole life story. He felt the weight he had been carrying around all this time lift off his shoulders. He knew he truly did love Kallie. There had been lots of times when he'd thought he was in love, throughout his long life. But this time he knew he was, or else he would not have been able to talk to her so easily. He looked into her green eyes as the sun disappeared.

"I love you," he told her.

She smiled. "I love you, too," she said.

Jamison brushed the hair out of Kallie's face, then leaned in and kissed her. Kallie pulled Jamison in closer. Then Jamison lay her down as he moved on top of her. His hand caressed her inner thigh as their lips locked together. Kallie pulled Jamison's shirt over his head. Jamison pulled her up as he untied her dress and pulled it off of her. His hand traveled up between her legs, and Kallie's lips ran down his neck and over his chest. They removed the rest of their clothing from each other's bodies. Then Jamison kissed Kallie in a place that she had never been kissed before.

Tucker was the first to ever touch her in that area, but Jamison was the first to ever put his mouth there. Kallie felt like there was fire spreading throughout her veins. He moved his hands up her body and over her breasts as his tongue continued what it was doing. Moments later his lips moved all the way up her body and rejoined hers as they moved forward with their passion and their bodies connected.

Afterward, they held each other close as it became black outside. They could hear a howl in the distance.

"There's Tucker," Jamison said. Kallie wished Tucker were there. She felt if he knew Jamison's story, he could understand him better.

"You didn't deserve to go through all that, Jamison," Kallie said as they looked up at the night sky.

"You didn't deserve all the things that happened to you, either," he said. They could hear more howls in the distance.

"Do the other wolves know yet?" she asked Jamison.

"I would think so."

Kallie fell asleep in Jamison's arms as she listened to Tucker howling. Jamison realized that he and Kallie were leaving their horrible pasts behind, and were going to give each other the best future they possibly could. He loved holding Kallie as she slept. He wished he could do this every night. But he needed Tucker. It was why he gave in so easily to the idea of sharing Kallie. He knew his "family" would never leave him alone. For the last twenty years, they showed up at least twice a year, trying to convince him to help them out. He denied them each time. He feared that the next time they showed up, they would try to hurt Kallie again. Jamison could never harm them. But Tucker was always able to scare them away. And so Jamison needed Tucker. Kallie would only be safe from Jamison's family if Tucker was around.

CHAPTER THIRTEEN

June 4th, 1821

Sunrise was approaching, and the moon began to disappear. Tucker was back to a human. He took one look at his brother Thomas and knew exactly what was about to happen. He knew it would be pointless to try and come up with some sort of excuse as to why Kallie was with the vampire. The tribe was going to find out the truth someday, so it might as well be today.

"Why is the vampire with Kallie, and why is she in his territory?" Thomas asked as he approached.

"Because she wants to be," Tucker answered. He was avoiding looking his brother in the face. Instead he stared at the edge of the cliff.

"She left you for the vampire?" Thomas asked. Tucker shook his head no as the rest of the tribe gathered around them.

"Then why is she with him, Tucker?" Thomas was becoming angry.

Tucker didn't answer; he continued staring off in the distance.

"Both of you," Edudu whispered, a look of shock spreading across his face. All of the men heard what Edudu had said. Thomas moved in closer.

"What the hell, Tucker!" he shouted. "Have you gone fucking mad? How could you let that bloodsucking creature anywhere near an innocent person?"

Tucker remained silent. Thomas's voice echoed.

"Do you not understand that you have to have a son? How are you going to raise a family with her when there's a vampire around? If you don't have a son, the tribe will never have another alpha. Is that what you want for our future?"

Tucker looked over the crowd. The young men looked back at him, disgusted, but the older men looked at him like he had just done something so incredible that it would be talked about for centuries to come.

The crowd began to thin as they all made their way back to the reservation. Tucker suspected that his father would have a few words to say about all this, but instead all he did was give a small smile and nod and walk away. Edudu was the last to leave.

"Don't listen to what Thomas has to say about this, Tucker. I trust you know what you are doing," Edudu said.

"She's going to need saving . . . and for some reason I won't be able to save her. Only he will," Tucker confessed to Edudu.

While Kallie was still having to decide between them, Tucker could sense that eventually something was going to happen to her, and whatever it was, Tucker would not be able to save her. Only Jamison would, which is why he came up with the idea for her to be with both of them. He knew that at some point Kallie was going to need Jamison.

"Kallie has a special soul. Maybe her one soul was created perfectly for two separate souls," Edudu explained to Tucker.

Tucker stared back at him, confused. "What do you mean by that?" he asked.

"What seems to be happening here is that yours and Jamison's instincts must both be telling you to follow Kallie down whichever path she leads you. And if that path happens to be that she needs both of you to form some sort of mutual agreement and work together, then you must trust that. Kallie is different, she is not like other humans. Let her guide you to where you are meant to be."

Tucker was trying to make sense of it all, but he wasn't sure how to respond.

"We are building her a home. I need to get some tools and supplies," Tucker said.

They returned to the reservation. Edudu gathered everything for Tucker. Tucker decided to wait at the edge of the forest, as he didn't want to risk seeing his brother again. Once he had everything he needed, he said good-bye to Edudu and ventured back into the forest, to return to their new home.

Kallie woke up. She almost forgot where she was. When she saw Jamison's arms wrapped tightly around her, she remembered. She lifted her head and glanced at him. She looked twice just to be sure. His eyes were shut. He actually looked like he could be asleep.

"Jamison," she whispered in his ear. He didn't do anything.

"Are you asleep?" she said more loudly.

His eyes opened suddenly. Kallie laughed.

"I guess I was due for a nap," he said as they both sat up, still naked.

"How often do you sleep?"

"Probably a few hours, every other month. But as time goes on it becomes less."

They got dressed. Jamison gathered all his books, clothes, and other belongings, and stuffed them into different sacks.

Kallie climbed down onto the ground. She was standing in the middle of the huge flower patch Jamison had made. He began untying his hammock. He sat up in one tree and untied the knots. Half the hammock came falling down onto the roses. Then he jumped over to the next tree and untied the other side. The whole thing floated to the ground. He came down and rolled up the hammock. Then he picked up all his things, and was ready to go. He had his hands full.

"Do you want me to carry anything?" she asked him.

"Pick a rose. You can carry that," he told her. She looked at all the roses. She picked up a bright blue one. Jamison smiled at her.

"I knew you were going to pick that one . . . it matches the sky today."

"It matches your eyes," Kallie said. She could have sworn she saw his gray cheeks turn red for a moment.

"When we get there, plant it wherever you want. In a few weeks, there will be thousands of roses all over . . . just like this."

They began their adventure to their new home, where Tucker was waiting for them. Kallie kept asking Jamison if he wanted her to carry anything, but he said no each time. He wasn't struggling to carry all his stuff, he only wanted to be holding her hand. Then he smelled something amazing. It took him a while to realize where it was coming from.

"Are you bleeding?" he asked. She looked at him, confused.

"Umm . . . no?" she answered. Then she glanced down at the rose in her hand. There was a little spot of blood on her finger.

"It must have been one of the thorns," she said, and wiped the blood on a leaf hanging off a low branch she was passing. She looked at Jamison, whose eyes were beginning to turn red.

"How did you know?" she asked.

"I could smell it."

"What does it smell like?"

"Think of it this way. Say you're really hungry, and you can smell someone cooking food, and it smells amazing, and you can't wait to eat it. That's how I feel when I smell blood, especially human blood."

Kallie felt fear wash over her as Jamison explained his hunger to her with his eyes turning freakishly red.

"Are you going to be all right?" she asked him.

"Yes. I can control myself. I've had many years of practice. I'm not weak." His eyes began to turn blue again.

Tucker made it back before Kallie and Jamison. He unpacked all of the supplies. He started to think of a plan for how to start building the cabin. He walked around, trying find the best trees to use.

It was midafternoon when Kallie and Jamison entered the field. Kallie walked toward the pool of water to plant the rose nearby. Tucker came up behind her and wrapped his arms around her waist.

"What is that?" he asked her, looking down at the rose.

"It's called a vampire rose. Soon there will be hundreds of them," she explained, then turned to kiss him.

Kallie watched from afar as Tucker and Jamison discussed how to get started on the cabin. It just seemed so odd to her, watching them have a normal civilized conversation with each other, she couldn't help but find it funny. Then they both went around knocking down trees that had a trunk the perfect width they agreed on. Kallie sat as the ground shook every few seconds from them knocking a tree down. Then they would drag it to the field. By the end of the afternoon, they had made a pile of trees. They began sawing them, trying to make all the trunks the same length.

Kallie was impressed to see them moving so fast. It would usually take months to build a cabin, but these two looked like they could get it done in a few days. They were both very quiet as they worked, but Kallie knew that if they were to speak to each other, they'd most likely begin arguing instead of working. She felt so loved in that moment, knowing that both of these men were doing their best to build a shelter for her. They hated each other so much, but they were trying to get along, for her.

Kallie couldn't picture her life without either of them. She had fallen so deeply in love with both, and she couldn't believe they felt the same way about her. It was in that moment that she realized she was truly the luckiest woman in the world.

Once they were done with their task, they decided to continue where they left off the next day. Jamison disappeared into the trees, and Tucker walked to the waterfall to rinse off. Kallie found herself aroused by Tucker as she watched the water flow over his muscles. She removed her own clothes as she joined him. She kissed down his back and ran her hands down the front of him. When she moved around to face him, she could see that he was not amused.

"What's the matter?" she whispered as she ran her fingers through his hair.

"I'm not in the mood right now."

"Did the tribe find out?" She took a step back.

Tucker nodded.

"How angry were they?"

"My brother is not pleased with me at the moment."

"But you're the alpha. Why does it matter what he thinks? Out of anyone in the tribe you know best. You should stand up for yourself, tell him he has no power over you."

Tucker left the water. He knew Kallie was right, he did need to tell his brother to stop trying to overpower him. He was the alpha, the most powerful his tribe had ever had, and no one was going to try and tell him what he should or should not do.

Nighttime fell, and Tucker and Kallie were sound asleep inside the tent. Jamison wished he could trade places with Tucker. Then he ventured out to hunt. He traveled far through the forest. He had passed by Tucker's old camp a while before, when he had sensed something. He could sense that there were other humans in the forest besides Kallie. He traveled in their direction.

He got to their destination, where a fire had just been put out. Four tents were set up, and everyone was asleep. There were two horses sound asleep, and a carriage. Jamison investigated the carriage, to figure out who these people were and why they were camping in the middle of the forest.

He quietly searched through their belongings until he came across some papers. They were the posters with Kallie's face on them.

Jamison knew who these people were and why they were here. He rushed back to the field.

CHAPTER FOURTEEN

June 5th, 1821

Jamison returned to Tucker and Kallie as the sun was rising. He spotted Tucker already awake when he entered the field. Tucker stared down Jamison as he waited for him to confess what he had found.

"You discovered something bad . . . didn't you?" Tucker whispered to Jamison as they approached each other, making sure Kallie couldn't hear their conversation if she was awake.

"They are searching the forest for Kallie," Jamison finally said. "I'm almost positive it must be that Christopher . . . they have the same posters you showed me."

"Why won't that man just give up on her already?" Tucker sighed.

"Can you blame him?"

Tucker laughed. Jamison felt surprised. He never thought that he would make a werewolf laugh.

"Where did you see them?" Tucker asked.

"Northeast, past where your camp was."

"It should take them a day to make it over here. We have time."

Tucker decided to stay up and get an early start on the cabin, so Jamison chose to go and lie down with Kallie. He noticed all her freckles. Her face was even more covered now and they were more noticeable on the rest of her body. For some reason, her freckles reminded him of the night sky, like it was a map to the universe. Then he thought maybe she was whatever these star people were supposed to be.

Jamison ventured outside after a while, and Tucker wasn't in sight. Jamison started a fire in the fire pit. It was a chilly morning, and he knew Kallie would be cold when she woke up. He found a big piece of wood and began carving a door out of it.

Once Jamison started making noise while he was working, Kallie woke up. She crawled out of the tent and saw Jamison chucking away at the piece of wood. He stopped once she approached him.

"Sorry, did I wake you?" he asked.

"It's all right. What are you doing?"

"Making a door." He pulled her into his arms and kissed her on the forehead.

"Why are you making a door already? We don't even have any walls yet." Kallie smirked.

"Just thought I'd get it out of the way." Jamison shrugged.

"Where's Tucker?"

"I can hear him doing something over by the hill. But I don't know what."

Kallie started walking toward the hill. Jamison followed.

When they exited the field, Tucker was standing at the top of the hill staring down. They joined him and looked in the same direction.

"You made a path?" Jamison asked, sounding surprised.

"Now it'll be a lot easier to go up and down."

Kallie was happy, now that she could go up and down by herself.

Tucker and Jamison looked at each other with looks of raging anger on their faces. Kallie looked back and forth at each of them, waiting for someone to say something.

"What's wrong?" she asked.

"Get back into the field," Jamison said.

"But why?"

"Just go!" Tucker shouted.

Kallie didn't budge, she waited for an explanation. Tucker picked her up and threw her over his shoulder, then carried her back into the field, Jamison behind him.

"Shit," Jamison mumbled as he stared back to where they had come from. Tucker put Kallie down, and she gave each of them a mean look.

"How did they get over here so fast?" Tucker asked.

"They did have horses with them," Jamison answered.

"Horses? You never said anything about them having horses!"

"I didn't think I had to! How do they even know where we are?"

"They could probably see the smoke from the fire you built and knew there would be people here!"

"Well, now they can come right up the path you made!"

Both men angrily paced back and forth, both mad at themselves for making it so easy for the other men in the forest to get to Kallie, thinking about how they were going to handle the situation.

"What is happening?" Kallie asked in a demanding voice.

Her question was answered immediately. Two horses came barging through the vines. She knew whose horses they were. They were followed by the carriage they pulled. And there he was, the man she hated with a burning passion.

The horses stopped. Christopher and the other men looked shocked to see her. Kallie recognized the other men. They, too, had tried to win her over a time or two, but had also failed. Christopher jumped off the carriage and ran up to Kallie.

"Kallie, my dear! You're alive! I can't believe I found you!"

Kallie rolled her eyes.

Christopher hugged her tight. Tucker and Jamison wanted to punch him right in the face, but if they did he'd be dead.

Christopher looked at both men. Tucker wondered if he recognized him. Then Christopher grabbed Kallie's hand as he tried to start walking away.

"Thank you for taking care of her. You're good men," he said as he turned around. Kallie didn't move. Christopher turned and looked at her, confused.

"I am not going with you," she said firmly as she pulled her hand away from him.

Christopher looked angry. "And why not?" he asked, looking at all three of them.

"I am staying here . . . with them."

"You don't even know them, Kallie. They're two strangers you met in the woods. Now let's go. Your aunt and uncle have been worried sick about you."

"I've only known these men for a month, and they already know me better than you ever will."

"If you don't come willingly, I will force you to come with me," Christopher said through his teeth.

Tucker and Jamison stepped in.

"She said she is staying here," Tucker said as he stepped between them and nudged Christopher back.

"She's with us now," Jamison said. He stood next to Tucker.

"No. She's my fiancé. She belongs to me."

"No," Jamison said.

Christopher made the big mistake of punching Jamison in the face. Jamison didn't even blink. He and Tucker busted out laughing.

Christopher then attempted to punch Tucker, but Tucker grabbed his arm to stop him before he could make contact.

They laughed harder. Christopher tried to push through them to get to Kallie. Before he almost grabbed her, Jamison threw him back. Jamison's eyes turned red and his fangs came out. Christopher looked at him, terrified. Then he looked at Tucker, who couldn't help but transform into a beastly wolf and growl.

Christopher yelled as he went running back to the carriage. The second he jumped on, the horses turned around with the carriage and took off. Christopher yelled back, "Don't worry, Kallie, I'll come back with an army to save you from these beasts who have captured you!"

They disappeared.

"Thank you for protecting me," Kallie said to them, then gave them each a quick kiss on the cheek. "What are you going to do when he comes back?"

But their attention was drawn elsewhere. They were staring at something in the woods. Kallie turned and looked, but there was nothing there.

"What are you looking at?"

Then she saw.

The men in Tucker's tribe came out of the forest and entered the field. Thomas approached him first.

"Now you're fighting humans with the vampire?" Thomas asked Tucker. Jamison took a step back, and Kallie stood by his side.

"We were only trying to protect her," Tucker mumbled.

"You also just let a group of humans see that you're a werewolf!" Thomas screamed.

"I couldn't help myself!" Tucker yelled back.

"We are meant to protect humans from vampires, Tucker! Not fight humans with vampires!"

"We were protecting Kallie from them! What was I supposed to do, let them take her away?"

"You were supposed to keep her away from that thing! She shouldn't even know any of this exists!"

Kallie grabbed Jamison's hand and held it in hers.

"He's good, Thomas! If I were to kill him, it would be for no reason at all!"

"Don't you remember how this whole thing works? Werewolves protect the humans, vampires hunt the humans, werewolves hunt the vampires. He can still kill at any moment . . . I don't understand why you are doing all this with him." Thomas lowered his voice.

"Because she needs him!" Birds took off flying, after Tucker's booming cry. Tucker spotted Edudu's smile as the truth finally came out. Thomas, Kallie, and Jamison looked at Tucker, shocked.

"She needs him for what?" Thomas asked in disbelief.

"I don't know! But my instincts are telling me that this whole crazy, fucked-up thing is supposed to happen. For some reason, this needs to happen! Thomas, I'm sorry you are not the alpha, I know how much it meant to you. But how long are you going to hold it against me?"

"I will never support what you have chosen to do," Thomas said.

"I'm the alpha of this tribe. I have more power than you ever will, and you know that. Whatever I say goes, and you can't do anything about it."

Thomas turned around and began to walk away. Few went to follow him.

"Don't you even think about turning against me!" Tucker shouted to Thomas, and he froze.

"If you turn on me, you will lose everything, Thomas! And so will anyone else who decides to join you," Tucker finished. Thomas proceeded to walk away.

Tucker's father approached him. Tucker couldn't tell what his mood was.

"I support every choice you make, Tucker, whether it's insane or not. I know you know what you are doing, and I will not question you," his father said, and patted him on the back. He walked away. Everyone but Edudu left.

"Now there's only one more thing you are hiding," Edudu whispered to Tucker while he looked at Jamison. They knew what he meant by that sentence. Then he, too, walked away, and it was just the three of them.

"My instincts are telling me the same thing . . . that she also needs you," Jamison confessed as Tucker turned to face them.

"I don't even know what to say right now," Kallie said.

"Don't say anything. Just kiss me," Tucker demanded as he took Kallie in his arms and grabbed her face.

"Well, I'm going to go . . . somewhere that's not here," Jamison said, then walked into the forest, to leave them alone.

Kallie pulled Tucker to the tent and started undressing him. Kallie knew Tucker was stressed, with everything that had just happened. She wanted to make him forget it all and only focus on her. She also felt very turned on by him, watching him take control and be the true man he was meant to be. She straddled him as they sat in the tent, then bit his bottom lip and ran her mouth down his strong jawline. She kissed his neck, he pulled her dress off.

Kallie pushed Tucker back so he was lying flat on his back with her on top of him. His hands ran down her backside, grabbing on to her skin. Kallie nuzzled her face into the crook of his neck, breathing in and out. She held on to his shoulders as their bodies came together.

Kallie easily left Tucker breathless, always. She made him forget that the rest of the world even existed. Like it was just the two of them, and nothing else mattered. He was most likely the strongest man in the whole world, and Kallie was the one and only thing that could make him tremble with weakness.

After her session with Tucker, Kallie went under the waterfall to wash up. Then someone joined her. They grabbed her down low as they snuck up behind her. She was excited when she saw her favorite blue eyes staring back at her.

Jamison crouched. His lips started above her knee, then traveled all the way up her inner thigh. Just when he was about to reach the destination Kallie was hoping for, he shot up and kissed her mouth instead. Then his mouth slowly went down her neck, over her breast, to her stomach, then finally to where she wanted him to kiss her.

He picked her up and carried her to the edge of the pool. He set her down on the grassy border around the pool, where a vampire rose grew right next to her. Jamison took her right there, against where the water met the land, as his eyes turned red for the second time that day. She squeezed onto his biceps, which sent a shock of adrenaline running through Jamison. He grabbed her hands and held them behind her back, as the feeling of his fangs popping out went away.

Tucker and Jamison built the cabin walls that evening. When the sun was setting, they had the walls and roof assembled. Now all that was left to work on was the inside of the cabin.

Kallie's last few thoughts, before drifting off to sleep that night, were about how good she felt. Any other woman would have been disgusted with themselves after having intercourse with two different men in the same day. She wondered what others would say about her if they knew what she was doing. But, she could not care less if she seemed to be acting like a "whore." The voices of the woman in her village echoed in her mind. She was happy, and felt like she was

exactly where she was meant to be, and she was going to continue doing what made her happy.

Tucker and Jamison sat around the fire as Kallie fell asleep in the
tent. Tucker knew Edudu was hinting for him to tell Kallie and Jamison
what had happened the night Kallie's parents died. And Jamison knew
Edudu was hinting for him to mention something about Kallie possibly being a star person. Jamison could hear Kallie breathing steadily,
so he knew she was asleep.

"What's a star person?" Jamison asked.

Tucker looked up from the fire. "Where did you hear that?" he
asked Jamison.

"When Kallie was sick, I overheard some of your people talking
about them."

"They are these mystical beings that come from the stars to help
and guide us, who are here."

"Help and guide us for what?"

"In the right direction. My grandfather and parents have told tales
of when the star people visited the tribe. They gave my grandfather
seeds for plants that could cure just about any illness, they warned
them about what the future could bring, helped them become more
advanced in life. Then once they finished what they needed to do,
they would leave."

"So, they'd come down from the stars? And then go back?"

"If they didn't have to be here long term. If there was something important going on and they were going to be needed, their souls were
made into humans and they would come into this world and leave this
world just like anyone else."

"What would they look like?"

"I have never seen one. But they would have very unique hair and
eyes. Physical appearances that you would never see any common
person with."

"What about their personality?"

"I'm not sure. My tribe has said that once they would leave, an unexplainable wave of loneliness would wash over the whole tribe, and it

would take months to go away. They were the kindest, most generous beings that any of them had ever met, and it felt good to be constantly surrounded by all the happiness they would give off. Then, once they were gone, it took a while to feel like that again."

Tucker had gone to bed, leaving Jamison alone with his thoughts. Kallie did fit the description of a star person pretty well. But if she was, then what would be her reason for being here?

CHAPTER FIFTEEN

June 6th–8th, 1821

Both Tucker and Kallie slept in the next morning. Jamison searched nearby for stones to use to make a floor in the cabin. By the time Kallie and Tucker woke up, Jamison had a collection of rocks stacked next to the cabin. Tucker and Kallie ate breakfast before helping Jamison.

"Any sign of Christopher?" Kallie asked when she was done eating.

"I don't sense anything . . .do you, Tucker?" Jamison asked.

Tucker shook his head. "They're not going to come today," he said with confidence.

They started making the floor. Jamison and Tucker laid out the stones over the dirt floor of the cabin. Kallie got a bucket of mud to fill in the cracks between the stones. She was happy to help. The floor was done by evening. Tucker and Jamison gathered wood to build furniture. Once the sun went down, they decided to finish the next day.

Tucker woke before sunrise the next day. He returned to the reservation to get more supplies. When he got to the end of the forest, he saw his mother and Edudu waiting for him. Tucker knew that Edudu must have told her that he was coming. His mother ran up and hugged him, once he stepped out of the forest.

"Edudu told me," she said as she embraced her son. "I trust you, Tucker. I know you would never put anyone you love in danger." She looked him in the eye.

"Thank you," Tucker said, sounding relieved.

"We got everything ready for you," Edudu said and pointed to a wagon full of everything Tucker was there to retrieve.

"I made a few dresses and moccasins for Kallie, for all seasons. I knew she wouldn't have the materials to make herself new clothes," his mother explained.

"She's going to love it." Tucker smiled.

"I also knitted some blankets. I know." His mother looked over her shoulder before finishing her sentence. "Vampires get cold, too," she whispered.

"Anything the three of you might need is in the wagon," Edudu said as Tucker looked through everything. He thanked both of them, got the wagon, and returned to the forest.

By sunset, all the furniture was built. They had a bed, tables and chairs, cabinets, cupboards, dressers. Kallie made the bed with the blankets and pillows Tucker's mother gave them. She folded all her new clothes and tucked them away in her dresser. She was thankful that Tucker's mother had thought of her. Then she remembered that she still had many belongings back at her aunt and uncle's she would like to have. She walked outside, where Tucker and Jamison were picking up the tools.

"I have a few belongings at my aunt and uncle's that I would like to go get," she said uncertainly.

Jamison and Tucker looked at her. Neither of them knew what to say.

"Do you really think that's a good idea, Kallie?" Jamison asked.

"It'll be easy. I'll climb through the window, get my belongings, climb out, and we will come right back."

"I don't think we should, Kallie. What if someone sees you?" Tucker said.

"We can go at midnight, everyone will be asleep." She looked back and forth at both of them.

"Maybe. Either I can go, or Tucker can go. We'll retrieve your things and return," Jamison suggested.

"Neither of you knows where everything is." Kallie sounded frustrated.

Tucker groaned. Jamison wondered how Tucker was going to respond. Jamison was ready to give in and take her the moment he could sense she was getting upset. Tucker opened his mouth to speak, but Kallie interrupted.

"Fine, I can go by myself," she said and began to walk away, knowing that they would have no other choice but to give in to her.

"What could possibly happen that we won't be able to take care of, Tucker?" said Jamison.

Kallie smiled as her back was to them. Tucker stared up at the sky as it was changing to night. He knew that Kallie hated her village, and if she wanted to go back this badly, then whatever she wanted must be important to her.

"We'll leave at midnight," he finally said. Kallie turned back around.

"That'll be fine," she said and walked back toward the cabin.

While they awaited midnight, Tucker hunted and cooked supper, and Jamison even ate a little. Afterward, Kallie was standing in the cabin, looking around. The door was wide open behind her as the warm spring night breeze blew through. The fireplace was on the far-left wall, two armchairs in front of it. There was a stack of firewood against the wall. The bed was ten feet from the fireplace. On the right side of the cabin was a table with chairs; the cabinets and cupboards were along the wall. Everyone's belongings had their places. Kallie couldn't believe that this was now her home, and Tucker and Jamison were now her family.

Midnight had arrived, and the sky was full of stars. Tucker transformed into a wolf, Kallie and Jamison climbed on his back, and Tucker took off running through the dark forest. Kallie couldn't see a thing the whole time, and she was surprised when they had made it out without running into anything.

They were near the town square when they left the forest. Kallie could see that there was something going on in the center; she rushed over and peeked down one of the alleys to see.

"Kallie, come back here!" Tucker shouted in a whisper. He looked at Jamison and said, "I knew this was a bad idea."

They started walking toward Kallie.

"You think any idea that is not yours is a bad idea," Jamison said as they joined Kallie. She was so distracted by what was happening in the town square that she didn't even notice them bickering.

Christopher was in the town square with a large group of men. There were papers all spread out on a wooden table, and a few lanterns to see by. He seemed to be trying to convince the men to join him in fighting the beasts in the forest and save Kallie. None of the men seemed to be willing to do so.

"Oh, come on! Every last one of you is a pathetic excuse for a man!" Christopher shouted.

"Some of us are married and have children, Christopher. We can't risk our lives to try to defeat some creatures we know we don't have a chance at beating," one man said.

"Fine, get out of here! All of you!"

Christopher's voice echoed throughout the square. All the men left, gossiping about how Christopher had lost his mind while they exited the square. Christopher was left alone in the center of town.

"I'm going to have a word with him . . . I'll be back," Jamison said as he began walking into the square.

"What are you doing?" Kallie whispered.

Jamison kept on walking.

"He's going to kill him . . . isn't he?" Kallie said, looking up at Tucker, whose eyes glowed in the night.

"Possibly." He watched Jamison approach Christopher.

Christopher was turned around, looking down at the papers on the table, which were maps of the forest. He had no idea the vampire from the forest was just a few feet behind him.

"Having trouble finding men to fight alongside you?" Jamison said to the back of Christopher. Startled, Christopher turned around. He thought he knew who that voice belonged to.

"What do you want?" Christopher said with a shaky voice.

"I want you to leave Kallie alone."

"But she's my—" Christopher began to say.

Jamison interrupted: "No. She's not your anything! She does not belong to you. She never has and never will. You don't deserve her. No one does. I don't even deserve her . . . but for some crazy reason, she loves me."

As Jamison said this to Christopher, he reached for his gun, which lay on the table behind him.

Christopher shot at Jamison. Kallie was about to scream, but Tucker quickly covered her mouth. Jamison caught the bullet in his hand and dropped it on the ground like it was nothing. Christopher was in shock.

"I'm going to make this simple for you, all right?" Jamison said as he stepped closer to Christopher.

"Take one step into the forest, or come anywhere near her, and I will have no problem making yours the first life I ever take. Do you understand?"

Jamison's eyes began to turn red. Christopher nodded.

"Good." Jamison eyed the lanterns on the table. He walked to the table, and Christopher flinched the moment Jamison moved toward him.

"I'm going to take these," Jamison said and grabbed the lanterns. He walked back to Kallie and Tucker. "Found some lanterns for the cabin," he said when he returned to them. Tucker laughed. Kallie ran to Jamison and threw her arms around him.

"I thought you were going to die!" Kallie said as she hugged Jamison as tightly as she could. He leaned down and kissed her on the lips. He felt good knowing that for the first time in a long time, someone really did care about him.

They walked down the dirt road to Kallie's aunt and uncle's house. A warm breeze blew past them as they walked through the sleeping town. Then Kallie stopped in front of a house. A light shone in one of the windows.

"Is this it?" Jamison asked.

Kallie shook her head no. "This is Minnie's house." There was sadness in her voice. "She's probably heard what Christopher has been saying. She should know I'm safe."

"Go on and tell her," Tucker said.

Kallie walked forward, and turned to look at them.

"We'll wait here," Tucker whispered.

Kallie walked up the wooden steps to the front door and knocked lightly. Tucker and Jamison saw a woman peek out the window to see who was at the door. The woman's mouth dropped open when she saw Kallie, then the door swung open and the woman pulled Kallie into her arms.

"You're alive." The woman's voice cracked. Then she saw Tucker and Jamison standing in the road. Her expression changed.

"Is that—" the woman began to say as she let go of Kallie. Kallie turned and looked at them, then interrupted Minnie before she could assume anything.

"They're good. I promise," Kallie told her.

"So, you're safe?" she asked. Kallie nodded. "Are you happy?"

Kallie smiled and whispered, "Yes."

Minnie smiled and pulled her into another hug.

"I'm going to continue my life with them. They built me a home in the forest."

"Take good care of her," Minnie whispered to the men waiting for Kallie.

"We will," they whispered back to her.

Kallie hugged her one last time before walking away. Once Kallie was no longer in front of Minnie, the men could see her big stomach and that she was going to have a baby, any day now.

Kallie sighed with relief as she joined Tucker and Jamison. They continued to walk down the road. Before she knew it, Kallie was standing in front of her old home.

"We're here," she said.

"Which window are you going in?" Tucker asked.

Kallie started walking around to the side of the house.

"That one," she said, pointing up. The window was open. Tucker jumped up, grabbed the windowsill, then pulled himself up and inside. Jamison put Kallie on his shoulders, then Tucker pulled her up and she crawled through the window. Kallie looked around her old room, everything exactly as she left it. She opened the big trunk at the foot of her bed.

"It's all still here," she whispered. Tucker looked in the trunk. There were jewelry, a pocket watch, a journal, and a few dresses. A tear ran down Kallie's cheek.

"This is my parents' stuff . . . I thought my aunt and uncle would have sold everything."

Tucker wiped away her tears.

"Is this what you came for?" he asked her. She nodded. Tucker picked up the trunk, walked over to the window, and dropped it outside. It made a loud thud as it hit the ground. Kallie crawled out the window, Jamison standing underneath it with his arms wide open, ready to catch Kallie. She released her grip on the windowsill and landed in Jamison's arms.

"I must really trust you, " she said as Jamison put her down. "I didn't think twice about whether you were going to catch me or not."

Tucker jumped out the window. The ground shook. He made an even louder thud when he hit the ground.

"Oops," he said, laughing. Kallie saw a light go on in her aunt and uncle's bedroom.

"What was that?" she heard her uncle shout.

"It's the beasts that captured Kallie!" her aunt yelled.

All three of them snickered.

"I'm going to look outside," they heard her uncle say. Tucker changed into a wolf, and Jamison helped Kallie climb on his back. Jamison picked up Kallie's trunk, then both Tucker and Jamison took off running back to the forest.

They soon returned home. Jamison put Kallie's trunk at the foot of the bed in the cabin, then set up the three lanterns he stole from Christopher. Neither Tucker nor Kallie was tired enough to go to bed.

The trio sat around the fire outside. A random thought popped into Kallie's head.

"Tucker . . . when is your birthday?" she asked.

"August twenty-fifth," he answered.

"You're not going to ask Jamison when his birthday is?" Tucker asked, laughing. Jamison didn't age.

"It's January fifth," she answered confidently. Jamison was impressed by what a good listener Kallie was.

"I don't really have a birthday anymore, Kallie. I'm stuck at the age of twenty-five forever."

"So as long as you are with me, you will celebrate your birthday," Kallie said. Jamison couldn't believe how lucky he was to have her.

"When is yours?" Tucker asked her.

"April eighteenth," she answered. Both men stored that date into their minds.

Kallie was tired. She stood and went to walk to Jamison to kiss him good night. When she went to take a step, she tripped and bumped her face on a rock. She bounced right back up. She laughed at her own clumsiness.

"You all right?" Jamison asked as he helped her.

"Yes." She was still laughing. Then she leaned in and kissed Jamison on the lips. The second that her lips touched his, he smelled that amazing smell. He went to pull away, but it was too late. Her lip was bleeding and the blood had gotten onto Jamison's lips.

Kallie pulled away and looked at him, confused. He couldn't help but lick his lips. Once he tasted that human blood, he finally understood why others went crazy over it, and now he wanted more.

Kallie took a step back. "Jamison?" she said as his eyes turned red and his fangs came out.

"Your lip's bleeding," he mumbled. He was looking at her in a way he never had before. And for the first time, Kallie was afraid of him.

Tucker stepped in front of her. "Jamison, go!" he shouted.

Jamison didn't move. He kept staring at Kallie.

"Jamison, you know I will kill you if I have to. Now, go!"

Jamison finally started walking away.

"Don't come back until you've calmed down!" Tucker yelled as Jamison disappeared into the night.

Tucker took Kallie inside, where they lay down. He covered her with a blanket. She was crying.

After calming down somewhat, she tried to sleep but her heart ached for Jamison. Tucker could sense Jamison getting farther and farther away, until he could no longer sense him at all, which meant he was no longer in the forest.

Once Kallie's eyes finally closed and her breathing and heartbeat slowed, Tucker finally relaxed and fell asleep.

Jamison did not come back the next day. Kallie hardly ate or said a word. Tucker tried his best to make it seem like Jamison was still in the forest, and that he would be coming back, but Tucker honestly had no clue where Jamison was nor if he would return.

CHAPTER SIXTEEN

June 9th, 1821

When Tucker woke up, Kallie wasn't lying next to him, but he could hear her sniffling. He turned over and saw her sitting at the table, looking down at a book. Tucker stretched, then climbed out of bed. He walked over to the table and sat next to Kallie.

"What's that?" he asked, pointing at the book.

"Jamison's drawings," she answered.

"I didn't know he drew," Tucker said.

"There's a lot you don't know about him."

Tucker pulled the book toward him and began flipping through it. Most of the drawings were of the forest, or the vampire roses, and some were of Kallie.

"I miss him." Kallie began to cry harder.

Tucker wiped her tears away and pulled her in close. She could hear their hearts beating in synch with each other, as her ear was pressed up against his chest.

They sat in silence. Tucker held Kallie as she tried to stop crying. He played with her hair and rubbed his hand on her back as she tried to calm down. He kissed her on the forehead and looked into her sad, green eyes.

"I love you," he whispered.

"I love you more," she whispered back.

Kallie washed up under the waterfall. She stopped to admire the vampire roses when she was done. There were easily more than fifty of them. Tucker came up behind her and wrapped his strong arms around her. He looked down at the roses.

"That one matches your hair," he said, pointing to a bright red-orange one in the center. Kallie smiled, and Tucker's heart melted. Kallie turned around and kissed him. They held each other as tightly as they could, until a familiar voice broke them apart.

"Tucker," the exhausted voice said. Kallie and Tucker pulled away from each other.

Kallie gasped. "Jamison!" She tried to run to him.

Tucker pulled her back and whispered, "Please go in the cabin until I know he's safe."

Kallie knew he was right, so she went inside and closed the door. The biggest fight ever between Tucker and Jamison could possibly happen right now, and Kallie didn't want to witness it.

Tucker walked toward Jamison. Jamison's hair was a mess, his clothes were ripped. He looked worn out.

"Did you get in a fight, Jamison?" Tucker asked with his arms crossed.

"With myself," Jamison said in a tired voice.

"Did you kill anyone?" Tucker asked, staring him down.

Jamison looked at him, disgusted, and said, "No."

"Well . . . where were you?"

"As far from civilization as I could get. I need to talk to her." Jamison began walking toward the cabin.

Tucker put his arm out and pushed Jamison back. "No. How do I know you're all right now?"

Jamison rolled his eyes. "I'm fine!" he said.

"How am I supposed to know this won't happen again?"

"I only got like that because I tasted it. I've smelled human blood thousands of times, and I've never lost control. I should have never tasted it, I know that! I regret what I did! I'm not going to let you stop me from seeing her."

Jamison pushed past Tucker. Tucker grabbed him and threw him across the field.

Jamison's body slammed against a big tree and he slid to the ground. Then Jamison stood and charged at Tucker, who knocked him down to the ground and stood over him.

"What if you were in my position?" Tucker asked Jamison as he tried to get up. Tucker slammed him back down. "What would you do if it were me who almost killed Kallie?"

"I'm never going to kill her!" Jamison shouted as he grabbed Tucker's legs and knocked him over. They both rose to their feet.

"I saw the look in your eyes!" Tucker shouted. "I knew what was going through your head!" He shoved Jamison back.

"Do you have any idea what it's like to love the one thing you are meant to kill?" Jamison said, his voice lower. "Yes, I am a fucking vampire. Yes, I am supposed to kill humans. But I have made it 192 years without ever killing anyone! It's not who I am! And it's something I never will become. Being away from her for more than a day was the worst experience of my life. I need her, and you need her just as much, and she needs both of us. And if I ever come close to hurting her . . . go ahead and kill me! I'll deserve it!"

Tucker didn't respond. He couldn't imagine what Jamison was going through. He stared at Jamison, his expression being a mix of emotions. Tucker stepped aside.

"Thank you." Jamison walked to the cabin.

Kallie was sitting at the edge of the bed, her leg shaking up and down. She could hear both of them fighting outside, but she couldn't hear exactly what they said. All she wanted was to be in Jamison's arms again.

The door slowly began to open. Kallie anticipated who was on the other side. A touch of sunlight shone on Kallie's face as the door opened, making her eyes blue, then they met the only other pair of blue eyes she cared about. Jamison gently closed the door, then instantly fell apart.

"I hate myself," he whispered as tears streamed down his face.

Kallie didn't know what to say. He dropped to his knees in front of her.

"I'm so sorry," he said as he looked up at her. Her eyes filled with tears. He threw his face down in her lap and began to sob.

"Please forgive me . . . I never want to hurt you. Please don't hate me, Kallie."

She could hear the pain in his voice. Tears were running down her cheeks.

"I hate myself," he said again.

Kallie lifted his head and stared deep into his eyes. "Don't ever say you hate yourself," she began to say. "I love every single part of you."

"I love you so much, Kallie." He moved in to kiss her.

"I love you, too." Their lips touched.

Tucker was listening to every word. Even he was feeling emotional about all this. He couldn't imagine wanting to hurt Kallie. And for a split second, he knew Jamison had been debating it. Tucker looked off into the trees, he could see his brother standing there, he knew Thomas had to have seen and heard everything that just happened between him and Jamison. Thomas shook his head looking disappointed, then left.

Jamison didn't leave Kallie's side all day long. Once it was night, they lay down together, and Kallie fell asleep. Jamison went to get up, once Tucker came in to go to bed.

"You can stay there tonight. She needs you more right now," Tucker said as he grabbed an extra blanket.

"Really? Are you sure?" Jamison asked.

"It's fine. Besides, that's the most peaceful she's looked in two days."

Tucker lay the blanket on the floor and spent the night sleeping in front of the empty fireplace.

Jamison didn't let go of Kallie all night long.

CHAPTER SEVENTEEN

June 10th, 1821

"All right, that's it! I have had enough of this!" Tucker yelled in the middle of the afternoon. Kallie looked at him, puzzled after his random outburst.

"Let me take care of it," Jamison insisted, then walked out of the field.

"Well this is not going to be good," Tucker mumbled to himself.

Kallie approached him.

"Now what happened?" she asked, sounding annoyed.

"Jamison might kill someone," Tucker answered casually.

"What?" Kallie said, sounding both mad and scared.

"He has a good reason." Tucker shrugged.

"Explain please."

Jamison was a blur traveling at high-speed through the forest. That man had a lot of guts to be entering the forest after what Jamison had told him. Jamison found Christopher in seconds, knocked him right off his horse. He grabbed Christopher by the neck and lifted him off the ground. Christopher looked down to Jamison's raging red eyes, trying to pry his hand from around his neck. Jamison's fangs came out; Christopher tightly shut his eyes, struggling for air.

"I warned you. I told you not to come here. I told you what would happen to you. And you **still** won't give up." Christopher was making awful choking sounds, his feet dangling high off the ground.

"And now you are going to die because of your own stupidity." Jamison brought Christopher close to his fangs.

Jamison was going to do it. He was going to kill someone. He was doing it for Kallie. "Kallie," Jamison thought to himself. The look of disappointment on her face after she would find out he killed someone flashed in his mind. He loosened his grip on Christopher.

"Her aunt is sick," Christopher could hardly say. Jamison dropped him on the ground. He lay there gasping for air.

"I only came to tell her," he said wheezing.

Jamison stared down at Christopher, his body shaking with fear. Jamison couldn't believe what he had almost done. Even though Kallie hated Christopher she would still be angry at Jamison for killing him and he would regret it for the rest of his life. Jamison walked away, leaving Christopher on the ground, still struggling to catch his breath.

Jamison came barging into the field, angry with himself for almost doing what he promised himself he'd never do, but also angry with himself for not following through with what he warned Christopher he would do. Kallie and Tucker approached him.

"What happened?" they both asked eagerly, Kallie hoping Jamison didn't kill anyone, Tucker hoping he had finally gotten rid of Christopher.

"Christopher is on his way here."

"Why?" they both said.

"He has news for Kallie." Jamison walked inside the cabin, slamming the door behind him. Kallie and Tucker exchanged confused expressions.

Not too much longer Christopher came into the field riding on a horse. His neck was completely bruised. Kallie groaned at the sight of him; Jamison came back outside. He and Tucker watched as Kallie walked up to him.

"Looks like you almost killed him," Tucker said to Jamison.

"I just couldn't do it . . . but something's telling me I should have."

"Yes, you should have."

"What do you want, Christopher?" Kallie crossed her arms.

"Your aunt has become very ill. No one knows how much longer she has," said Christopher, his voice sounding raspy and eyes wincing with pain as he spoke.

"Oh," Kallie said as she almost felt bad for a second.

"Has she seen a doctor?" she asked him.

"Yes, but the only treatment that could possibly save her is very expensive."

Kallie looked back to Tucker and Jamison; she could tell that they were listening very intently.

"They could really use the money, Kallie. You could save her life; you know what you need to do."

She knew what Christopher was talking about. All she had to do was agree to marrying him and he would give her aunt and uncle the money they needed. Tears filled her eyes.

Her aunt was never much of a mother to Kallie, but she was the closest thing Kallie had to a mother. Kallie thought hard about what to do. They did take her in when she had nowhere else to go. If it wasn't for her aunt and uncle she probably would have ended up in an orphanage. Her aunt was her mom's sister. But both her aunt and uncle almost always ignored her; she felt invisible as a child, only being spoken to when they wanted her to do something. But her aunt was not a bad enough person to deserve to die. Kallie knew she had to be the bigger person and do what it took to help out the only family she had left.

"Fine, Christopher," she said, her eyes full of tears.

She shook her head. "You win."

Kallie looked back at Tucker and Jamison, disbelief written all over their faces.

"I'm so sorry," she whispered to them, as tears began to run down her face.

"No." They each gasped.

Christopher hoisted Kallie up onto his horse. She took one look back at them, then she was gone.

Tucker looked at Jamison, gray clouds moved over the sun, rain began to fall from the sky.

"We have to go after her," Tucker said to Jamison. Tucker was just about to run after her when Jamison stopped him.

"Tucker, stop!" he yelled at him.

"She chose to do this, you can't try and stop her."

"Yes I can."

"You have to let her go."

"I can't just let her go! I'm in love with her!"

"Well, so am I! I want to do the exact same thing as you. But we can't, we have to let her go, and let her come back on her own."

"So, now what? She goes back to her miserable, awful life. And we return to our opposite sides of the forest and go back to hating each other?"

"For now, I guess that's all we can do."

And that's what they did. They gathered their belongings, took one more look at the home where they were supposed to have a wonderful future, one last look at each other before going back to being enemies, then went their separate ways in the pouring rain.

Kallie's mind was going in a million different directions. Every time she thought about how heartbroken Tucker and Jamison both looked it seemed to start to rain harder. She just couldn't stop picturing them, and it made her feel like a monster. As they left the forest she could feel a big empty hole form inside of her. She wanted to go back, she belonged with Tucker and Jamison. Before she knew it they were back in front of her old home. Kallie rubbed her tear- stained face; they climbed down off the horse.

"Look who finally returned home!" Christopher tried to yell as he yanked Kallie inside.

"What in the world happened to you?" Kallie's uncle Frank said to Christopher when he saw his black-and-blue neck.

"I don't want to talk about it."

Kallie tried not to crack a smile.

"Well Kallie, nice to see you're doing well," Uncle Frank said to her.

"How's Aunt Angie?"

Uncle Frank took a while to answer. "Not very well," he said.

"Can I see her?"

"No. She doesn't want to see you. She's too ashamed that her one and only niece, who she treated as her own daughter, up and left in the middle of the night."

"So Christopher, I take it we can have that money now?" Uncle Frank asked him. Kallie could already feel herself becoming invisible.

"Not until it's official. After we walk down the aisle and it's all said and done."

Kallie wanted to vomit. She went to walk up the steps, but Christopher stopped her.

"Where do you think you're going?" He gripped her arm tightly.

"We have a wedding to plan," he said to her.

"When is it going to be?" Uncle Frank asked.

"As soon as possible, so tomorrow," Christopher answered.

Tears filled Kallie's eyes once again as Christopher dragged her back outside into the pouring rain. They rode Christopher's horse into town, and Christopher stopped in front of the seamstress's shop. They walked in together. The seamstress looked shocked to see Kallie.

"Can you give us a minute?" Christopher asked the woman, she nodded and went into the back room. Christopher looked at Kallie and laughed, but then started to choke in pain from his injury, which made Kallie laugh.

"I don't know why you're laughing, I got what I wanted, just as I always do. And you didn't. You honestly thought you could run away from me? You're a very stupid woman if you thought running away would get me to leave you alone."

Kallie raised her hand to slap Christopher but he grabbed her wrist.

"I would be nice to me from now on, especially without those two things around to protect you."

"They're not things, they're real men, and you'll never be half the man they are."

"Oh is that right? Because in the end . . . I'm the one that got the girl, not them."

Kallie was furious, she wanted to wrap her hands around Christopher's neck and finish what Jamison had started.

"We're ready for you now," Christopher tried to yell toward the back room.

"What can I help you with today?" the seamstress asked them as she entered the room.

"We are getting married tomorrow afternoon. I need a suit and Kallie here needs a wedding gown."

They stood on the pedestals as she got their measurements. Christopher's eyes didn't leave Kallie the whole time. She could feel him staring at her, and it made her want to crawl out of her own skin. She kept her eyes on the window, watching the rain as she tried to keep herself from falling apart.

"Don't make her gown too complicated to take off. I want to consummate the marriage as quick as possible," he said with an evil look on his face. Kallie cringed at the thought of him trying to make love to her.

The seamstress got what she needed. Christopher pulled out a handful of money to persuade her on getting everything done on time.

The rain had stopped shortly before they left the shop, but the sun was still nowhere in sight.

"What are you doing?" Christopher asked. He was sitting on his horse waiting for Kallie as she looked up at the sky. Then she began to walk away.

"I'm going to see Minnie."

"Get on the horse and I'll take you there." He ordered the horse to go in Kallie's direction.

"No. I can walk."

Christopher laughed. "You are going to be fun as a wife. Challenging me every day. The more stubborn you become, Kallie, the more I want you."

She ignored him.

Christopher and his horse stayed next to Kallie as she walked to Minnie's. They waited in front of the house as she walked up to the door. Kallie couldn't help but think about how the last time she was here the loves of her life were standing where Christopher was. She knocked on the door. A man opened it, a blank expression on his face.

"I am seeing a ghost?" he said with a small laugh. Kallie smiled for the first time in a while.

"Hi David," Kallie said to the man who was Minnie's husband. She could hear the cry of a baby come from one of the rooms. Kallie gasped.

"Minnie had the baby?"

"Just yesterday. Come on in," David said, moving aside for her.

Kallie rushed to the room the cry had come from. Minnie was sitting in a rocking chair, the baby wrapped up in a blanket in her arms.

"Kallie? What are you doing here?" Minnie asked as soon as Kallie entered the room, David following behind.

"Yeah, what are you doing here? And why is Christopher outside?" David asked, looking out the window.

"Let me see the baby," Kallie said, ignoring their questions.

Minnie moved the blanket so Kallie could have a better look at the baby. She smiled big when she saw it. The urge to cry snuck up on her; she was going to have to have children with Christopher.

"Boy or girl?" Kallie asked, trying to distract her mind.

"Girl," Minnie answered.

"She's beautiful . . . what's her name?"

Minnie and David looked at each other and smiled.

"Kallie," Minnie said.

"What?" Kallie asked, confused.

"The town just wasn't going to be the same without a Kallie. She's named after the woman who ran off on her own to find the life she deserved."

Kallie felt completely disappointed in herself now.

"So, why is Christopher outside?" Minnie asked again.

"I'm marrying him tomorrow," Kallie finally said. It killed her to say it.

"What happened? You were so happy with those other two."

"My aunt is sick; they need the money."

"You never said anything about Angie being sick, David," Minnie said, looking at her husband.

"I didn't hear that she was. I just saw her last week, and she seemed fine," said David.

"I haven't even seen her. My uncle has barely spoken to me," Kallie added.

"So, you gave up a life full of love and happiness to help a woman who could not care less about you," said Minnie.

"I at least owe this to them—they took me in when I was three."

"You don't owe them or anyone else anything. But you owe a lot to yourself. You deserve nothing but complete and utter happiness, Kallie. Don't do this to yourself, he doesn't deserve you."

"I have to do this though," Kallie whispered as she fought to hold in her tears.

"No you don't. Go back to them."

"I don't think they would take me back after this. Anyway, your baby is adorable." Kallie leaned down to hug Minnie, and she placed a kiss on the baby's head.

"Congratulations," Kallie said before walking out of the room.

"I wish I could say the same for you," Minnie mumbled.

"I'll walk you out," David said, following her.

David opened the door for her once they reached it. Christopher was still standing in front of the house, his arms crossed as he impatiently waited for her.

"Minnie is right you know," David began to say before Kallie could walk away.

"He doesn't deserve you," he finished.

"Well, my aunt doesn't deserve to die."

"Kallie, you want to know the real reason why every man has been chasing you for years, and why every woman has envied you all this time?"

"You and Minnie never did either of those." She smiled. David also smiled.

"Because we have something that's real. But the reason is, because of the way you carry yourself. You have such a strong self-confidence and truly believe that you can do anything; you want what's best for yourself and wouldn't settle until you had it. But, now you're settling for someone the whole village worships because they fear him. He's always gotten everything he wanted. You are the one and only person who would never let him get his way. You are the only one who has been brave enough to stand up to him. Don't let him win." David closed the door. Kallie walked to Christopher as David's words sank in.

"Took you long enough," Christopher grumbled. "Get on, we're going home," he demanded.

"What do you mean?" Kallie didn't even want to know the answer.

"You're staying with me now. I'm not letting you out of my sight."

They had arrived at Christopher's home. It was big and empty, and Kallie hated it. All his servants kept asking about his injury; he lashed out at all of them.

They sat down for dinner, only the two of them at the big table. Christopher was having difficulty swallowing. If he was someone Kallie cared about she would insist he see a doctor but, she could not care less about his pain.

"Stop thinking about them," he said to her as she stared out the window that had a perfect view of the forest.

"You don't belong to them. You're mine now."

Kallie scowled at him. "I will never be yours, Christopher."

"Well by this time tomorrow you will be my wife—" Kallie cut him off.

"It doesn't matter, you will never have my whole heart. You will never even have a piece of my heart. All of me is in that forest and it always will be. We may walk down the aisle and say "I do" but you mean nothing to me. I will never love you, I'll never even like you. You will be chasing me your whole entire life. Even if I am your wife, you can chase and chase me all you want, but you will never win me over! They will always be on my mind and in my heart and there's nothing you can do about it!" Kallie abruptly got up from the table and stormed out of the room and up the stairs, before Christopher even had a chance to lose his temper.

Kallie remained hidden upstairs in a spare bedroom for the whole night. Christopher had some of his closest friends over to celebrate his victory. Kallie could hear them laughing and drinking all night long. She sat on the bed as she stared out the window at the forest. She felt as if her heart was tugging her in the direction of the forest, trying to lead her back to Tucker and Jamison. She knew she belonged with them, everything always felt right with them, and now everything felt completely wrong.

"Aunt Angie better get better after all this," Kallie whispered to herself.

The house became silent. Kallie knew everyone must have left. She could hear Christopher stomping up the steps, then walking right toward her door. She prepared herself to be ready to fight him off, knowing he was going to attempt to sleep with her. The door flew open, and Christopher stood there with a half-drunken smile. He slowly approached Kallie. She looked into his deep brown eyes; they were so dark they looked like empty black orbs. He moved in close to her, their bodies slightly touching.

"I don't understand why you are doing this, Christopher. Why are you so obsessed with having me? Why can't you just give up already?"

"Because, there is just something about you that I want. You have something that every man craves. Something you give off that I can never get enough of and I constantly need it." He ran his hand up her thigh. Kallie shook her head.

"Every time you touch me or kiss me, or even try to be romantic with me, you will be the last thing on my mind. All I will be thinking about is them. It'll never be you."

Christopher raised his hand to hit Kallie, but she pushed him out the door. He stumbled backward. Kallie slammed the door in his face and locked it as fast as she could.

It was a sleepless night for Kallie; she wouldn't allow herself to close her eyes. Because once she would open her eyes she hoped to be in the cabin, with Tucker sound asleep beside her and Jamison occupying himself across the room. But instead the awful feeling of reality would hit her all over again.

Tucker and Jamison both returned to their areas of the forest. Jamison laid in the vampire roses, not caring that the thorns were piercing through his skin. It wasn't nearly as painful as Kallie leaving him. He regretted not killing Christopher; if he would have just done it he could have been with Kallie right now. But instead he was lying on the ground staring into the dark as the familiar feeling of loneliness sank in, but this loneliness was the worst he ever felt. He had never felt this lonely before in all of his 217 years.

Tucker was also on the ground. He didn't even bother putting his tent back up. He was looking at the night sky, the clouds like a blanket over the forest. He felt like nothing mattered anymore. He was completely empty inside without Kallie next to him. The forest was the most silent it had ever been. Tucker remained wide awake all night long, engulfed in the emptiness.

Chapter Eighteen

June 11th, 1821

Jamison finally stood up off the ground as the sky grew lighter, even though the sun was still hidden behind the gray clouds. He wondered what Kallie was doing, who she was with, how she was handling all this. Anger filled him as he pictured her unhappy face. He dug through all his belongings that he stuffed into one of the sacks, looking for his notebook. He sat down against a tree and began to draw the woman that would never leave his mind.

Tucker had eventually fallen asleep at some point during the night. He woke up hoping yesterday was just a nightmare before he had even opened his eyes. He stood up and paced back and forth. He craved Kallie's presence there with him; he was ready to run to the village and bring her back, killing Christopher in the process.

Jamison stared back at his drawing, and tears formed in his eyes as he wondered if he was ever going to see that face again. He made a promise to himself to keep drawing Kallie even if she wasn't around, that way he would never forget how beautiful she was. Jamison noticed that the ground was slightly shaking and it wasn't from Tucker. He stood up and stared off into the distance as he listened for what was coming, then he took off running.

Three werewolves were running right toward Jamison. He was running as fast as he could, the werewolves struggling to keep up with him. Jamison decided to take it easy on them, make them think that they may actually be successful for a moment. But his plan backfired on him.

They had caught up to him in seconds and now all three of them were circling Jamison, growling at him. Jamison wondered if Tucker had put them up to this. He would handle these wolves with ease and then move on and deal with Tucker. The three wolves were ready to pounce on Jamison, and Jamison was ready to fight them. The ground shook even more. Jamison knew Tucker would be showing up any second. And Jamison was ready to fight him now too.

Tucker appeared in wolf form. He jumped in front of Jamison, blocking him from the other wolves. Tucker let out the most angry growl he had in him. It even struck fear into Jamison for a split second. The other three wolves began to whimper and shake, then all of them changed back into their human forms, including Tucker. One of the men was Tucker's brother, the other two looked familiar from the tribe. All three of them dropped to their knees in front of Tucker, getting ready to beg for his forgiveness.

"What the hell do you think you are doing?" Tucker shouted at them; he didn't even sound like himself. Jamison couldn't recall ever hearing so much anger in one voice before.

"We were just . . . " Tucker's brother Thomas began to say but Tucker didn't let him finish.

"Did I tell you to go after him?" His voice boomed. All three shook their heads.

"I warned you what would happen if you turn against me."

"We weren't going against you," one of the men said. Tucker looked at him like he was about to kill him.

"I'm the alpha! When the time comes, I'm the one who orders you what to do and when to do it! But you refuse to trust me! You did something that I did not approve of and you know I would never approve of it! That counts as disrespecting and turning on the alpha."

"Tucker, we're sorry," one man begged. Jamison could see that Tucker had struck fear into their hearts.

"All of you know what happens to a wolf when they try to overpower the alpha."

"No, Tucker, you can't," Thomas pleaded.

"You should have thought about that before you decided to go behind my back. No one goes behind the alpha's back. You are supposed to respect me, and none of you have done that. You continually try to overpower me. Nobody does that to an alpha. You are all out of the tribe! Say good-bye to your families, wives, and children. You are on your own now."

"You can't just throw us out. The vampire population is growing more and more, and you can't expect us to be able to fight off a group of them on our own."

"That's just too bad."

Thomas rose from his knees. "You're going to throw out your own brother?" he said, moving toward Tucker.

"You turned on your alpha, your own brother."

The other two men rose to their feet, they all took one last look at Tucker, and then they left.

Tucker turned to Jamison. Jamison almost wanted to applaud Tucker for finally rising to claim his crown.

"I'm sorry about my men, Jamison, you won't have to worry about them anymore."

Jamison shrugged. "You didn't have to step in. I was doing just fine," he said jokingly. Tucker let out a small laugh.

"Sorry your brother turned on you," Jamison said to him.

"I knew it was going to happen one day, just always hoped I was wrong. My mother is going to be furious with me."

"You just about scared the shit out of them, and you're afraid of your mother being angry with you?" Jamison said, laughing. Tucker smiled. They looked at each other, and it was almost as if they were staring into their own reflection. Same sad eyes, their souls being consumed by emptiness, the horrible lonely feeling that was making them mad.

"Well, guess I'll go back over to my side now," Tucker said as he began to walk away.

"Let's go get her back," Jamison quickly said before Tucker could leave. He looked at Jamison, shocked.

"What about the whole, 'let her go, she'll come back on her own.'" Tucker mocked Jamison, and he looked at Tucker unamused.

"Well, I don't know what the hell I was talking about. She should be with us."

Tucker nodded. "Then let's go."

They traveled east. Neither knowing what was going to happen when they saw Kallie, neither of them could even think of what they were going to say to her.

"What are you going to do about the vampire population?" Jamison asked once they were about halfway to the village.

"It'll be awhile until it gets out of hand, there's nothing to worry about right now."

Tucker and Jamison arrived at the village around noon. They could see the townspeople rushing around the square. They could also hear a man's voice yelling about how everything better be at the church in time.

"She better not be getting married today." Tucker nervously looked at Jamison.

"We just have to hurry. She's probably at home."

They walked through town trying not to draw any attention to themselves as they searched for Kallie's home. They walked down the dirt road until things began to look familiar.

"I think it's this one," Tucker said, pointing at the house coming up.

"No, it's the next one farther down."

"I'm telling you it's this one."

"I'm telling you you're wrong."

People began coming down the road, some walking, others in carriages being pulled by horses. Men in suits, women in fancy dresses. All of them were heading toward the church that sat upon a hill down the road.

Tucker groaned. "We don't have time for this. I'll check this one, you go check that one." They split up.

A strong wind blew, taking any of the wedding guests' hats with it. Tucker laughed to himself as he watched the men chase the hats down the road. Tucker glanced at the sky as he walked up to the home he hoped Kallie was in. A storm was heading right for the village.

Tucker stood right under a window as he eavesdropped on the conversation going on inside.

"When is he going to give you the money?" he heard one voice say.

"Right after they say 'I do,'" a different voice answered.

"I still can't believe she fell for it."

"Christopher was right, she would be dumb enough to believe him."

Tucker was ready to jump through the window and tear them apart. Jamison came walking up to him.

"Alright I'll admit it, you were right. I don't think anyone has lived in that house over there for years," Jamison began to say.

"Sh!" Tucker pointed to the window.

"I don't think her aunt is sick," he whispered to Jamison as they both continued to listen.

"You better hurry and get to the wedding, I'll finish packing everything. Come back as soon as you have all the money. We can leave right away."

"Alright, I'll be back soon."

"Make sure you make it seem like I'm still sick. You don't need her to run away at the last minute."

Jamison's jaw dropped. "We can't let this happen."

"I don't think she's here," Tucker said.

"She's probably at the church by now."

They each took off running down the road toward the church, both trying to run at a normal speed and not cause a scene. They could see someone in white with red hair pacing back and forth in front of the church. As they got closer they could hear her heart pounding as if it was about to jump right out of her chest. She was trying to take deep breaths, her face looking toward the sky. A bouquet in one hand, her other hand on her side.

Kallie felt like she was about to fall over as she paced in front of the church. Nothing had ever felt more wrong to her. Her hair was blowing wildly in the wind. Any moment now she was going to have to walk in that church and be forced to spend the rest of her life with her worst nightmare.

"Kallie!" she heard two voices yell. She thought she had officially lost it, hearing Tucker and Jamison shout her name, because why would they come back for her? They had both sacrificed so much for her, and she repaid them by leaving, saying nothing but sorry.

But then, there they were, standing right before her.

"You can't do this!" they shouted at her.

"I know that, but I have to. Did both of you really show up here just to make me feel even worse than I already do?"

"Your aunt is not sick," said Tucker.

"How would you . . ." Kallie stopped. She could see someone at her old home who looked an awful lot like her aunt, and she was loading up the covered wagon with all their belongings.

"What the hell?" Kallie threw her bouquet down on the ground. Thunder rolled off in the distance as Kallie stormed down the hill. Tucker and Jamison exchanged looks. They had seen Kallie frustrated before, but they had never seen her angry. Her uncle stepped in front of her as she reached the bottom of the hill.

"We don't have time for your shenanigans; go inside now."

"Why should I listen to you?" She pushed past him, the train of her gown blowing in the wind behind her. She kept her eyes on her old home, and she was finally able to confirm that the person outside was indeed her "sick" aunt. Rage filled Kallie's whole body. Lightning flashed across the sky.

Kallie approached her from behind as she loaded the wagon. "Well Aunt Angie, if I didn't know any better I'd say you are feeling much better," she said with a fake smile.

Her aunt froze. "I'm still—"

"Do not even try to lie to me right now!"

Her aunt turned to face her. "Was this your plan all along? You'd pretend to be sick, then I'd agree to marry Christopher, then you and Uncle Frank would finally get your money, and then you would both disappear to live an extravagant life while my life became a living hell!"

"No, Kallie. That's not at all what is going on."

"It's exactly what's going on!"

Uncle Frank came up behind Kallie and grabbed her arm. "That's enough! Get back to the church now!" he said through his teeth. Kallie shoved herself out of his grip. She turned around, and the whole entire town was gathered on the front lawn watching the drama unfold. Christopher pushed his way through the crowd.

"Kallie, I had no idea your aunt was lying. They will no longer be getting any money from me; come on, we can still get married."

Tucker and Jamison watched from behind the crowd. Jamison was about to go intervene until Tucker stopped him and said, "She can handle this. Let her stand up for herself, she needs to prove to them that no one can overpower her."

"We had a deal! She marries you, we get the money!" Uncle Frank yelled.

"She will still marry you, and you still give us our money," Aunt Angie said, pushing Kallie toward Christopher.

"I am never going to marry him! You cannot tell me who to marry! You cannot choose who I will spend the rest of my life with! Neither of you have ever cared about what I want! All you have ever cared about is yourselves! You are all greedy, selfish people! The whole damn town is!" Kallie yelled. Turning to face everyone, she spotted Tucker and Jamison almost towering over everyone.

"I care about what you want, Kallie, I promise I didn't know about their awful plan. Can we just go get married already." Christopher reached for Kallie's hand. She swung her fist and punched him right in the face.

"You don't think that I know this whole thing was your idea?" she said to him. He was hunched over, holding his face. The crowd gasped from shock of a lady acting in such a way. Kallie shook her hand and rolled her eyes at how much the town was overreacting. Christopher stood up straight and stared at Kallie with the most evil look in his eyes.

"You are going to pay for that— no one disrespects me," he said slowly, moving toward her.

"No one disrespects *me*! You are the most manipulative, careless, coldhearted person!" She pushed Christopher away from her.

"Kallie, think about all we have done for you, we took you in and treated you as if you were our own daughter, and this is how you repay us? By causing a scene in front of the whole town?" said Aunt Angie.

"By treating me like your own daughter, you mean by making me feel like I didn't even exist? All either of you did was give me a room to sleep in, that's it! Why should I do anything for you? If you had to choose me or money, you would both take the money without even having to think. You took advantage of my kindness and the good person that I am. And this will be the last time any of you will ever see me. You can all rot in hell for all I care! Now if you'll excuse me, I have forgiveness to beg for, from two real men, who actually care about me and would like to see me happy."

All three of them began bickering, yelling all sorts of stuff at Kallie. She walked away, ignoring every word they said. The crowd began to thin. She looked at the sky, and the storm looked like it was going to pass.

"If it makes you feel any better, I don't think there is anything you could possibly do that would make either of us stop loving you," Jamison said to Kallie as he and Tucker walked up behind her. She turned around, tears forming in her eyes.

"I'm really—"

Tucker stopped her before she could apologize. "Don't you dare apologize for trying to be a good person and helping someone you cared about. It's part of who you are; don't ever apologize for being you."

Kallie smiled. "Can we go home?" she asked. They each nodded and began to walk back to the forest.

Christopher ran right in front of them.

"I am not going to let you get away with this," he said, looking at all three of them. They each scoffed at him.

"I will get you back for this." His gaze burned into Kallie. "All three of you," he said, looking up at Tucker and Jamison.

"Not if we kill you first," Tucker threatened.

"I will find a way to get my revenge," Christopher said, trying to hide his fear. He took one more long look at Kallie, then finally walked away.

Jamison sighed as they all watched the crazy man walk away. "Alright, let's get out of here," he said as he put his hand on Kallie's back, guiding her toward the forest.

"Wait," she said to them. "I have to get out of this." She ripped off her wedding gown, leaving it to blow away in the wind, then walked away in nothing but the shift she had on underneath, leaving all of the village's men in awe. Huge smirks spread over both Tucker and Jamison's faces.

Once they were back in the forest, Tucker changed into a wolf; Kallie and Jamison climbed on as they made it back home in no time. Kallie smiled and sighed a sigh of relief as she climbed down off of Tucker, the sun coming out with her smile. Jamison looked up at the sky as it cleared, then to Kallie's face.

"Have you ever noticed that the sky almost always matches your mood?" Jamison asked Kallie, as Tucker went back to human.

"I think it's just a coincidence, Jamison," she said, looking around the home she never wanted to leave.

"No, even the sky wants to see you happy," he said to her.

Late at night, Christopher carried his drunken self down the road as he struggled to remember where he lived, rambling on about some dumb whore.

"Aw, look at the poor human. Drunken with rejection, starving for revenge," Nessie said as she and the rest of the family watched Christopher stumble down the road.

"He could use our help," said Samuel.

"Well, who is going to be the one to help him?" asked Fiona.

"I'll do it!" Nessie and Samuel both shouted eagerly.

"No, I'll do it. We need him to become one of us, not die," Andrew said as he made his way toward Christopher. He stood in front of him.

"Out of my way!" Christopher yelled. Andrew moved in close to him.

"I am only doing this to help you. You'll get the revenge you're aching for. But first, there's a few things you must do for us." Then Andrew sank his fangs into Christopher.

CHAPTER NINETEEN

June 12th–August 3rd, 1821

The last month had been the greatest month of Kallie, Tucker, and Jamison's lives. Although Tucker and Jamison were forced to be around each other, they were slowly forming some sort of friendship. Kallie noticed this, but knew that if she were to say something about it to them, they would deny it.

It was the first few days of the month of July. The long hot summer had just begun, and there was a full moon that night.

"Are you excited to finally be alone tonight?" Jamison asked Kallie. He bit his bottom lip as he thought of the amazing time they would have, knowing Tucker wouldn't be near.

"Actually," Kallie said, "I think I'm going with Tucker tonight."

Tucker's eyes widened. "Really?" he asked Kallie.

"I want to see what it's like."

Jamison sighed.

Moments before sunset, Tucker took Kallie up to where he and his tribe went during the full moon. It was a large cliff that overlooked most of the forest. It was up high enough that you could see where the forest ended and met with civilization on both sides. Tucker set up his old tent for Kallie to sleep in, and finished as the sun began to set. He kissed Kallie right before his body forced him into a wolf. Seconds later, his tribe showed up in wolf form.

They all looked very similar to Tucker, with shades of gray and black spread over their fur. They were all slightly smaller than Tucker, except one, who was the same size as Tucker. Kallie knew that wolf must be Edudu.

All the wolves lined up on the edge of the cliff. The sky grew darker as the sun disappeared and the full moon took over. The howling began. There were over thirty of them, all howling at the big, bright moon, as loud as they could. And Tucker was right; the moon did hypnotize them, and it was impossible for them to tear themselves away from it. Kallie could tell they had grown oblivious to their surroundings. She looked them in the eyes, and didn't think they were even blinking. She sat next to Tucker and stared at the sky. The moon took up most of it, though there were stars all around, and a few clouds.

Kallie stayed there for the rest of the evening. Once she became tired, she went inside the tent. She felt weird, lying there by herself. She wondered what Jamison was doing—most likely sitting near the fire and drawing in one of his notebooks, like he did every night while she and Tucker slept.

Kallie found it difficult to fall asleep with all the howling going on outside the tent. She began listing all of the werewolf and vampire facts she knew inside her head, in hopes it would help her fall asleep.

Werewolves have the ability to transform into powerful wolves whenever necessary, insanely strong and fast even in human form; eyes glow in the dark; always warm, never sweat; strong instincts; protective toward humans; hate vampires; bodies seem to try and force them into wolf form when their adrenaline rushes; always aware of their surroundings; full moon hypnotizes them; they are born like this, but it does not occur until they are fifteen years old; age slowly later in life, happens to all the males in the tribe; injuries heal in seconds; alphas are discovered after they turn eighteen; alphas are the leaders of all the wolves in the tribe; they are stronger and faster than the others; have stronger instincts; can sense specific traits in people.

Vampires are also insanely strong and fast; have fangs that can descend, eyes that can turn bright red; gray skin; drink any kind of blood; hate werewolves; normal body temperature; hardly sleep or eat; live forever; remain the same age forever; you can only become a vampire if you get bitten by another and they release their fangs before too much blood is drained; strong instincts; aware of surroundings; supposed to kill humans; eyes turn red and fangs come out when around blood, also when adrenaline is rushing; do vampires also heal quickly?

Kallie was impressed with herself. She had learned a lot about these magical creatures within the past two months. She still felt like there was more to learn.

She eventually fell asleep to the sound of howls, but she only remained asleep for the next few hours. The howling became louder and woke her up; now she was wide awake. She crawled outside and sat next to Tucker.

The moon had traveled across the sky, and Kallie thought the night would end soon. She thought she heard something behind her, but with how loud the wolves had gotten she wasn't sure. Kallie glanced over her shoulder to see a huge black bear. She wondered for a second if it was the same bear that came after her on her first day in the forest, but then she realized that was not important.

The bear stood on its back legs and let out an angry roar. Then it dropped to all fours and started running toward Kallie. It was still far from her, but it was going to reach her within the next few seconds. Kallie shook Tucker, trying to get him to snap out of it.

"Tucker, please," she whimpered as the bear got closer. She knew it was no use, there was nothing Tucker could do.

"Jamison!" she screamed. But she had no hope that Jamison would make it all the way to her before the bear did. She kept inching back, getting closer to the edge of the cliff, and clutched Tucker's front.

Jamison was lying in the grass in front of the cabin. A bad feeling washed over him; he felt like something was going to happen to Kallie. But Kallie was surrounded by over thirty werewolves, and there was nothing they couldn't protect her from.

Then he remembered what Tucker said when he explained what happens to werewolves when there is a full moon.

It's like the moon hypnotizes us . . . it's physically impossible for us to tear ourselves away from it.

Tucker's voice echoed throughout Jamison's head. He could have sworn the wolves had started howling more loudly, all of a sudden.

Then he heard the love of his life scream his name like her life depended on it. And it did. Jamison followed the scream as fast as he could, hoping he wasn't too late. The scream led him to the edge of a cliff, where a pack of werewolves were serenading the moon. And a terrified Kallie hid by Tucker. She was trying to protect herself from a bear that was inching closer to her.

Jamison jumped onto the bear, trying to get it away from Kallie. The bear shook Jamison off and went after her. Jamison grabbed it and threw it into the trees, then ran after it. Kallie could hear horrible noises coming from the woods. She couldn't see anything, but she could hear it all. Jamison yelled in pain, and the bear growled. It went on for a while, then it stopped. And the only noise was coming from the wolves.

Kallie watched the woods, waiting for Jamison to come out.

"Come on, Jamison," she begged in a whisper.

He finally stumbled out into the open. He was covered in blood.

"No," Kallie whispered as she ran to him, hoping he wasn't hurt. His body was covered with claw marks. He looked down at her, an angry look in his red eyes.

"You should have stayed with me tonight!" he shouted.

Kallie looked up at him, surprised. That was the first time he'd ever yelled at her.

"You could have gotten yourself killed, Kallie!" he yelled again.

Kallie threw herself into him, hugging him tight and crying into his chest.

"I'm so sorry! This is all my fault!" she sobbed.

Jamison felt bad for yelling at her; it made his throat burn. "Shh . . . I'm alright. It's mostly the bear's blood," Jamison said, trying to get her to calm down. Kallie looked up at him, then right before her eyes the claw marks on Jamison began to disappear.

"See? It's like it never happened." Jamison wiped the tears off Kallie's cheeks as the sun began to shine on her freckled face.

All the howling had stopped. The wolves were human again. Tucker knew this was the moment his instincts warned him about, when Kallie's life would need saving and only Jamison could save her.

Tucker approached his brother who was not supposed to be there. "What are you doing here?" he asked Thomas.

"To apologize for my actions. You were right, Tucker, he is good. A vampire would never save a human's life. I should have believed in you. Please let me back into the tribe," said Thomas.

"No, I'll never allow you to come back. Find somewhere else to go where there is a full moon—from now on, you are not welcome here."

Thomas looked around the tribe—no one would make eye contact with him—then he left. Everyone seemed relieved that Jamison had made it to Kallie in time; they couldn't stop staring at him as they left. Edudu stayed behind, wanting to witness what was about to happen. Tucker approached Kallie and pulled her into his arms.

"I'm sorry I wasn't able to do anything." He kissed her forehead.

"What happened with your brother?" she asked him.

"I removed him from the tribe."

"Why would you do that? He's your brother."

"Because he and two others attempted to kill Jamison."

"Oh . . . " was all Kallie said.

"You should have gotten here faster." Tucker looked at Jamison.

"Wait, all of you knew what was happening . . . and none of you did anything about it?" Jamison asked Tucker.

"I told you it becomes impossible for us to take our eyes off the full moon . . . it doesn't matter what is happening around us."

"She almost died with you right next to her!" Jamison shouted.

"Why do you think we started howling so loudly?" Tucker yelled back. "We all knew something was coming . . . everyone began howling more, hoping it would get your attention and you would realize you needed to get here.

"You claim to have instincts, Jamison . . . but it seems you are not using them. You should have been here before the bear even noticed Kallie. But instead you got here when it was right in front of her face.

And I'm actually going to admit it . . . you are just as physically strong as I am. Your instincts have got to be as strong as mine are. Maybe you should stop daydreaming and start focusing on your surroundings."

Kallie was disappointed that they were back to arguing again. They had been getting along, and now they were in another fight, just because she was curious about what werewolves are like during full moons.

Edudu stood by and watched the argument. He could see how upset Kallie looked. He wondered what was going on in her mind. He knew that her soul knew why all this was happening. She had all the answers as to why a werewolf and vampire had made a crazy agreement, and why they were equals. She knew it all, but right now she had not the slightest clue. She had no idea what she was, what she knew, or what she could do.

Tucker guided Kallie in the direction of the cabin. Edudu turned and left when they began walking toward him. All three of them noticed Edudu and thought that he was going to have something to say to them, but he didn't, he was only observing. He did in fact have a million questions for Kallie, but she was not going to be able to answer them.

The month of July had come and gone. It was now the beginning of August, also the night of the next full moon. Kallie had made a promise to herself to never leave Jamison's side every time there was a full moon.

Jamison had gone off to drink some blood before Tucker had to leave. Ever since Jamison had killed that bear and drunk every drop of its blood, it was enough to satisfy his cravings for a month. Once he returned, Tucker left.

It was a hot night. Jamison and Kallie sat next to the empty fire pit, Kallie sat herself in between his legs. She leaned her back against his muscular chest as they gazed up at the night sky.

"I don't understand how anyone could be hypnotized by the moon," Jamison said as he stared up at the full moon. They could hear the wolves in the distance.

"That would be like Tucker saying he doesn't understand how anyone could drink blood," Kallie said, sounding annoyed.

"The full moon to him is how human blood is to you . . . you both lose control . . . can't tear yourselves away." Kallie paused for a moment before saying, "I know neither of you likes to admit it, but whether you like it or not you are very similar. Besides, I think the howling is beautiful—their singing to the moon."

"Dance with me, then," Jamison said as he rested his chin on her shoulder and looked over at her. Kallie giggled and shook her head.

"Come on," Jamison said. He lifted both of them to their feet.

Kallie stood in front of him. He grabbed her hands and put them around his neck, then placed his own on her waist. He spun her around and dipped her right there under the stars, the moonlight like a spotlight on them, as they listened to Tucker serenade the moon. Jamison couldn't take his eyes off of Kallie. She kept looking back and forth between him and the sky.

"You really love the sky, don't you?" Jamison asked.

Kallie smiled and shrugged her shoulders. Jamison wanted to tell her that she most likely came from somewhere up there, but he didn't know if he was allowed to say anything about it. If Kallie knew what she was, then she was keeping it a secret. If Tucker knew, then he too was keeping it a secret. And if Tucker's grandfather and father knew, they were not mentioning it to either of them. So then maybe, if a human had the soul of a star person it was supposed to remain hidden. Jamison decided on keeping it to himself, unless someone else brought it up.

"What do you love more . . . me or the sky?" Jamison asked with a chuckle.

Kallie smiled. "I don't think I could ever love anything more than I love you," Kallie confessed as she moved closer and leaned her head against his chest. Jamison continued swaying them back and forth as they rotated.

"What about Tucker?" he asked.

"I love you both the same . . . I have told both of you that more than once."

"You can tell me the truth, Kallie. Just admit it. You love me more. I won't tell him. I promise." Jamison chuckled.

"If I were to ever say that to either of you, the first thing you would do would be to run to each other to rub it in the other's face," Kallie said through her smile.

They continued dancing in the moonlight all night long—laughing, smiling, and kissing under the stars. Tucker had had his full moon tradition for many years, and now Jamison and Kallie had a full moon tradition of their own. Every night of the full moon, Jamison and Kallie would slow dance in each other's arms as the wolves sang their song to the moon.

CHAPTER TWENTY

August 4th–25th, 1821

It was the night of the twenty-fifth, Tucker's birthday. He was now twenty-four years old. All three of them were sitting around the fire. Kallie was sitting on Tucker's lap as his hand lightly gripped her thigh. Jamison was finally getting used to watching Kallie and Tucker be affectionate toward each other in front of him, as was Tucker with seeing Kallie and Jamison do the same. The impulse to rip each other off of her was slowly fading as they got used to seeing the love of their lives with another man. She had a smile on her face and a look of happiness in her eyes. They didn't want to be the one to make it go away.

Tucker couldn't see Kallie's face as her head was leaned back on his chest, but he could feel her laughing to herself. Jamison stared at her as she looked down at the fire with a smile across her face.

"What's so funny?" Tucker asked

Kallie sighed before she said, "Everything really does happen for a reason, doesn't it?"

"What's that supposed to mean?" Tucker asked, trying to get a look at her pretty face.

"Think about it. If Christopher wasn't such a jerk and made me want to run away, none of us would be here together right now."

Tucker and Jamison looked at her with wondering eyes. Kallie shifted her position on Tucker. She sat sideways, so she could look at him as she explained. "And if that bear never came after me the first time . . . then I might have never met you."

"And if those rocks never came tumbling over me, then I might have never met you, Jamison. And if I never got scarlet fever . . . then I would have been at the west village when Christopher arrived, and that would have been awful.

"And if neither of you took the time to get to know me, and make me fall in love with you, over and over, every day, and agree to see your archenemy constantly, I wouldn't be as happy as I am. I don't know what I did to deserve either of you in my life. I never thought I could feel a love so great and passionate, and I'm fortunate enough to have that with both of you.

"Each of you mean more to me than you could imagine. I know you hate each other and you're supposed to kill each other, and so many times I thought you were going to kill each other. But you haven't. Thank you for everything you have both done for me. I don't know how I could repay you. I am not worth everything you both have gone through. I really am the luckiest woman in the history of the world. Thank you for loving me.

"Everything that has happened to all of us was leading us to this moment. We are all meant to be here, right now. I know there is not another soul in the world that could understand this crazy triangle that has formed between the three of us. But it makes sense to me. And I know if it didn't make sense to either of you, then you would not be here right now."

Kallie held back the tears that threatened to spill over her eyelids. Tucker and Jamison were at a loss for words.

Tucker kissed Kallie on the cheek. He knew now was the time to tell Kallie and Jamison one of the secrets he had been hiding from them. He knew Kallie would be furious with him for withholding this important information from her for so long, but now was the only moment that felt right.

"I think Jamison is the most important reason why we are all here right now," Tucker confessed. Kallie and Jamison looked at him, puzzled.

"I don't understand," Kallie said.

"How did your parents die?" Tucker asked her.

A look of heartbreak came over Kallie's face.

"Don't make her talk about it if she doesn't want to," Jamison said.

"It's all right. I should talk about it eventually." She rested her head on Tucker's shoulder. Tucker didn't take his eyes off of Jamison throughout Kallie's story. He wanted him to finally realize what was going on.

"I was only three years old, the night it happened, so I don't remember it very well. But I know it was a cold night. My parents and I were sleeping on the floor in front of the fireplace. I was curled up between them, sound asleep. I remember being woken up suddenly. Some man had picked me up . . . the entire house was on fire. I didn't even think I was in the same place anymore."

Tucker saw Jamison's eyes dart from the fire to Kallie; his brain had finally registered why Kallie's eyes seemed so familiar. Kallie paused for a moment and sighed before continuing.

"The man carried me outside. I remember I was screaming and crying for my parents. He ran back in the house after putting me down . . . then I remember the house coming down."

Tears rolled down her face, and Jamison stared at her in complete shock.

"I can't remember what happened after that. I don't know who it was that saved me that night. All I can recall are his eyes. Through all the smoke and darkness, all I could see were these two extremely bright, blue eyes."

Kallie's gaze met Jamison's through the fire. Her jaw dropped. She was finally on the same page as Tucker and Jamison. Tucker waited for one of them to say something, but they were in too much shock to speak.

"Jamison, did you ever save a little red-haired girl from a burning house?" Tucker asked.

Jamison nodded. Kallie left Tucker and was in Jamison's arms within seconds. She wrapped her own arms around him as tight as she possibly could.

"That's why I always feel safe when I look into your eyes," Kallie whispered. Her gaze met his.

"Thank you for saving my life," she said as her voice cracked from wanting to cry.

"I'm sorry I couldn't save your parents." Jamison looked at her, disappointed.

"So, you knew about this, Tucker?" Jamison asked, Kallie's body still latched on to him.

Tucker nodded, waiting for one of them to yell at him.

"How did you find out?" Kallie asked, her head buried in Jamison's shoulder.

"My grandfather told me while you were sick. He knew it was you the moment he saw your eyes. He said that was the night when the rest of the wolves finally realized Jamison was a good man. They understood why Edudu let him stay in the forest."

"Why didn't you say anything till now?" Jamison asked him. Tucker shrugged.

"Would you tell him something that would make him seem better than you?" Kallie asked Jamison.

"I guess not," Jamison answered.

Tucker was surprised that Kallie wasn't angry with him. He felt relieved that they both finally knew it was Jamison who had saved her from the fire. Now he only had one more thing to discuss with them, but now was not the time. He could see the passion burning between them.

"I'll let you two be alone," Tucker said as he stood.

"Wait!" Kallie yelled as she got off of Jamison and ran into the cabin. She came out seconds later and handed Tucker a folded piece of paper. He looked at her with a confused expression.

"You really thought I wasn't going to give you anything on your birthday?" Kallie said with a smile. He smiled back at her, then walked toward the cabin as he unfolded the paper.

"Happy birthday, Tucker," Kallie said and walked back to Jamison.

Tucker entered the cabin and sat on the bed as he read the piece of paper.

Dear Tucker,

When I chose to run away that night, I never would have thought this would be the outcome. If I knew there was a werewolf in the forest near my home and that he was the most caring, gentle, understanding soul, I would have run away a very long time ago.

You saved me from that bear and refused to let me leave until I healed. You listened when I spoke and understood without judging. You were patient with me and let me go when you thought it was what I wanted. You were the first to truly know me in many different ways. I would have never thought in a million years I would experience a love like yours. You gave up your territory, your home, and selfishness, all for me.

I don't deserve you, Tucker, but I will prove to you day after day how no one could ever love you as much as I do. You were the first man to capture my heart, and you have given the other half to the one man you have ever wanted to kill. If that's not a sacrifice, then I don't know what is. You are an amazing person, Tucker, and I am so proud to call you mine. I will love you for eternity, no matter what happens. Happy 24th birthday!

Love always,

Kallie

Tucker felt even more in love with Kallie after reading the love note from her. He fell asleep with a smile on his face. This was by far his happiest birthday yet.

CHAPTER TWENTY-ONE

August 26th–December 18th, 1821

Summer had ended, and the beauty of autumn had come and gone. The forest looked empty and bare. Kallie did not like the winter, mostly because the sky was always a dreary gray and the sun hardly ever shone, but also because she despised being cold. Lucky for her, Tucker was never far.

It was the coldest day all three of them had spent together. Jamison was drawing in his notebook. Kallie looked over his shoulder and watched him, finding it amusing. She would watch him do lines and shading, wondering what it could possibly be. Once he began to connect everything, Kallie could see it was a beautiful wintry scene.

It was almost evening. Tucker had something important to discuss with Kallie. They had been together for over seven months, and he knew it was time to figure out their future. He cleared his throat before he said, "There's something you should know. Well, both of you should probably know. The only way the tribe could have another alpha is if I have a son."

Kallie sighed with relief. She thought Tucker had bad news, but when she looked at Jamison's facial expression, she realized that it was.

Jamison didn't say a word. He slammed his notebook shut and stormed outside. Tucker and Kallie exchanged glances.

"Well?" Tucker said, not taking his eyes off of her. She smiled a big smile.

"I would love to have your children one day, Tucker . . . but I need to discuss this with Jamison." She began walking to the door.

Tucker felt annoyed and angry. He didn't like that Jamison got to have a say in Kallie being the mother of Tucker's children. He wanted to yell and throw things, but that would only make Kallie upset. And the whole world seemed to be upset, if Kallie was.

"I'm not saying we need to start a family today. All I'm saying is that one day I would like to give you the family you have missed out on having. And if that's what you want, then we can start whenever you are ready." Tucker tried to make himself seem calm. Kallie smiled at him before she walked outside to find Jamison.

Snowflakes began to fall from the sky. Jamison was staring off in the distance.

"Jamison," she said as she walked up behind him.

"There's nothing I would love more than to give you a family one day, too, Kallie." His back was turned to her. Kallie knew he had heard what Tucker had said to her.

"Well, maybe," Kallie began to say, but Jamison cut her off. He turned around and looked at her.

"I can't have children, Kallie," he said.

She could see the sadness in his eyes and hear it in his voice. "How do you know?" she asked in disbelief.

"Because you would be pregnant by now. For that matter, I would probably have over a hundred children by now, if I could," Jamison mumbled.

Kallie gave him a mean look.

"Oh don't look at me like that," he said. "I am over two hundred years old. You couldn't have thought you were my first."

Kallie often did wonder how many women Jamison had been with throughout his long life, but she always knew the truth would hurt her.

"I'm sorry you can't have children, Jamison," Kallie whispered.

"Don't be sorry. Monsters like me shouldn't reproduce." He moved in closer to her. Bigger snowflakes started falling.

"I always wanted to be a mother. Are you going to leave if Tucker and I have a child together?"

"Listen to me," he said as he cupped her face in his hands, both of them feeling their cold skin. "You are going to be a great mother, you deserve to have children. I'm just upset because I wish it could be with me, and I don't see where I would fit in if you start a family with him. But I want you to be happy and have the future you deserve. I've always dreamed of being a father one day. I would never try and stop you from becoming a parent."

"I want you to be like a second father to mine and Tucker's children," Kallie said to him.

"He would not allow it. He wouldn't want me anywhere near them."

"I'm his only hope for a son . . . so he's going to have to do what I say." Kallie sounded determined. Jamison smiled at how in control she was. He kissed her, but then turned and stared into the woods.

"What's wrong?" Kallie asked.

"Get inside," he demanded.

She stared back at him blankly.

"Go!" he yelled.

Kallie turned around and made her way back inside.

Tucker began making hot cocoa over the fire. A while ago Jamison went to a market in the west village and came back with a whole cart full of chocolate for Kallie, and they had been trying to use it all up before it went bad. Tucker kept glancing outside. Once Kallie returned, he did his best to distract her from looking out the windows. He handed her a cup of hot cocoa and pulled her into him as they cuddled in front of the fire.

Then he sensed it. They were back. They were right outside. They were too close to the cabin and to the one thing he must always protect, his one true love.

Jamison knew they were bound to show up sooner or later. He groaned and rolled his eyes when he saw them enter the field.

"I'm going to have to ask you to leave," Jamison said, looking at the family he had abandoned. All four members looked around.

"What are you . . . living with the werewolf now?" Andrew asked him.

"And that girl," Samuel said with an evil look in his eyes.

"Don't even think about it!" Jamison said, trying not to be so loud that Kallie would hear.

"You seem to have become very fond of this girl, Jamison," the older woman, Fiona, said.

"Would be a shame for something to happen to her. Then you would have no reason to stay here anymore," Nessie said.

"Tucker! Can you come here for a moment!" Jamison yelled, trying to make it sound like everything was fine.

Kallie looked up at Tucker.

"I'll be right back," he said. He lifted Kallie off him, and kissed her on the forehead, trying to act natural.

He walked outside with a steaming cup of hot cocoa in his hands.

"Everything all right, Jamison?" he asked.

All the vampires looked at Tucker, terrified, except for Jamison.

"Everywhere the girl goes, the werewolf is also there. If you come anywhere near her, he will kill you. In fact, if I have to, I will kill you," Jamison said.

Tucker placed his cup on the now snow-covered ground, showing the vampires he was ready to take them on.

"You're bluffing!" Samuel said as he got in Jamison's face.

Tucker growled and made a move toward them. All four vampires flinched.

"We will be back one day, and with someone else," Andrew threatened.

"Oh, did you finally find someone to replace me with?" Jamison asked, sounding uninterested.

"We did and he's not a coward like you. He enjoys human blood, just like vampires are supposed to."

"Well then where is he?"

"Once he's strong enough and has done everything we have asked of him, we will return. And the day we finally return will be the day that we will all get our ultimate revenge."

Tucker changed into a wolf and the four vampires vanished immediately. Tucker and Jamison stayed outside until they could sense there were no other vampires in the forest.

They returned to Kallie, hoping she did not notice what was happening outside. She was staring deep into the fire. Tucker and Jamison exchanged worried looks.

"Do you think," Kallie began to say, her eyes on the fire, "we could let the animals sleep inside tonight?" She was referring to the animals that Tucker had got from another market awhile back.

Tucker and Jamison chuckled and said, "What?"

She looked up from the fire to them. "It's snowing and it's really cold out, and the animals are going to be freezing in the barn. I think we should let them sleep inside, with us."

"No. They're animals, Kallie. They will be fine," Tucker assured her.

"That's coming from the man that's never cold!" Kallie said.

Jamison snickered. "Yeah . . . you're an animal, and we let you sleep inside," Jamison said. Tucker looked at him, unamused.

"So, what did your family want, Jamison?" she asked. Both men tried to act casual.

"What do you mean?"

"I'm not blind, I saw you arguing with them."

"They were just trying to convince me to return to them once again," he lied.

Kallie had trouble falling asleep that night. She felt bad for the animals in the barn, and now it looked like a blizzard outside. Tucker was sound asleep. Kallie stared down Jamison as he sat in a chair in front of the fire reading a book.

"Stop trying to burn a hole through me with your eyes . . . I am not helping you bring the animals inside," Jamison said without having to look at Kallie. She laughed at how he knew what she was thinking.

"Think of how mad it'll make Tucker," she whispered, hoping that would persuade him.

He looked up from his book and thought for a moment. "Let's do it," he said and stood.

They put on their boots and coats and sneaked outside without waking Tucker. They walked to the small barn that had been beside the cabin for the past few months and opened the doors. Jamison tied a rope to the cow and put one chicken under his arm. Kallie carried the two other chickens.

Jamison slowly entered the cabin, tugging the cow behind him, Kallie following and trying to contain her laughter. Then the cow had the perfect timing to moo extremely loud right as it walked through the doorway.

Of course Tucker woke up. One of the chickens flew out of Kallie's arms and rested on the edge of the bed. Kallie and Jamison could no longer hold in their laughter. An angry look came over Tucker's face.

"Seriously. You let her do this?" Tucker asked.

"Oh, like you could ever say no to that face," Jamison said as he pointed to Kallie.

"This is the only night I am allowing this," Tucker said, then buried his face in the pillow. Kallie lay down beside him and fell asleep. The animals got situated and remained mostly quiet through the night.

CHAPTER TWENTY-TWO

December 19th, 1821–August 25th, 1822

It was Jamison's birthday. Tucker was outside, gathering firewood. Jamison was sitting on the floor in front of the fireplace, his back against one of the chairs. Kallie walked past him, but he pulled her down and she sat herself between his legs. She got settled and rested her back against his chest. He wrapped his arms around her torso and sighed with happiness.

"So, out of *all* your birthdays . . . which one is your absolute favorite?" Kallie asked as they watched the roaring fire. Jamison snickered. The last time he celebrated his birthday, he was only twenty-five years old.

"Definitely my 218th birthday," he said. He held one of Kallie's hands in his, brought it to his lips, and kissed it. He left kisses all the way up her arm, leading to her shoulder, then her neck.

"And why this one?" Kallie asked through a smile.

"Because I finally have a love that was worth waiting this long for. I finally have you, Kallie." He moved her hair out of the way and left a kiss behind her ear. He could see her beaming smile.

He kissed her cheek and down her jawline. He squeezed behind her knee, his hand traveling up her inner thigh and up her dress. Kallie sighed as he kissed along the back of her neck and his hand teased her between her legs.

Jamison began undoing her dress. She stood as it fell to the floor. Jamison tossed it aside. Kallie pulled his shirt over her head and dropped herself on his lap. She was straddling him. Jamison kissed that special spot on Kallie's neck, right below her ear. He squeezed her backside, hoping to get a moan out of her loud enough for Tucker to hear and know not to come inside.

Tucker got the message, loud and clear.

Jamison played with Kallie's hair as she left a trail of kisses on his chest and abs. He noticed her hair was becoming a dark shade of red from being inside so much. She looked up at him and began taking off her undergarments. He also saw that her freckles had almost vanished and her skin was becoming plain.

All their clothing lay on the floor around them. Kallie moved her hips up and down as her body connected with Jamison's. She pressed her hands against his chest, but he grabbed her wrists and held them behind her back with his one hand. The other cupped her face as he kissed her, his eyes growing redder by the second.

They sat side by side on the floor once it was all over.

"I just want to clarify something," she said to Jamison as he kissed her neck. "Why do you like to hold my hands back?"

Jamison smiled, surprised by her question. "'Cause every time you touch me you light my skin on fire, which makes it very hard to stop my fangs from coming out while I'm kissing you."

"That's what I thought . . . do you think Tucker does it for almost the same reason?"

A look of disgust came across Jamison's face. "I did not need to know that."

Kallie laughed.

"But, yes. You probably wouldn't like it if he turned into a wolf right then," Jamison said, laughing. "You know you could just not touch us during it."

Kallie shrugged. "Eh . . . " She smiled at him and pressed her lips on his.

Tucker came inside once he knew they were finished with their business. He lay down on the bed next to an exhausted-looking Kallie. Just as her tired eyelids were about to close, she shot up. She walked to her dresser and pulled a folded piece of paper from the top drawer. She approached Jamison, who sat in one of the chairs in front of the fire. She handed it to him, kissed him on the cheek, and whispered, "Happy birthday, Jamison." Then she crawled back into bed with Tucker and fell asleep instantly.

Jamison unfolded the paper, thinking it was probably like what Kallie gave Tucker on his birthday.

Dear Jamison,

I never thought someone like you could exist. Even though you may not see it, there is so much good inside of you. Please don't forget how much good you truly have. You have been through so many challenges in life, but they have only made you a stronger man.

I wish I could have been at your side throughout your life. You did not deserve to go through any of that, let alone go through it alone. You are not a monster, nor a creature. You are a human being with an amazing, brave, loving, strong soul.

How could a monster be the only thing that can make me smile at times? I am completely in love with you, and I will remain in love with you until the end of time. I could never thank you enough for all you have done for me. You share my love with a man you once and possibly still do despise, and for that I am forever grateful. Thank you for letting me be a part of your long life and for being my whole life. There will always be room for you in my heart.

I will always need you, Jamison. Happy 218th birthday.

Love forever,

Kallie

Tucker opened his eyes for a moment and saw Jamison wipe a tear away. Tucker smiled as he pulled Kallie's sleeping body into his.

The long, cold winter finally ended. Kallie couldn't have been happier when spring had arrived. On the first warm day of the year, she went bursting out of the cabin like a caged animal, and gazed up at the bright blue sky she had missed for far too long.

It was the eighteenth of April, Kallie's twenty-first birthday. Tucker noticed the blondish highlights that the sun returned to her hair.

She was leaned against the willow tree that shaded the natural pool of water, looking down at the duck eggs that had been laid that morning. The vampire roses were slowly making their way down along the stream that continued throughout the forest. Tucker came up behind Kallie and placed her birthday present on the ground, waiting for her to notice. She turned and looked at him once she heard him put something down.

Tucker had carved a beautiful wooden bench, with a vine design that ran throughout the wood. Kallie gaped in awe.

"Would you like to sit?" he said with a big smile.

"You made this?" she asked as they sat together.

He nodded. "Happy birthday," he said and kissed her on the cheek.

Kallie sighed. "I am happy." She looked deep into Tucker's golden-brown eyes.

"That's all that matters," Tucker said. "My life's purpose is to never let that beautiful smile disappear." He ran his thumb along her lower lip.

Kallie felt butterflies take over her body.

Later that day, she sat on the bench and gazed at the night sky.

A chilly breeze was in the air. Jamison joined her. She could see he was hiding something behind his back.

"What are you hiding?" Kallie asked.

"You have to kiss me first," Jamison insisted. He sat next to her. Kallie rolled her eyes and kissed him on the lips.

"More passion, please," he said, knowing she was annoyed. She laughed and tried to kiss him with more passion.

"I guess that'll do," Jamison said, sounding unimpressed.

"I'll kiss you better after you show me what you're hiding." Kallie snickered.

Jamison finally gave in and revealed what he was hiding. He handed Kallie a drawing, of the both of them in a passionate kiss, holding each other tight in front of a night sky. He'd even made a colorful frame out of vampire rose petals.

Kallie was stunned. "It's amazing," she whispered and ran her fingers over the drawing.

"Thank you." She looked into Jamison's eyes.

"Happy birthday, Kallie. You owe me a really good kiss now."

She laughed and kissed him with all the passion her body held. He deserved it, after all. And then, without either of them noticing, they had created the exact moment Jamison had drawn.

The season of spring was over. Summer would soon come to an end. It had been more than a year since Kallie ran away from home. She had known Tucker and Jamison for over a year. It had been more than a year since Tucker and Jamison made their crazy agreement that neither of them thought could possibly work.

But it did. Their cabin had been standing for over a year. The past year was filled with many happy moments and memories that none of them would forget. Everything was great and perfect. Nothing could be better than this, but things were going to become even greater.

"So, is Tucker the same age as you now?" Kallie asked Jamison, a puzzled look on her face. It was Tucker's twenty-fifth birthday.

"I'm not sure," Jamison said, looking back at her with the same expression.

Kallie laughed. "So, next year, will he be older than you?"

"I have no idea," Jamison said through laughter. "What did you get him this year?" Jamison was trying to steer the subject away from the confusing question.

Kallie bit her lip as she tried to hold back her smile. "I guess I should probably tell you before I speak to him," she said, her gaze pointed at the sky.

Jamison looked at her freckled face with concern. "What is it?" he asked.

"I'm going to tell him I'm ready to try and have a baby with him." She hoped Jamison would be as happy as she was, but he wasn't. His eyes started turning red. The anger and jealousy running through his body made his adrenaline skyrocket. He tried to walk away, but Kallie stopped him.

"Don't be like this, Jamison. Don't assume the worst. The three of us are a family. You are my family. And it doesn't matter if the children are not yours, you will be a part of their lives. You will help raise them and be just as important to them as you are to me."

Jamison wanted to wreak havoc on the forest. He could see it in Kallie's eyes that she was begging him not to ruin something that was so important to her. And he didn't want to ruin it. He never wanted to do anything that would take away her happiness. But he was insanely jealous of Tucker in that moment.

"I'm going for a walk. I'll see you later," Jamison said. He kissed her on the forehead and exited the field. He knew exactly what Tucker was going to do after Kallie told him. And Jamison did not want to be in earshot for it.

Kallie walked around to the back of the cabin. Tucker was making a few repairs to the cabin from the winter's harsh weather.

"Do you want your birthday gift now?" Kallie asked, trying to contain her excitement.

Tucker looked at her. "You don't have anything," he said. He went back to what he was doing.

"Well it's a . . . sentence?" Kallie said, sounding unsure.

Tucker looked at her with the most confused expression. "What?" he asked, still focusing on what he was fixing. "Just say it."

She took a deep breath, trying to remain calm. Her knees went weak and her hands were shaking.

"I am ready to make you a father."

Tucker's eyes lit up. His expression filled with utter happiness. He dropped the tool in his hand. It made a thud as it hit the ground.

"You mean it?" he asked, almost whispering.

Kallie nodded. Tucker smiled from ear to ear.

He walked up to her. Kallie was expecting him to hug her and kiss her, but instead he picked her up and threw her over his shoulder. Tucker rushed around the cabin and made his way inside.

He threw her down on the bed and practically ripped her clothes off, and then his own. He hovered above Kallie's body, kissing her most sensitive areas as lightly as he could. His fingers traced her smooth skin, running along her chest and stomach. One hand made its way down her legs while his other hand held her arms down above her head. He didn't want the chance of transforming into a wolf to become a distraction during this moment.

His fingertips tickled the back of her knee as goose bumps rose all over her skin. Tucker smiled when he noticed and kissed her lips, his hand moving far up her thigh and rubbing the area between her legs. Tucker could hear Kallie's heart begin to race. Her breathing became unsteady. He pressed his midsection between her legs. His bronze skin pressed against her pale, white skin. He laced his fingers between hers and kept her hands next to her head.

Sexual tension and excitement rose between the alpha moon wolf and his one true love. Their hearts beat in overdrive, and they gasped for air between kisses, their bodies melting together, closing the space between them.

Jamison had run to the very north end of the forest. He sat on a cliff, his feet dangling over the edge. He was daydreaming about Kallie, as always, thinking about what a perfect little family they could have had together: adorable, red-haired children with bright blue eyes running around. It brought a smile to his face. He hated that becoming a vampire had made it impossible for him to have children, but he was almost thankful for being one. If he weren't one, he would have never met Kallie.

Kallie was going to be a great mother, and even though Jamison would never admit it to his face, Tucker was going to also be a great father. Jamison laughed as he thought about how he could be the crazy uncle, or something.

He hoped the child would like him. Then he realized he was probably more nervous about this baby than Kallie and Tucker were.

He was going to do what Kallie had said. He was going to be like a second father to her and Tucker's children, and Tucker was going to have to deal with it. Jamison was going to love this baby like it was his very own. His heart filled with happiness.

CHAPTER TWENTY-THREE

August 26th, 1822–July 18th, 1823

It was the middle of March. It was between winter and spring. Kallie was over six months pregnant with Tucker's child. And Jamison was surprisingly all right with everything. Edudu had been visiting at least once a month to check on her, and lately, Tucker and Jamison could have sworn they heard three heartbeats coming from Kallie. One heartbeat belonged to her, which meant there must be two babies on the way, but neither of them spoke a word about it.

There was a light powder of snow on the grass. Edudu entered the cabin, removing his hood as he walked through the door. He kindly smiled at Kallie, already sensing what Tucker and Jamison were aware of. He examined her, and once he was positive there were two babies he laughed.

"Well, I know twins don't run in Tucker's family. What about you, Kallie?" Edudu asked. She looked at him, puzzled.

"My father was a twin," she replied.

"That explains it." He looked back and forth at Tucker and Jamison's happy but apprehensive expressions.

"It explains what?" Kallie asked, feeling left out.

"You're having twins," Edudu finally answered.

Kallie smiled brighter than the sun, which made Tucker and Jamison do the same. Jamison snickered to himself.

"She would be having a litter," he mumbled quietly. Everyone looked at him.

"That was not supposed to be out loud," Jamison said innocently.

Kallie tried to hold back her laughter, but laughed right along with Jamison. Tucker and Edudu ignored his rude comment.

It was the middle of a warm spring night. Kallie and Tucker were both wide awake, sitting up in bed.

"I hope it's a boy and a girl," Jamison blurted out.

"I just hope it's not two boys," Tucker added.

"I couldn't care less what they are, I'm happy with anything." Kallie smiled.

It was the middle of the night, and Tucker was wide awake staring off into space. Jamison looked up from the book he was reading and gazed at Tucker.

"Why don't you want two boys?" Jamison asked him.

"Because if one of them becomes the alpha, the other will most likely become insanely jealous."

Jamison knew what Tucker was talking about. He didn't want his children to have the same relationship with each other that he had with his own brother.

The last day of May arrived. Kallie was sitting on the wooden bench that Tucker had made her for her twenty-first birthday. She was watching the new family of ducks swim around in the water under the big willow tree. Jamison and Tucker were admiring Kallie from afar.

"It's going to happen today, isn't it?" Jamison asked, his arms crossed over his chest.

"It sure is," Tucker answered.

Kallie looked at both of them, her eyes wide. "It's happening!" she shouted.

Tucker and Jamison looked at each other in excitement and fear.

Edudu came rushing out of the woods.

"It's happening! I'm here!" Edudu shouted as he rushed to the cabin.

"Hurry! Get her inside!" he yelled to Jamison and Tucker.

Just a few hours later, Kallie and Tucker were sitting up in their bed, each holding a baby boy. Both boys had their father's tan skin, and a birthmark in the shape of a wolf's paw print that took up most of their tiny chests. Tucker kissed Kallie on the head.

"I'm so unbelievably proud of you," he said, and rested his head on her. She cracked a smile as she stared down at their two beautiful children. The babies looked alike, except for their eyes. The baby in Tucker's arms had big, golden eyes with flecks of blue, and the baby in her arms had big, golden eyes with flecks of green.

Jamison entered the cabin, dragging two cribs made of wood.

Kallie gasped. "Did you make those, Jamison?"

"We both did," Jamison said, pointing to Tucker.

A tear slipped out of Kallie's eye. "I've been meaning to tell you he will be just as involved with our children as we are," Kallie said, looking up at Tucker.

"Why else do you think I let him help me build the cribs?" Tucker whispered.

Jamison sat on the edge of the bed and admired the babies. "Do they have names yet?" he asked them.

"I think one should be Hunter," Tucker said.

"I like it," Kallie said. "Which one should be Hunter?"

Tucker looked back and forth at both boys. "This one," he said, looking down at the baby in his arms.

"You need one more name," Jamison reminded them.

"You pick the other name, Kallie," Tucker said.

"Hmmm . . . " Kallie stared down at her baby as she thought.

"What was your father's name?" Tucker asked her.

"Isaac."

Tucker smirked. "I like it."

"I think that would be a good fit for him," Jamison said, looking at the baby in Kallie's arms.

"Isaac it is, then," she said, as more tears fell from her eyes. She thought about how happy her father would be.

"Hunter and Isaac," Jamison said.

"Good, strong names." Tucker beamed.

Tucker had been at the reservation for the past few days. Jamison had been a great deal of help for Kallie with the babies while Tucker was away. A thick fog rolled in early one morning just as the sun was rising. And Jamison could also sense what would also be arriving shortly. He stood in the middle of the field staring, waiting for him to show himself.

In the blink of an eye Andrew was standing there. Jamison charged right for him, pushing him back.

"I only came to warn you, Jamison, not get in a fight," Andrew said as he stumbled backward.

"Warn me about what?" Jamison asked, doubting Andrew held any important information.

"There's another vampire out there."

Jamison looked at Andrew with a blank expression. "That's not something to warn me about!" He held Andrew by the collar of his shirt, his fist ready to ram into Andrew's face.

"Let me finish," Andrew pleaded as he scrunched his face, waiting for Jamison to punch a hole through him. "A vampire that could be just as strong as you are one day, maybe even stronger, he's becoming more and more powerful."

Jamison let go of Andrew, and he fixed his shirt once he was released. "I came here under his orders to try and negotiate with you."

"What do you mean, under his orders?"

"I said he's powerful. He wants all the vampires, all over the world, to join forces and take down every wolf there is; he's starting to call himself the king of vampires, thinks he can form an army and be the leader."

"He sounds insane."

"He very much is."

"So what are you supposed to negotiate with me? I am not leaving, I am not going to join some crazy vampire army, especially when I could easily kill the leader with my bare hands in seconds."

"I know that, and I told him that. So, he suggested an ultimatum."

Jamison scoffed. "And what would that be?"

"Either you kill the alpha, or we kill the girl. And I can also sense that there are children involved now; if either of them happen to be a male, they will also be killed. The wolf population is large enough. If you do kill the alpha, then the girl and her children will remain untouched. No vampire will ever come after them for as long as they live."

Jamison didn't even know how to respond, his mind was trying to come up with some way around this. Whoever would come after Kallie and her sons would have no chance against him and Tucker.

"You don't have much time, Jamison. Someone will be sent here to see if you have gone through with it in the near future. And if you haven't, then she will be killed, even if he has to come here and do it himself."

Jamison opened his mouth to speak, but Andrew quickly interrupted. "Just think about it. If you get rid of him, you can finally have everything you have ever wanted, all to yourself. You wouldn't have to share her anymore, you wouldn't have to be jealous of the family they have created together. He trusts you, I'm sure you could kill him without him even seeing it coming. All you have to do is break his human skin with your fangs, and he will no longer be in your way."

Andrew turned around and left before Jamison's mind could even process all his words. "Shit." Jamison swore under his breath. He turned and looked in the opposite direction. Tucker was on his way.

"Is everything alright, Jamison?" Tucker asked as he came out of the trees.

"I handled it. He's gone." Jamison tried to read Tucker's expression, trying to find out if he had heard what Andrew was saying, and it didn't seem like it. Tucker nodded, then left to return back to the reservation.

Jamison walked inside the cabin. Kallie and both babies were still sound asleep during the early morning. He looked at all three of them, and he never wanted anything to happen to them. But how could he murder the one person that meant so much to each of them? He couldn't possibly cause them the pain of losing Tucker, forcing those boys to grow up without even the memory of their father.

CHAPTER TWENTY-FOUR

July 19th–August 19th, 1823

It had been a few weeks since Jamison was visited by Andrew. Tucker had also been back from the reservation for a while. Jamison stood over Tucker as he slept one night. His fangs were out, ready to go. Jamison realized that Tucker did truly trust him. Jamison was standing right over him, about to kill him, and Tucker had no clue. Jamison fought with himself in his head, Andrew's words repeating themselves over and over. He couldn't believe how stupid Tucker actually was. He was dumb enough to let a vampire be a part of his perfect little family, the vampire that could possibly be the reason why his whole world might be taken away one day if he didn't go through with this.

He looked back and forth, from Tucker, to Kallie, to their children. He needed to do this in order to keep Kallie and her children safe. Maybe Tucker would understand, Jamison thought to himself. Maybe if Tucker knew his family would never be bothered by any vampire, he would sacrifice himself, for the sake of his family. Then the image of Kallie's face popped into his mind. The image of her heartbroken expression once Tucker would be gone. It made him shatter to a million pieces. Tucker was one of the main reasons behind her smile; how could he possibly do that to her? Take something from her that brought her nothing but the pure happiness she deserved.

And he knew Tucker didn't deserve any of this. He didn't deserve to die, especially by someone he had so much trust in. He deserved to be with Kallie and her children, he deserved to be there for them. But what if they are killed because of this? Tucker didn't deserve to lose all three of them, and Jamison didn't want to lose any of them either.

He was going mad, his mind was racing at a million miles a second with all the horrible things running through his head. He let out a loud groan, then stomped outside, slamming the cabin door behind him. He instantly hated himself once he heard the babies wake up and cry from the loud noise.

"Jamison." He heard Kallie groan.

"Sorry, it was the wind," he shouted in a whisper toward the door.

Tucker glanced out the window. "It's not even windy," he said, watching Jamison take off into the trees. Kallie shook her head in annoyance as they both walked over to the babies and soothed them back to sleep.

A few days had passed. Jamison was being very standoffish and quiet the whole week. Both Kallie and Tucker noticed, but didn't speak a word of it. Both of them figured he would be over whatever it was that was bothering him in the next few days. But they had no idea that he was currently at war with himself.

Tucker walked outside into the blazing heat. There hadn't been any rain in over a month and it was the dead of summer. All the field grass was brown and insanely dry; it crunched under Tucker's feet as he walked over it. Jamison was leaned over the pool of water trying to splash some water on his face. The level of the water was extremely low and looked like it would be dried up by the end of the next week if no rain arrived.

"I'm going to be gone for the next few days, I've already told Kallie," Tucker said as he walked up behind Jamison.

"What are you leaving for this time?" Jamison said as he turned around to face Tucker, making it obvious that he was not interested in this conversation.

"We are going to search for my brother and the other two. Something doesn't feel right."

"You would go looking for the people who turned on you." Jamison's voice was full of sarcasm.

"What's that supposed to mean?"

"You know you can't trust them, yet you still want them around."

"I said I was only going to look for them, I didn't say I would let them back into the tribe."

"You're so foolish," Jamison mumbled.

Tucker rolled his eyes. "Oh, what is it now, Jamison? What could possibly be making you angry this time?" Tucker said sarcastically.

"You honestly thought this could work?" Jamison looked at Tucker with disbelief.

"That what could work?"

"This whole damn thing! How could a vampire and a werewolf possibly have the same woman? How stupid can you be to trust a vampire to be around your own flesh and blood? You're supposed to hunt vampires! I'm your fucking prey! Yet here I am, pretending that this whole thing works and makes perfect sense!"

The cabin door squeaked and Kallie came outside. She stared down Jamison, her arms crossed over her chest.

"I don't have time for your nonsense right now, I'll let her deal with you," Tucker said right before he left.

"So, you're just pretending now?" Kallie said, trying to disguise how hurt she felt.

"No, that's not what I meant, Kallie."

"That's exactly what you just said!" she shouted.

"There's just a lot going on in my head right now, you have to understand that. I'm sorry."

"Then talk to me about it, Jamison."

"I can't."

"Then I can't help you." Kallie went back inside.

"You'll hate me," Jamison said to himself once the cabin door closed.

Kallie barely spoke to Jamison for the rest of the day. She wouldn't even let him kiss her or lay in bed with her during the night either. He felt even more awful that he had hurt her feelings; he never intended to.

Jamison was searching the forest for a larger supply of water, then he sensed who had just entered the forest. He had to get back to the cabin fast, before they did.

Once he finally reached the field he spotted Samael, just about to open the cabin door. Jamison had him pinned down to the ground in a flash.

"I told all of you what would happen if you get too close to her! You honestly thought I was bluffing? I spoke the damn truth! I told all four of you that I would kill you if I had to! But you still don't believe my words! You can just be an example to all the other vampires out there of what will happen if any of you try to harm her!" Jamison spat in Samael's face through gritted teeth.

"He ordered me to. You didn't kill the alpha and we gave you enough time. Andrew told you what would happen." Samael could barely speak as Jamison was cutting off his airways, his knee pushing deep into his gut.

"I don't care who ordered you to do what! No one, and I mean no one, tries to give me an ultimatum! I don't care how powerful this said vampire is supposed to be! No one tries to have power over me! I will never kill anyone who does not deserve it!" Jamison gripped his hands around Samael's neck, strangling him.

"I don't deserve to die, Jamison," Samael begged.

"You have any idea how many innocent lives I've watched you take? And you say you don't deserve to die? I watched you kill over and over and over again. You picked the wrong man to mess with and the wrong woman to go after. This is for every life you have stolen and the true monster that lies within you. You are getting everything you deserve!" Jamison sank his fangs into Samael, drained every last drop of his vampire blood out of him, even though vampire blood was as tasteless as water.

Kallie watched from the window, horrified, the awful scream that left Samael when Jamison bit into him still echoing in her ears. She saw it all. She saw the look of regret wash over Jamison once he realized what he had done. He disposed of the body and then walked off into the trees.

After watching what Jamison had done, it didn't make Kallie look at him any differently, she still loved him just as much as she always did. She knew Samael was not a good person; this was the second time he had attempted to kill her, and Jamison knew he had to go. He did it to protect her. She hoped he would let out his anger and then return, but he didn't.

Kallie had been alone for a whole three days. No Tucker, no Jamison. Just her and the twins. She did her best, trying to take care of both of them on her own, but running on no sleep wasn't helping. When the babies were sleeping she would just stare at the door, hoping and waiting for one of them, or both of them, to just come walking in the door already.

It had been four days since Jamison left. Each day was hotter and drier than the last. The waterfall was a mere trickle, the pool almost completely dried up. Kallie wondered if Jamison had ever found more water, and if he did if it was close by.

She put the twins down for their nap, she turned, a direct view out the window. She saw them, Jamison's three other family members. They each kept looking around, a shocking look on their face. Kallie's heart was racing crazily. She and her children were in danger, and no one was there to protect them. None of Tucker's men would be at the reservation, they would be with Tucker. And if any of them did stay behind it would be impossible for them to make it that far when the vampires were just a few yards away.

Kallie knew she had to do whatever it took to protect her children. Her mind was racing, trying to think of something, anything. It was the middle of the afternoon, but it had become a strange kind of darkness outside. Black clouds were moving shockingly fast across the sky, and a crazy strong wind sent tree branches flying through the air. The thunder boomed so loud it shook the ground. That's when the vampires sprinted toward the cabin.

A bolt of lightning struck the ground, just a few feet in front of the cabin. Wildfire began to spread across the dry grass, then another bolt of lightning struck, the fire continued to grow, then another bolt. A wall of fire had spread all around the cabin. Kallie could see through the flames that the strong wind was pushing the fire closer and closer to the vampires.

Kallie looked off in the distance, and a tornado had formed in the east, charging right toward them. She now not only had to worry about the vampires and the fire, but now also a tornado. Trees were sent flying through the air, some landing right in front of the vampires as they attempted to move through the thick wall of flames. The tornado swept up everything in its path, and the vampires struggled to stay in one place as the wind and fire pushed against them. As the tornado got extremely close, the flames began swirling all around the cabin, spreading the fire farther and farther out as it grew to an extreme height.

Kallie could no longer see a thing out the window, all she could see was the fire. It still remained just a few feet away, still not touching the cabin. The babies were still sound asleep through it all, but Kallie knew that it wouldn't be long till the cabin would be consumed by the fire. But the flames were all around them; there was no way out of it.

Then the most harsh rain that Kallie had ever heard began to fall from the sky, the huge droplets pounding down on the roof, splashing onto the windows. The fire slowly shrunk down its height. Kallie kept pacing, checking each window for any sight of the vampires. The fire was no longer at a ridiculous size, and it stopped spreading. The tornado was gone, the wind calm. The rain pouring from the sky would eventually cause the fire to die out. Kallie did not see anyone in the field. The vampires were either chased away by the tornado, or sucked into it.

"Kallie!" She heard her name being called. It was Tucker.

Tucker could see the tornado and all the smoke near his home from miles away. He ran there at lightning speed. He went right through the remaining flames and flew through the door.

"Is everyone alright?" he asked as he looked at the babies, still sound asleep. He pulled Kallie into his arms, drops of rain still on his skin.

"I'm so happy you're safe, I don't know what I'd do if anything happened to you or the boys." He could feel Kallie shaking.

"What just happened?" she said with disbelief, trying to catch her breath, realizing she wasn't breathing the whole time.

"Shh. You're alright, everyone is safe," he said in a calming tone.

"Where's Jamison?" he asked her.

"He left four days ago."

"What? What do you mean, he left?"

"His . . . vampire brother showed up, I think he was planning on killing me. Right when he was about to come inside . . . " Kallie swallowed before finishing her sentence. "Jamison killed him. He hasn't been back since." Tears welled up in her eyes.

"The rest of his family was just here. Just as they came running toward the cabin, the storm started, and a huge fire was just surrounding the whole cabin. And then the tornado came, and then they were gone. It was the most insane thing I have ever witnessed. I was so scared, Tucker!" Kallie cried into his chest.

"I can't believe he left all of you here, unprotected. He should have known better." Tucker was becoming warmer as the rage grew inside of him.

Jamison came running into the field. "What have I done?" he said to himself as he looked around. He ran his hands through his hair, guilt washing over him. He stood in the pouring rain, the grass was completely charred, smoke filled the field, and fallen trees were all over. But the cabin was untouched, no damage had been done to it, and not a single thing was out of place.

He ran inside. Tucker's eyes grew wide with anger when he saw Jamison.

"Where the hell were you?" Tucker raised his voice, letting go of Kallie.

"I . . . " Jamison began to say, but Tucker interrupted.

"I trusted you to protect my family! And when they needed you most you were not around! Where could you have possibly gone that I got here before you?" Tucker's voice filled the cabin. The twins both woke up crying. Before Jamison could yell back at Tucker, Kallie pushed both of them out the door into the rain.

"Do not come back in till you are done yelling at each other." Kallie's voice was stern and she closed the door in front of them.

"Tucker, I'm sorry. But you don't understand what has been going on in my head. I am on the verge of insanity."

"Do you even know that your family of murderers was just here? If it wasn't for that storm, Kallie and the twins would be dead, because of you!"

"They were here?"

"That's what Kallie said. She said they were running right toward the cabin, but the storm and the fire got in their way."

"This is all my fault . . . If I would have just killed you already this wouldn't be happening!"

"And if I would have killed you this wouldn't be happening either!"

"No one has threatened you to kill me!"

Tucker stared down Jamison, wondering what he was implying. "Who has so much power that they could have possibly threatened you? Other than me."

"Some crazy vampire out there who is trying to form an army to take down every man like you! He keeps ordering them to come here and kill Kallie, and the children, because I haven't killed you yet! This is actually all your fault! It's your fault I killed Samael! It's your fault they are after Kallie! If I would have just gotten this over with already then no vampire would ever come near her or the twins!"

"Alright, Jamison. If that's how you feel then go ahead and do it. Just get it over with. All you have to do is break through my human skin with your fangs and I'll drop dead instantly. I won't even try to change into a wolf, I swear." Tucker surrendered, his hands in the air. "I'll even make it easier for you." He turned around. "I won't even see it coming. Go ahead Jamison, do it, kill me."

Jamison stared at the back of Tucker; he didn't even have to think twice about what to do. "I don't want to kill you, Tucker. I could never do that to Kallie, or her children. I just killed the closest thing I had to a brother and I hate myself more than ever right now. I don't even want to imagine how much more I'd hate myself if I killed you. That's why I was gone for so long, I couldn't face her after she just watched me commit murder. But, at least I had good reason for not being here, while you were off trying to find the men that betrayed you."

Tucker turned back around. "Well turns out they all killed themselves."

Jamison saw a new kind of emotion come across Tucker. Like Tucker hated himself just as much as Jamison hated himself.

"What?"

"My brother and the two others I forced to leave the tribe are all dead." That was the hardest sentence Tucker had ever said.

"What happened?"

"The regret of how disloyal they were to their alpha must have been too much for them. I drove my own brother to suicide." Tears formed in Tucker's eyes. Jamison was shocked.

"Sorry . . . "

Tucker shrugged and blinked his tears away. "My grandfather said that that is usually what happens to a wolf when they are forced to leave, they can't live with themselves anymore. That's why we went looking for them. I can always feel some sort of connection with all my wolves; even after they left, I still felt it. Then one day, I couldn't. I knew we had to find them, but it was too late. I'm also . . . sorry about your brother."

They stared at each other in silence for a while. The same emotions were portrayed on each of their faces and in both of their eyes. They were both the reason why their brothers were dead. Regret was eating away at the two of them, but they knew they did what they had to do.

Tucker glanced at the cabin window. He could see Kallie rocking one of the babies in her arms, smiling down at him. "We brought her into a very messed-up situation, and we don't deserve her." Tucker shook his head.

"But who else could possibly give her the love she deserves other than us?" Jamison looked around the field again. A few flames still burned on the ground, and the rain had slightly slowed down. He couldn't believe how much damage had been done to the forest, but not the cabin. "I'm telling you, Kallie has some sort of influence on the sky," he said, looking up at the dark gray clouds.

Tucker laughed. "Whatever you say, Jamison."

"So, can we move past this now? We both recently lost our brothers, we both don't want to kill each other. And as long as we work together, no vampire could ever come near Kallie and the boys."

"Agreed," Tucker said, holding his hand out for Jamison to shake. Then they walked inside.

Kallie put down the baby she was holding once they walked in. "Just thought you'd both like to know that I heard everything." A heavy sigh left both of them. "Look at me," she urged both of them as she stood in front of them. "I know you are both dealing with a lot right now and you're questioning your past decisions." She looked back and forth at both of their eyes. "But, you did what you had to do, you did what you thought felt right during those moments. I don't want to watch either of you hate yourselves. Teach Hunter and Isaac how to love each other, be there for one another, and support each other's decisions, like a family is supposed to. Make sure they have the brotherhood you both missed out on. And don't ever say you don't deserve me, because I will spend the rest of my life proving to both of you how worthy you are of the love I have to offer." Tears spilled over the rim of her eyes. Tucker and Jamison refused to let their tears slip out, they looked at each other, then back at Kallie.

"How did we get so lucky?" Jamison asked.

Kallie shrugged. "Must have done something right." She smiled with teary eyes.

CHAPTER TWENTY-FIVE

August 20th, 1823–May 31st, 1841

Years passed. Tucker and Kallie were even better parents than Jamison had predicted. Both made sure that their sons grew up to be good, kind people. And just like Kallie had said, Jamison was like a second father to those boys. He was just as involved in raising them as Kallie and Tucker were.

The boys resembled their parents. Their tan skin was covered with dark freckles in the summer, and their dark, brown hair had streaks of reddish-orange. The flecks of blue and green remained in their big, gold eyes.

Hunter's personality was much like Kallie's and even a little like Jamison's. Hunter was laid back and full of adventure and curiosity. He had a great sense of humor. Isaac was a lot like his father, always thinking ahead, taking everything very seriously, and yelling at Hunt er to stop daydreaming and focus on whatever it was they were doing. Every time they fought and argued, Kallie couldn't help but laugh because they sounded like Tucker and Jamison.

It was the first week of June. The boys' fifteenth birthday was a few days before. They were both growing into the same build as Tucker.

It was the middle of the night when Jamison entered the field. He wiped the blood off his chin as he noticed both boys standing in the middle of the field, staring straight ahead.

"What are you looking at?" Jamison asked as he stood next to them and looked in the same direction. He didn't see anything. He looked at both boys. They had strange looks on their faces. Jamison waved his hand in front of their faces, trying to get their attention, but nothing was happening. Then he remembered something.

Jamison rushed inside. He began shaking Tucker awake.

"Tucker, wake up!" Jamison shouted in his face.

Tucker's angry, sleepy eyes opened wide. "What?" he growled.

"What happens to a boy right before he turns into a werewolf?" Jamison said.

Tucker thought for moment. "It's like what happens when there's a full moon. They stare straight ahead and—"

"It's about to happen!" Jamison shouted.

"Which one?" Tucker asked. He sat up and saw the boys' empty beds.

"Both!" Jamison ran outside.

"Both?" Tucker said.

Kallie flew past him and ran out the door.

"They're twins! Of course it would happen at the same time!" Kallie yelled as she made it outside. Tucker joined them there.

All three of them eagerly stared at the boys, waiting for it to happen.

"How much longer?" Kallie asked.

"It's going to happen any second," said Tucker.

The boys' eyes began to glow in the night, just like Tucker's. And then their baby boys, who were becoming men, transformed into two wolves before their parents' eyes. Tucker smiled, his eyes filled with happiness. He felt so proud to be a father in that moment. Then Tucker himself changed into a wolf and took off running through the forest with his sons. Jamison held Kallie as she failed to hold back her bittersweet tears.

Three years later, the twins were in the exact same spot. They had grown much stronger and taller over time. Jamison thought that they looked stronger than him and Tucker. They both anxiously watched the boys, waiting for one to turn into the alpha.

Tucker hoped it wouldn't be either of them. He hoped it would skip over them and be passed on to one of his grandsons instead. He didn't want to see his sons envy each other.

Tucker rushed inside to get Kallie. He walked to her side of the bed and gently shook her awake.

"Kallie, sweetheart . . . it's about to happen . . . come outside," he whispered.

She picked up her tired body. She still looked much the same as the day she first met Tucker. She was forty years old, now, and only a few things about her appearance had changed. Her hair was a few shades lighter and she had few freckles left. Other than that, she looked ten years younger than she really was.

Tucker's age had not begun to slow yet. He looked forty-three, which he was. He still had the same muscular body he'd always had.

Kallie stood between Tucker and Jamison, just as both of her sons changed into their wolf forms. Kallie was expecting them to be the same wolves they always were, and Tucker was hoping to see that. But what all three of them saw was something that had never existed, until then.

Kallie gasped. Jamison almost looked frightened, and Tucker was in shock. He was trying to search for the words to say, but all that would come out of his mouth was, "Both." Jamison and Kallie looked at him, hoping he would explain what had just happened.

"Both? They're both alphas?" Jamison asked in disbelief.

Tucker nodded. The two wolves standing in front of them didn't even look real. They towered over their parents, looking down at them. They were easily larger than any breed of horse, possibly doubled. It was almost like each of them had the strength and size of two Tuckers. So it was as if there were four Tuckers, in wolf form, standing before them. Jamison was immediately more than thankful to be on their good side, because if he wasn't, he wouldn't stand a chance against them.

"Woo!" Tucker yelled up to the sky as he threw his hands up. Words couldn't do justice to how proud he felt in that moment.

He changed into a wolf. The rest of the wolves in the tribe had sensed something going on and came to investigate. Tucker took off through the forest with his sons as the rest of the wolves followed.

Tucker had a hard time trying to keep up with his sons. He actually looked small, for once.

Jamison pulled Kallie into his arms.

"I cannot believe this," she said, smiling.

"I fear for any vampire that gets in their way." Jamison chuckled.

The wolves returned to the field, and the other wolves made their way home as they howled in excitement for their new alphas.

Tucker changed back to human form, and lifted Kallie off the ground.

"Thank you for giving me two incredible children," he said and kissed her through their smiles.

The boys changed back to human form as well, and looked at each other.

"Both of us!" they yelled, and hugged each other.

History was made that night. Tucker and Kallie's children had become known as the Alpha Twins, the only ones ever to exist.

CHAPTER TWENTY-SIX

June 1st, 1841–October 6th, 1843

Tucker was no longer the alpha of his tribe. The twins had successfully taken over, and everyone couldn't have been prouder.

The abilities the twins presumed were incredible, their instincts keeping them aware of everything going on even past their surroundings. They were the strongest and fastest men the world had seen.

Kallie, Tucker, and Jamison's story had begun traveling throughout the werewolf and vampire worlds. But the twins had still not gotten their chance to show off how much power they had. Jamison was the only vampire they had ever encountered, and danger was nowhere to be found.

It was a crisp autumn day, and the sun shone bright in the cloudless sky. Jamison was chopping firewood to prepare for the winter. Kallie was pulling out the dead plants in the garden she started many years before next to the stream. The vampire roses were all around, spreading through the forest.

Tucker and the twins were back at the reservation. A tribe they had a close relationship with was in need of an alpha. The trait had slowly died out of their families. Since Tucker's tribe had two alphas, they were discussing whether one of the boys would be willing to go to the tribe in need.

Jamison dropped his axe. Kallie was across the field. He could hear her heartbeat escalate. He turned around and began running to her. Both of their heartbeats pounded in his head, until one began to slow down and then it stopped completely. Jamison watched her body go limp in the arms of the monster.

The evil vampire dropped her to the ground and looked at Jamison; he had never seen that man before. Jamison then spotted his family, which hadn't shown up once for the last twenty years.

"Now you have no reason to stay," Nessie said.

"I told you we would return," Andrew said.

"No . . . no . . . no . . . no" was the only sound coming out of Jamison as he rushed toward Kallie. All the vampires vanished. Jamison held her drained body in his arms.

He kept waiting for her to wake up, begging and pleading that this wasn't the end.

Tucker and the twins were in wolf form when they barged into the field. Tucker stopped and changed to his human form. The twins continued running right through the forest. Tucker and Jamison knew where they were going.

"Please tell me this is a nightmare." Tucker's voice broke. He knelt next to Kallie's body. He and Jamison held her hands in theirs, waiting for her eyes to open, but they never did.

"Kill them, boys," Jamison whispered as they could hear the wolves taking on the vampires at the opposite side of the forest.

Tucker and Jamison were numb. They couldn't feel a thing, not the ground below them nor the breeze blowing past them. They couldn't take their eyes off of Kallie's lifeless body.

"Is she gone?" Hunter asked. Tucker and Jamison looked at the boys' heartbroken faces. Tucker didn't know how to tell them their mother was dead. As they both got closer to the scene, the blood on their mother's neck answered the question.

"We killed all five of them," Isaac said as they joined their father and Jamison.

Tucker looked at Jamison to see his reaction.

"It's all right, Tucker. They killed my one true love. They deserved to die," Jamison said.

The boys looked at both of them, confused, with teary eyes.

"They were Jamison's family," Tucker explained. The boys looked at Jamison, even more confused.

"No, they were never my family," Jamison said. "*This is my family.*"

The four men stood, wiping their tearstained faces. Then they were in a group hug over Kallie, nothing but the sound of hearts breaking and voices sobbing.

"She was perfect," Jamison whispered between sobs.

"Amazing." Tucker's voice trembled.

"Boys . . . you want to start digging her a grave?" Tucker asked his sons. They nodded.

"Jamison." Tucker paused for a moment. Jamison expected Tucker to lash out and kill him, since this was all his fault.

"Why don't you make her a headstone? I'll build a coffin," Tucker suggested.

Jamison nodded. They finished their tasks quickly. They filled the coffin with vampire rose petals. Tucker gently picked up Kallie's body and lay her in the coffin. Tears blurred his vision. Jamison placed a bouquet of bright blue vampire roses in her hands. The boys refused to close her coffin; neither could accept the fact that their mother was never going to meet the women they would spend forever with, and that their children would never know their grandmother. Both took a long, deep breath and shut their mother's coffin. All four lowered it into the ground. Tucker and Jamison both debated jumping in there with her.

Jamison picked up the headstone he had made, and placed it in the ground. He carved the words, *Here lies the most beautiful soul in the universe.* They covered her grave with dirt and stood around as the world stopped.

As realization set in about everything that had just happened, anger washed over all of them. They went in four different directions and wreaked havoc on the forest, taking their anger out on all the innocent trees. They tore them out of the earth and tossed them away.

Jamison had just ripped out what seemed to be the hundredth tree in under ten minutes when Edudu appeared before him.

"Taking your anger out on nature is not going to bring her back," Edudu said in a calming tone. Jamison sighed as he dropped the huge tree on the ground.

"That's just how we deal with anger, here in the forest," Jamison said to Edudu. It had been a while since Jamison had seen him. He was over a hundred years old and looked to be in his eighties. Jamison had never seen Edudu look old before. Edudu smiled kindly at him.

"I'm sorry about Kallie," he said.

"She can't be gone."

"It was time for her to go. She accomplished what she came here to do. Her work was done, so she left. Did you ever tell Tucker that Kallie was a star person?"

Jamison shook his head.

"A feeling of unexplainable loneliness is going to fall over both of you. But Tucker is going to take losing Kallie a lot harder than you."

"Why?" Jamison almost sounded angry. He felt like Edudu was implying that Tucker loved Kallie more.

"Because you knew you were not going to have forever with her. I'm guessing you have always been preparing yourself for this day. Tucker was hoping that he would go before her."

"What about the boys?" Jamison asked.

"They'll be all right. After all, they did know what their mother was."

"How did they know?"

"When they first heard the story of the star people that visited us many years ago, they realized it right away that their mother fit the description. That's why they are as incredible as they are. Their father is Tucker, the greatest alpha of all time. And their mother is Kallie, the star person who came here and got a vampire and werewolf to stop trying to kill each other and form a friendship. It's no wonder their children are invincible."

"But why? Why was it so important for us to get along?"

"I have been wondering that since Tucker brought her to me when she got sick over twenty years ago. And I still don't have the slightest clue. I have wondered what she was doing here since the night you saved her from the fire. The answers will come to you one day, Jamison. You have many more days left than the rest of us."

And with that, Edudu left. Jamison returned home. Tucker's tribe filled the field, his mother holding her sad grandsons. Everyone was leaving Kallie flowers on her grave. Tucker was sitting under the willow tree on the wooden bench that he made many years before. He gazed up at the sunset, thinking how much Kallie would love it. He thought about every conversation and passionate kiss they shared where he was sitting. He refused to think there wouldn't be more of them. He heard Jamison come up behind him.

"I'm sorry, Tucker," Jamison mumbled.

Tucker turned to face him. "For what?"

"It's my fault she's gone." Jamison hung his head.

"Remember that one night during our first few months together and Kallie was saying how everything happens for a reason?" Tucker asked as he stood up.

Jamison nodded.

"She was right." Tucker moved toward Jamison. "It's because of *you* we got to have her in our lives. If you never became a vampire, Kallie's life would have ended long ago. And if she were to have still survived the fire without you, that bear would have killed her on her first day in here. Because if you were not here in the forest, I wouldn't have been here. I would have been at the reservation, and I never would have made it in time. And if it wasn't the bear that killed her, it would have been something else. Or that jerk would have married her. But, all of this, everything from us falling in love with her and her falling in love with us, to her amazing children, and every single moment in between, all happened because you became a vampire.

"When we shook hands and made that agreement so many years ago, I honestly did not think it was going to work. I really thought I was going to regret it. But, here I am, twenty-two years later, and I don't regret a single thing. I would do it all over again, and the only thing I would change is the ending. I'm glad you were in her life, and my children's lives, and my own life.

"You are more like a brother to me than my own brother was. It must have been her time, because none of us knew she was going to die until the moment her soul left her body. Our instincts didn't think there was a need to warn us of what today would consist of. Maybe if she didn't go like this, something worse was going to happen."

Tucker couldn't believe what had just come out of his own mouth. Jamison stared at him.

It was like a stronger force had pushed them together. Neither of them was sure how they ended up embracing each other and patting each other on the back, but it was happening.

"You see that?" the twins' grandfather asked as he pointed to Tucker and Jamison. They nodded and tried to recall if they had ever seen their father and Jamison hug before.

"Your mother did that," he said with a teary-eyed smile.

Tucker entered the cabin late at night. He expected to see Kallie smile up at him as he walked through the door, but he shattered to a million pieces instead. He stared at her side of the bed, waiting for her to appear.

Jamison was at the same spot where he was when Tucker and Kallie conceived the twins. He sat at the edge of the cliff, his eyes on the night sky.

"Why, Kallie? What was all of this for?" he mumbled, wondering which star belonged to her.

"Why couldn't you have stayed longer? I still need you!" he said between sobs.

A bright shooting star flew across the sky. It filled Jamison with love and hope. No matter how long Jamison would end up living, he was going to carry Kallie in his heart forever.

CHAPTER TWENTY-SEVEN

October 7th, 1843–February 26th, 1844

Tucker was no longer Tucker. He hadn't been himself since the morning of the day Kallie passed away. He sat in the cabin all winter long. He barely ate, slept, or said a word. He had fallen into a dark depression after losing the most important thing to him. Jamison and the twins tried to cheer him up, but it was useless. His soul couldn't go on without her.

Winter seemed like it was never going to end. Hunter and Isaac were at the reservation, waiting to meet with the other native tribe that was in need of an alpha. Both of the boys were hoping Tucker would accompany them and give them guidance, but they knew it was impossible to get him to leave the cabin.

"You're really not going to help them out?" Jamison asked, when he came inside and saw Tucker lying in bed. Tucker didn't say a word.

"They need your advice," Jamison said sternly.

"They'll be fine as long as they listen to their instincts," Tucker mumbled.

"That's not what matters right now! They are about to decide their futures, and they need their father by their side . . . but instead you're going to lie here and feel sorry for yourself! This isn't what Kallie would want. She would want you to be there for them."

With that, Jamison left the cabin and made his way to the reservation. He knew someone should be there for the twins.

Tucker buried his face into the pillow. He had what seemed to be his millionth breakdown since Kallie left. Just the sound of her name had that much power over him.

He eventually drifted off to sleep and began dreaming of Kallie. They were together again, and everything was perfect, like it was meant to be. But his wonderful dream came to a screeching halt when the cabin door flew open.

A man stood in the doorway. Tucker had never seen him before. But he knew exactly what this man was, when he saw his gray skin. He looked at Tucker with red eyes and fangs. Tucker didn't even move, he just stared at the man, not even caring who he was and what he was doing there.

"You're supposed to be the greatest werewolf of all time?" the man asked with an evil laugh. "Look at you! A vampire just entered your home and you're not even trying to fight him!" The vampire walked toward Tucker. "So, the stories I've heard about you aren't true, then, are they? You're weak!"

The man roughly picked Tucker up out of bed and tossed him outside.

Tucker didn't even attempt to get up and fight back. He knew what was coming and he couldn't wait. He knew the boys were going to be fine without him. But he could not be anywhere near fine without Kallie.

The vampire kicked Tucker, yelling at him, "Get up and fight! Come on! Change into the wolf that's supposed to be so mighty and powerful!"

But Tucker didn't. He could have had that vampire dead in seconds, but he chose not to. He was ready to go.

The vampire finally did what it came there to do. He sank his fangs into the past alpha's neck. Tucker died instantly.

Jamison, Hunter, and Isaac ran as fast as they could. But once again, they were too late. The vampire who killed Tucker stood over his body. He looked over at the three of them, terrified, once he heard the ferocious growls escape from the alpha twins' mouths.

"Kill him," Jamison said to Hunter and Isaac.

"Please, Jamison . . . we're the same . . . don't turn your back on your own kind!" the man begged, knowing it was the Jamison he had heard about.

"No, we are not the same. I'm with the wolves, now, and we don't kill good souls." Jamison glanced down at Tucker's body.

The boys launched themselves at their father's murderer and tore him apart in seconds.

Jamison knelt down next to Tucker. He didn't even realize he was crying. He couldn't help but notice how at peace Tucker looked. Jamison knew this was what Tucker wanted. The boys joined him.

"Shouldn't he have been able to heal?" Hunter asked as tears streamed down his face.

Jamison shook his head. "The second a vampire's fangs rip through a werewolf's skin while they are in human form, they die instantly." He wiped his tears away. The boys looked at him, confused.

"Your father never told you that?" Jamison was shocked. The twins shook their heads no.

"I guess he didn't think we would ever have to worry about it," Isaac said.

Jamison pulled both of them into a hug.

"He's with Mom, now," Hunter mumbled.

"That's what he's been wanting." Isaac's voice trembled.

"They will always be proud of you and the choices you make," Jamison whispered to them.

They went through the same process with Tucker's body as they did with Kallie's. Hunter dug a hole, Isaac made a coffin, and Jamison made the headstone. The coffin was filled with vampire rose petals. Hunter picked up his father's body and placed it in the coffin as he sobbed. A bouquet of blue and green vampire roses was placed in his hands. They lowered him into the earth, next to Kallie's grave, and covered it. Jamison placed the headstone in the ground. He carved, *Here lies the greatest leader to ever roam the earth.* The twins began to cry even harder as they read it.

"Your father was my best friend," Jamison admitted.

No one knew what to do with themselves. Kallie and Tucker were gone. Their children and Jamison felt lost without them.

The tribe showed up. Thanks to the other wolves' instincts, everyone was aware of what had happened. Tucker's parents seemed to be in shock. Edudu didn't look at all surprised. He approached Jamison with a tearstained face, though. Jamison noticed he looked even older now and was slowing down quite a bit. The boys stood by Jamison's side as they watched everyone leave flowers on Tucker's grave.

"He didn't attempt to fight back at all, did he?" Edudu asked as he got closer. They shook their heads no.

"She was calling him to her," Edudu said. Jamison hoped that wasn't true, because why wouldn't Kallie call him, too?

"Why would they leave us?" Hunter asked his great-grandfather with tears in his eyes.

"Because they knew you were going to be all right without them . . . if they didn't already know that, they wouldn't have left."

"We never even got to tell him what we decided to do," Isaac said as his voice cracked from trying not to cry anymore.

The tribe returned home. Jamison and the twins stood around the graves that were covered in vampire roses and many other flowers.

"Jamison . . . " Isaac said softly.

"Hmm?" Jamison answered.

"Can you please make sure our parents' legacy lives on . . . even long after we are gone?"

"We want you to forever remain a part of our family. Every moon wolf everywhere will know to only trust Jamison . . . the vampire with eyes that match the sky," Hunter added.

"I would be honored," Jamison said, choking back tears.

"We don't know what you plan on doing now. But we hope you are going to stay here. You helped our father build the cabin for our mother . . . it would only be right for you to have it," Isaac said.

Hunter and Isaac went inside. They knew it would be impossible to fall asleep. Jamison went to the same area he was in the night after

Kallie died. He looked up at the night sky. He couldn't believe everything he had gone through. He never thought any of this was going to happen to him when he found this forest.

He had hated Tucker, and wanted him dead, so many years before. Then he met a woman who literally came crashing into his life, and everything changed. His life didn't feel worthless anymore, he felt alive, and loved, and cared about. And he gained an amazing friend who was supposed to be his enemy. He was finally part of a family; his life had a meaning and a purpose, and it was all because of Kallie deciding not to listen to Tucker and go across the river.

Jamison spotted two shooting stars traveling across the sky. He smiled as a single tear slipped down his cheek. Wherever Kallie's soul had gone after she passed, Tucker's had gone with her. Jamison chuckled to himself.

"Even when you're dead . . . you still make me feel envious of you, Tucker." He wished to trade places, once again.

CHAPTER TWENTY-EIGHT

February 27th, 1844–July 17th, 1996

It had been more than 150 years since Kallie and Tucker died. Jamison was repainting the letters on their graves. He sighed as he reminisced how the twenty-two years spent with them were still his favorite time. He would do anything to go back to it.

He looked up at the summer sky, wishing for Kallie to be there next to him. He had tried to find a love like hers, filled with passion and hope and intimacy. He almost found it, a few times. But it was still nowhere close to the love he had had with her.

Jamison recalled the moment Edudu said to him, "The answers will come to you, one day." It was just a few hours after Kallie passed away. And Edudu was right.

After Kallie and Tucker died, vampires kept appearing in the forest, seeking revenge on the alpha twins for every vampire they had killed. It had gone on for five years. And the twins defeated each and every one. The vampires formed their army and planned on attacking the alphas in separate groups at different times, hoping to take down the powerful alphas, but it was no use. The twins were unstoppable. Jamison never did find out who the powerful vampire behind it all was supposed to be.

The vampires stopped coming to the forest. It was believed that the twins had killed the whole vampire race—except for Jamison, of course. Jamison was known to be the last vampire. But a soul like his deserved to live forever.

It was after the twins had passed, which was about a hundred years after their parents, that the answers finally came to Jamison.

Kallie did more than just help a werewolf and vampire get along. She saved the human race. She fell in love with both the werewolf and the vampire. Her love was so strong and pure for each of them, that they had no other choice but to be with her. And if they didn't agree to both love her, she would have never been truly happy, and she would have felt empty inside.

Jamison also knew he was meant to be a vampire. Like Tucker had said, "All of this, everything from us falling in love with her and her falling in love with us, to her amazing children, and every single moment in between, all happened because you became a vampire."

The alpha twins needed to be born. They needed to be conceived by Kallie and Tucker in order to have been so powerful. They needed to kill the vampire population, or else the human race would have been killed by vampires or turned into them. The vampire population would have grown much faster than the werewolves, since vampires only need to be bitten and werewolves have to be born into it. And Jamison knew that back then the vampire population was already large.

Jamison also knew that Tucker and Kallie only would have met and fallen in love if he was there. Either she would have died in the fire along with her parents, or Tucker wouldn't have been able to save her in the forest. She was right when she said, "Everything really does happen for a reason, doesn't it?" Jamison now lived by that saying.

But Kallie did more than save the human race. She was there to save Tucker and Jamison from each other, but most importantly, themselves. She gave their lives more meaning than just trying to kill each other for the safety of their own kind. She gave them a purpose; she filled their empty hearts with love, and became their only weakness. She tamed the monsters inside of them and helped them show their true selves. She was everything and more. She was perfect in every way, and she didn't even have to try. Even though she wasn't physically aware of how her choices were going to impact the future, her heart and soul led her exactly where she was meant to be.

Jamison's thoughts were interrupted when he heard Kallie and Tucker's sixth-generation grandchildren playing in their backyard, which was not far from him.

The forest had changed a lot since then. It wasn't nearly the size it used to be; only a small percentage of it remained, which Jamison owned. The river and streams were mostly dried up. The perimeter of the forest was surrounded by suburbs. The closest home to his belonged to the descendants of Kallie and Tucker.

Just like Jamison had promised the twins, their parents' legacy lived on, even though they did not. Everyone who had native blood running through their veins knew the story of the Love Triangle, where a star person named Kallie, an alpha named Tucker, and a vampire named Jamison, formed the most uncommon, craziest, strongest love triangle of all time. Most people believed the story was just a story. There was only one group of people who knew the story was true, and that was the family that had a vampire as a member. Jamison made sure that every generation of Kallie and Tucker's family knew everything.

The werewolf population was slowly dying out. Since there hadn't been any vampires for over a hundred years, there was no need for moon wolves. Some men could only transform into wolves that were the size of a regular wolf, some men couldn't even get their body to transform, and some had no trace of werewolf abilities at all. Tucker's family seemed to be the only ones that were not affected. They hadn't had an alpha in a long time, but they could still change into the powerful animals.

Jamison grew tired after wracking his brain about all of this. He went inside to his modern home that was built over the cabin. He lay on the couch and shut his eyes. He woke a few hours later. Something felt different.

He tried to recall any dreams he may have had, but he remembered nothing. Every time he slept, after Kallie and Tucker were gone, he dreamed about them. They were together again, and happy. The last time he slept, which was a few years before then, Tucker wasn't in his dream, it was only Kallie. And now this time Kallie wasn't there, either. Jamison dreamed about nothing but darkness.

"Holy shit," he mumbled to himself as it finally hit him. His story with Kallie and Tucker wasn't over. It wasn't even close to the end. He suddenly felt like Kallie and Tucker were no longer gone. They were back. And the whole thing was going to happen all over again. But when?

Made in the USA
Lexington, KY
22 March 2019